Christmas at Serenity Bay

Titles in the Serenity Bay series:
Summer at Serenity Bay
Christmas at Serenity Bay

Christmas at Serenity Bay

Helen Bridgett

Stories that inspire emotions!
www.rubyfiction.com

Published 2022 by Ruby Fiction
Penrose House, Crawley Drive, Camberley, Surrey GU15 2AB, UK
www.rubyfiction.com

A CIP catalogue record for this book is available from the British Library

ISBN: 978-1-91255-066-1

Printed and bound in Great Britain
by Clays Ltd, Elcograf S.p.A.

For my fabulous family, friends and readers
– have a very Merry Christmas!

Acknowledgements

My thanks, first and foremost go to everyone at Choc Lit and Ruby Fiction for giving me the chance to share another Serenity Bay story with you. In particular the Tasting Panel who passed the original manuscript and made publication possible. A special thanks to: Barbara Wickham, Debbie Southwell, Bee Master, Hilary Brown, Jenny Mitchell, Honor Gilbert, Michele Rollins, Carolina Castro, Jenny Mitchell, Carol Orpwood, Julie Lilly, Sharon Walsh and Gill Leivers.

I'd also like to give a particular mention to my editor for helping me get the story into shape and my cover designer for the gorgeous cover.

I'm a real animal lover and support a few charities who rescue or look after dogs. One of these is the Cinnamon Trust and through them I met two of the characters in the book – Poppy and Portia. They are actually named after two little Yorkshire Terriers I have had the privilege of walking for the past three years – so thank you to Elizabeth for allowing me to use their names. The Trust supports people who cannot get out to walk their own dogs and are worth looking up.

Thanks to everyone who gives their time to help animals – you make the world a better place.

Chapter One

'Do you think it's him?'

Maggie whispered excitedly over Chloe's shoulder for the umpteenth time that morning. Her breath hung in the cold morning air like a tiny soft cloud as they looked down the street with its sprinkling of untouched frost twinkling under the street lights. Chloe hugged herself against the chill as they both stood in the doorway of the pub peering down over the calm, empty streets of Serenity Bay waiting for the film crew to arrive. Along with the seagulls, it seemed they'd both been up since before first light pacing their respective homes. Chloe had been relieved to get a text from Maggie asking if she were awake yet and hoped she might rescue at least some of her fingernails if she waited with someone else. It was still dark when she'd headed to the pub and had breakfast with the landlady; Chloe had been too full of nervous anticipation for much small talk but fortunately it hadn't been needed. Maggie had filled the silence with "interesting" facts she'd found on the internet about the star of the show. Now at just before 8 a.m., the incredibly beautiful December dawn was beginning to break and a seam of soft rose gold was breaking through the blackness at the same time as headlights appeared around the corner. Chloe's body tensed and she could feel Maggie doing exactly the same.

'It's a transit van,' sighed Chloe as they both relaxed again. 'Somehow I don't think the lead actor will arrive in a battered old white van with "CABLE SUPPLIES" plastered across the side would he?'

'He might like to travel incognito?' The landlady

shrugged. 'I've read he's actually quite modest in real life despite being such a big star. It doesn't surprise me.'

Chloe's job was to persuade production companies that the village of Serenity Bay was perfect for filming TV shows, adverts and maybe one day, even films. Earlier in the year they'd landed the film shoot of the enormously popular show – *The Montgomery Mysteries*, and since then Maggie had endowed its star – her absolute favourite actor of all time apparently – with so many wholesome characteristics that everyone in the village was expecting a modern day saint to arrive. He was, according to Maggie: modest, honest, breathtakingly handsome, a supporter of orphaned puppies and more bizarrely, chaste – which was a strange virtue for the landlady to have given him considering her other plans for the actor.

'I hate to burst your bubble, but I really don't think he's noted for his modesty,' said Chloe getting a disdainful glare from Maggie in reply.

Chloe wrapped her coat tightly around herself and went out to greet the driver of the van; as she did so another car pulled up and the man stepping out introduced himself as the set manager, Max.

Time seemed to have passed very slowly in the months between winning this contract and the crew actually arriving but it was finally about to begin and Chloe couldn't help but feel a shiver of excitement. She directed Max and his guys to the old school yard which was out of action pending some work to build a new adventure playground and could therefore form the car park for the duration of the shoot. She then pointed out the grocery store which would soon be transformed into a bookshop and become one of the main locations.

More headlights appeared around the corner as camera

and lighting teams made their way towards the set manager pulling huge trunks of equipment as they went. It was all starting to feel like a real film-set. Maggie stood behind Chloe closely watching everyone who opened a car or van door. In fact she was standing so close that Chloe could actually feel Maggie pull her stomach in then exhale again as each vehicle dispensed a technician rather than a movie star.

'Try to relax,' said Chloe turning to face Maggie. 'You don't want to pass out with excitement when he does get here – that would really ruin your chances.'

'So he is arriving today?' squealed Maggie grabbing Chloe's arm. 'I knew you were keeping something close to your chest.'

A fortnight ago, Chloe had received the script and filming schedule. It told her which parts of the village they'd need access to each day as television shows were never shot in the order they appeared on TV. Sometimes the actor was only available for a day or two and so every scene involving them would be filmed together; equally, all shots involving the same set and some outdoor scenes might be filmed on the same day depending on the weather reports.

Although Chloe hadn't said anything to Maggie, she knew Dominic was arriving before the other stars because they were going to start filming his scenes during the afternoon and one of the first featured the super sleuth crime writer arriving at his coastal retreat and working on his latest masterpiece. For the rest of the day, the set designers would be busy dressing the promenade and creating the Serenity Bay Festival of Writing.

'So what's the story?' asked Maggie. 'What dastardly deeds does my hero uncover?'

'All I can say is what you already know,' replied Chloe. 'Dominic has been invited to take part in the writing festival – he's up for an award as are some of the other characters. Obviously some suspicious things happen and a few people die as they always do when he's around.'

'So what scenes will he be filming today? The actual murder? Who's the victim? Are they famous?'

Chloe just shook her head and smiled. 'Good try but that's as much as I can say. You know it has to be kept under wraps.'

'I'm as discreet as they come.'

Maggie ran an imaginary zip across her lips but Chloe knew that her version of discretion was only to tell a "few close friends" – which roughly translated meant every customer who crossed the threshold of the pub.

After arriving in Serenity Bay nearly eighteen months ago, Chloe had fallen in love with the sleepy seaside village but to stay here, she needed to build a career for herself – something that would benefit everyone. She worked hard to make Serenity a great place for film crews. Apart from the stunning Northumberland coastal scenery, the village had all the practical things many people didn't think about but the crew really needed: a big enough car park to house the catering trucks, enough holiday accommodation for everyone involved and a variety of settings, like the church, pub and cricket ground so that all the different scenes could be shot without losing days to travel.

Their first booking had been a reality show which was filmed at her friend Roisin's Wellness retreat. It really put the village on the radar and the village was suddenly abuzz with visitors. Holiday cottages were being booked up, day trippers bought local gifts and home-made produce, the pub was run off its feet with Sunday lunch orders and life was good. As an added bonus, the producer who worked on the reality show, Kareem, had loved spending time here and when he was promoted to the drama division he invited Chloe to tender for one of the nation's favourite Sunday night shows – a long running cosy crime – *The Montgomery Mysteries* – starring the fictional crime-writing sleuth Dominic Montgomery. When they won the tender, Chloe promised Kareem that she'd do everything in her power to make his first drama production run like clockwork.

Although the overall mood of the village was excitement at the forthcoming shoot, some residents were slightly less enthusiastic as the timing of the shoot was a bit of a nuisance. Kareem needed to shoot this episode in early December. The village was now popular out of season too but the timing meant that the villagers couldn't advertise their cottages for early festive breaks and were turning away enquiries from tourists in order to house the production team. Chloe tried to assure them that keeping the village on prime time TV was so important for their long-term security but a few counter-argued that the film shoot was putting too many eggs in one basket – they should be attracting tourists right now and not keeping them away.

Adding weight to their argument was the fact that because this show was actually not scheduled to go out until next year, there could be no Christmas decorations on display anywhere in the village; the residents with children were particularly dismayed by this, complaining that it felt as if Christmas had been cancelled. Chloe promised them that the fee they'd each be getting would more than compensate for this inconvenience and the crew would be gone by 20 December – just in time to have their best ever midwinter celebration and a fabulous festive week. She convinced them that this could make Christmas even more exciting if it didn't go on for weeks beforehand.

When the local media started to take an interest, even the dissenters started to look forward to the shoot and the possibility of having a photograph with one of the stars started to be the main topic of conversation. For several days before the crew arrived, the local hairdressers was packed as the villagers of Serenity booked full makeovers having highlights, re-styles, perms and beard shaping – even Maggie had gone from her usual salt and pepper to a shocking copper tone she'd called *autumn glow* just in case she saw Dominic. Chloe had smiled to herself as she'd looked around at the customers in the pub one night. Whereas previously, this was a village with its fair share of silver surfers, right now the villagers rocked every shade from raven black to golden glow – there wasn't a single touch of grey anywhere in Serenity.

Maggie headed inside the pub and instructed Chloe to tell her immediately if Dominic arrived. Shaking her head in amusement, Chloe returned to watching the production crew and spotted Andy striding down the street towards her – his broad shoulders in that down jacket silhouetted against the early morning sun. He glanced at the teams setting up and then stopped to help one of them lift an enormous reel of cable from the back of a van; with arms made strong from years spent teaching clients to kayak and surf he made the job look so easy. The team gave him a nod of thanks and he reached Chloe with a smile on his face. He kissed her before wrapping both of those warm arms around her as she snuggled into his chest and together they continued to watch the hive of activity. In complete contrast to the strong man of the sea image he portrayed, Chloe noticed he was also wearing a Christmas scarf with a snowman motive around his neck. Chloe smiled and tucked it in for him.

'It's finally happening. Are you excited?' he asked.

'Who wouldn't be?' she replied with a touch of hesitation in her voice. 'But it's Kareem's first big drama and he's placed a lot of trust in us giving Serenity this show. I don't want anything to go wrong for him or us.'

'It won't. You've done this before and survived.'

'This is different,' said Chloe pulling herself away from him. 'With the reality show, we could turn the disasters into drama and the audiences loved it. With this there's a fixed budget and a tight schedule so the actors can get onto other jobs. There's a penalty clause in the contract and if the shoot goes over because of location issues, it eats into our fee. Besides which, if the midwinter celebration is threatened in any way the villagers will have me hung up like a bauble from the nearest lamp post.'

Andy tried to pull her back even closer but now she'd voiced all the responsibilities she was shouldering, it felt less like an embrace and more like a vice, tightening its grip so she untangled herself from him. Despite all outward appearances to everyone else, Chloe suspected the tingle of excitement she felt was actually a tickle of terror.

'You can't control everything,' Andy was saying, reaching out to gently hold her hand. 'But it'll all be fine and I'll help you however I can. We will do whatever it takes and then enjoy a fabulous Christmas. What are the other conditions – not feeding the actors after midnight?'

'It's not funny. Kareem wants me to work with Max and ensure every location is ready when the crew want to move in for that day's filming, deal with any issues or village disputes threatening to derail the timetable and crucially I have to ensure the script and storyboard don't get into the public domain as the network are releasing the show over two parts and they don't want the murderer being known before the finale.'

'You mean you know who did it?'

'See, even you want to know, everyone does. Maggie offers to carry my files for me at least three times a day.'

'Well this does mean the world to her,' said Andy. 'If you think about the years of bad luck she had – her ex-husband left her and Nick to fend for themselves. She threw herself into managing the pub while coping with being a single parent to a teenage lad and then when this village was on its knees, the brewery told her they wanted to close it.'

Chloe knew Maggie's history and realised that during those years she must have felt as if she was losing everything but the determined woman fought to keep The Fiddler's Arms open for the locals and that wouldn't have been easy.

'So now, having her absolute favourite TV show being filmed here must finally feel like the universe is smiling on her,' continued Andy. 'But you're right – she wouldn't be able to stop talking about the plot if she ever got hold of it!'

'Precisely,' replied Chloe. 'But don't worry, I've locked it away and will only take out each scene as we shoot it.'

'See,' said Andy planting a kiss on the top of her head. 'You have this completely under control – it'll be a breeze.'

Chapter Two

The production crew worked quickly and efficiently so that by midday the main street and all of its shops had been transformed. At the entrance to the street was a fabulous canopy of lights in the shape of an open book and a banner inviting visitors to the Serenity Bay Festival of Writing. Every shop façade had been changed so as well as a grocery store that was now a bookshop, the Serenity Bay Publishing House had replaced the ice-cream parlour and along the promenade, stood a brightly decorated traditional gypsy caravan which Chloe knew would feature a character who could read fortunes. It might not be Christmassy but it still looked magical and Chloe had suggested they keep the name of the village in the script.

'Serenity Bay sounds exactly the sort of place Dominic Montgomery would go to write his books and it would help us so much,' she'd said knowing the show usually featured fictional villages. However, this would help hugely with tourism and the locals would be absolutely thrilled if they could see the real name on screen.

After a consultation between the script writers, the team had agreed with Chloe and had even tweaked the script so that the story featured a writer of historical fiction who was supposedly working on a book about the Viking history of the area. The whole village was delighted that their little corner of Northumberland would be beamed out in all its glory as the whole nation settled down on their sofas. Well, a strange version of the village would be anyway.

'Why did they have to change the name of the pub if

they're not even filming in it?' whined Maggie as she came back outside and stood beside Chloe. 'The Fiddler's Arms is as good a name as any – whoever heard of a pub called The Hanged Man? No one would ever eat there.'

'I thought you'd be pleased. In this episode, it's the title of Dominic Montgomery's new book so it fits better with the festival and they will feature the outside of the pub,' replied Chloe as they watched the team take down the pub sign and fix the new spooky looking one to the bracket.

'They can cut to the sign just after they find a body. It'll swing in the wind like the hanged man himself, creaking eerily,' she added, in a low spooky voice.

'Bit clichéd if you ask me.'

'Have you actually seen this show?' Chloe laughed. 'They tend to take cliché to the next level; the least famous person gets murdered first, most famous person is always the murderer and Montgomery always solves the crime thanks to his trusty dog – no one wants reality on a Sunday evening.'

'It would play havoc with the digestive system after all that Yorkshire pudding I imagine.'

The women turned to find the owner of that smooth voice and Chloe watched as Maggie took in every inch of his six foot frame. Open mouthed, Maggie's eyes ran from his battered suede desert boots, up his denim-clad thighs, across his broad chest and shoulders from which a long leather coat hung perfectly before stopping to stare at the stubbled jawline and dark brown eyes. On top of his salt and pepper curls sat his trademark leather fedora. Chloe saw Maggie swallow hard and wondered whether she was actually going to pass out.

'I'm Dominic,' he said, 'well the actor who plays him

but I do prefer to stay in character during filming as do my co-stars.'

The actor was already in costume as his on-screen persona and he held out his hand to Maggie but she was still spellbound and instead of shaking it, she curtsied then kissed it. Chloe dragged the landlady back up, afraid that she might start kissing his feet. Chloe took hold of Dominic's hand and shook it politely.

'Very nice to meet you and welcome to our village,' she said in her best professional tone. 'I'm Chloe, the location manager and the speechless person next to me is Maggie who runs the pub.'

He touched the peak of his fedora and took Maggie's hand. 'Then I'm sure I'll be seeing a lot of you,' oozed Dominic. 'I do like a nightcap at the end of a day's filming.'

'It wouldn't fit on your head unless you took that off.'

Chloe held back a snort of laughter at Maggie's dreadful attempt at a joke. It baffled Dominic until the landlady explained herself.

'I meant the nightcap, it wouldn't fit over the fedora,' she mumbled. 'Never mind, I think I'd better get back to work.'

Maggie retreated inside and they watched her slapping herself on the back of the head as she went.

'Is she always like that?' asked Dominic.

'Take no notice, she just loves the show and you're her favourite character,' replied Chloe. 'You must get that a lot, fans clamming up when they meet you?'

'Well I have to say, I prefer the ones who clam up to the ones who scream my name constantly, and quote lines from the show. They seem to think I've written them but it's the script guys who're the clever ones, not me.'

Chloe recognised a person fishing for a compliment when she saw one and decided to go along with it.

'But you bring them to life,' she replied getting a smile and nod in response. 'That takes incredible talent. Now has anyone shown you where you'll be staying?'

Dominic replied that he still had time before the first scene so would be delighted to have Chloe show him the village and his accommodation. Chloe pointed him towards the promenade and began the tour as all around them set designers scurried around continuing to transform the place. She knew the villagers were disappointed that they couldn't put up the Christmas decorations until the crew had left but the place already looked amazing as a writing festival and she had a surprise in store for them later. Serenity had been gifted an enormous Norwegian pine Christmas tree by the production company. It was far bigger than the one the village would normally be able to afford and it would simply dazzle everyone when it arrived.

But right now, the village was set up for filming with all the stalls reflecting the literary genres they represented: the historical fiction tent had a Viking helmet over the entrance, the romcom tent was pink with cheerful bunting, the sci-fi tent wasn't a tent at all – it was a glass dome with strobe lights flashing inside. It all looked such fun and once again, Chloe was amazed at how much a production team could achieve in such a short space of time. Dominic seemed to take it all in his stride so not wanting to appear overawed, Chloe tried her best to ignore the hubbub and focus on the actor.

'Well you've met out local landlady – there are rooms at the pub and Maggie is looking after some of the crew, plus the script team as well as Riley the director and Kareem the producer – but I guess you've worked with them lots of times?'

Dominic said that it was the first time he'd worked with Kareem but that he knew Riley well and was godfather to the director's son.

'This is the shop which becomes the Serenity Bay Museum and where the first deadly deeds take place,' she continued as they peered into the window of what had been the chocolate shop then strolled further. 'And here, above the gift shop, is my apartment. If you need anything at all while you're here, please do let me know.'

'It must have a fabulous sea view,' said Dominic looking up at the building. 'May I see it?'

The request took Chloe by surprise and in the moment, she couldn't think of a good enough reason to say no. To try and feel less awkward about taking a world famous actor up to her tiny flat, she first of all introduced him to Louise, the gift shop owner.

'Louise here can tell you anything you want to know about Serenity. It has a fabulous history and as you may have heard is where the Vikings settled when they arrived – that's why it's been built into the script,' Chloe told him as they lingered around the door that led upstairs.

Dominic said a few charming words to Louise and then looked expectantly for the next stage of his tour. Chloe smiled awkwardly at Louise then unlocked the door and trotted up the stairs, wondering what on earth Maggie would think of this. Or Andy for that matter.

She opened the door to the living room with its huge windows where the magnificent Northumberland coast could be seen at its best. The watery blue December sky was more gentle than its summer cousin but no less beautiful. The view had taken her breath away when she'd first arrived and now Chloe stood watching Dominic take it all in. He looked as overawed as she had been and she relaxed a little as she realised he'd genuinely only wanted to come up here to see the view. She felt slightly silly for thinking anything else but his reputation as a ladies' man was well-documented in the tabloids and there was no doubt he was very good looking.

Chloe took sneaky glances at the man in her living room as he gazed out of the window. Probably in his early forties, she could see how Maggie would be attracted to this guy and of course the character's wardrobe simply added to that strong, silent persona. Aside from the leather fedora, he always wore a thick fisherman's jumper and at some time during every show, a victim's mother, wife or girlfriend would bury her face into that strong chest to be consoled. He evidently worked out too as the muscles underneath the jumper didn't look fake.

Embarrassingly, when Chloe looked up from studying his legs she found Dominic staring at her.

'Easy on the eyes isn't it?' he said.

Chloe felt her face bursting into colour and was stumbling for words when Dominic just smiled and put one hand on the small of her back causing her to start slightly.

'Yep, it's one hell of a view,' he added looking directly at her. 'You're a lucky lady.'

His gaze felt like a set of spotlights on a stage – revealing her embarrassment and causing her cheeks to redden further from the heat of it. She turned away from him and looked out of her window, spotting Andy on the beach below. He was putting the paddles into the kayaks ready for the day's lessons and had his back to them. Imagining what the scene at the window looked like, Chloe prayed silently for him not to turn around but Murphy's Law prevailed and that's exactly what he did – he turned, looked up and saw his girlfriend in her apartment beside a film star who had his arm around her. Chloe edged herself away from Dominic slightly and gave Andy an exaggerated wave but he gave her a simple nod then went back to work. Chloe sighed. Andy hadn't seemed at all bothered. Maybe it didn't look as bad as she'd thought.

'Let's go and get you settled into your cottage,' mumbled Chloe scurrying to lead Dominic out of the flat as quickly as possible and get back into a public place. 'It's much nicer than this pokey place.'

Chloe marched the star through the rest of the village without hesitating to show him anything else and within ten minutes reached the door of the cottage they'd allocated to Dominic. Whitewashed with a blue wooden door and blue window frames, it was picture-perfect and set back from the village in a quiet cove. Chloe had often looked at it and imagined living there, snuggling up by the cosy fireplace inside.

'We thought this looked like the sort of cottage Dominic would retreat to when he wanted to write his books so it'll help you stay in character. There's a room with your typewriter in it and filming will take place here too,' said Chloe. 'I hope you like it. It's very peaceful here, with a view of the harbour but slightly out of the way so the hordes shouldn't be able to find you.'

The actor followed her as she showed him every room of the house; it had been furnished specifically for him following the dressing-room demands his agent had sent.

'The linen is one thousand thread count Egyptian linen, the church candles are on your desk beside the typewriter and there are no flowers in the rooms, just aloe vera plants as requested,' Chloe told him, reading the requirements from her list. 'I've stocked the fridge with alpine mineral water and your Television Award for Best Actor is already displayed on the mantelpiece.'

Chloe had been informed that the statue was Dominic's lucky charm and as he believed in feng shui he insisted that it be prominent in any place he stayed while on location. The actor simply nodded along as she spoke but said nothing. He walked around each immaculate room and then stood at the window looking down over the cottage garden where a holly bush was bursting with red berries, towards the village and the harbour beyond.

'Is everything okay?' asked Chloe already guessing the answer from his manner.

'It's simply stunning,' he said giving her his most charming smile. 'You have everything spot on. We actors must seem a bizarre bunch, with all our little superstitions.'

'I guess we all have them,' replied Chloe. 'I won't walk under ladders.'

'But as charming as it is,' Dominic continued. 'There's something missing.'

He paused as if waiting for Chloe to guess. She consulted her notes again but couldn't see anything that she'd missed and couldn't imagine what he was hinting at. He gestured for her to join him at the window and Chloe cautiously stepped forward. Her heart started pounding as she thought about what had happened at her flat and his hand on her back. Chloe really hoped he didn't think ...

'The action,' he declared, 'I'm here on a magnificent stretch of coast and in the middle of an exciting shoot and I can't see any of it. It's so far from the village, the hubbub. I'd much rather be where the people are.'

Chloe quietly sighed with relief then new anxieties

formed a huge lump in her throat; she had already failed in her job if the lead actor hated the accommodation she'd chosen for him. Dominic put that reassuring hand on her shoulder.

'But don't worry,' he said. 'It's easily solved. If you can bear it Chloe, we could swap places. I think I'd be much happier staying in your flat.'

Chapter Three

'Are you sure that he didn't say "I'd much rather move in with that devastatingly beautiful yet age appropriate cutie at the pub"?' asked Maggie on hearing the news. 'Because as much as it would inconvenience me for a minute or two while I threw someone else out I'd do it. For the good of the show obviously.'

Chloe managed a half-smile, half-grimace as she watched the landlady arrange her hair and reapply her lipstick in the mirror behind the bar. After Dominic's bombshell, Chloe promised to look into it and left him at the cottage while she cycled to the pub to try and find Kareem. She wasn't exactly sure of the protocol in these situations and although Dominic was the star, it was the production company who paid her fee and they might not be happy at having to move people around at this stage. Fortunately Chloe knew she could have an off the records conversation with Kareem so she sent him a text asking to meet and within a couple of minutes the producer emerged from his room upstairs at the pub and Chloe explained what had happened.

'Don't worry,' Kareem told her. 'I should have warned you. I've been told that he likes to test new producers so has a tendency to ask for changes wherever he goes and the real reason he arrives before anyone else is that he likes to check to see he has the best accommodation. I didn't expect anyone to be turfed out of their flat but I guess we have to keep the talent happy. And it's quite handy actually – we have a couple of assistants arriving and as the cottage has two bedrooms it's perfect for them. We can still film the study scenes in there so that won't be a problem. Can you arrange all the bag switching?'

The producer went on his way with a spring in his step – his problem had been sorted. Chloe's hadn't. She now couldn't even just swap places with Dominic – the lovely cottage had been commandeered too.

'Why don't you stay with Andy?' asked Maggie who'd been eavesdropping.

'He's let his place out to the catering crew and is bunking up with a friend,' said Chloe. 'Which is actually quite lucky because he was going to move into my flat for the shoot but we're on such different schedules over the next few weeks we decided against it. Otherwise, he'd have nowhere to stay either.'

Pretty much every bed in the village was taken up for the next couple of weeks as everyone had been keen to earn an income from the filming.

'My Nick's room is free if you don't mind his hideous posters and the smell of socks. I haven't found them yet but my nose tells me they must be hiding somewhere.'

Maggie's son had decided to have a gap year and was currently driving an old campervan across Europe with his friends. After that he'd be off to university but because Maggie had decided to keep his room exactly as he'd left it, sock smell and all, it was the only room that hadn't been let out. Chloe grimaced at the thought of sleeping in the bed of a hormonal teenage boy. Surely there had to be a better option.

'Thanks, I'll bear it in mind,' she replied. 'I think I'll check whether Roisin has any spaces first.'

Her best friend Roisin had been the one who originally invited Chloe up to Serenity Bay. Roisin was a true advocate of the power of fresh air and exercise and had created the village Wellness retreat from the farmhouse her gran used to own. Thanks to that appearance on the reality TV show, it had done well ever since and always got five star reviews. It had a reputation as the place to go for outdoor activities and a natural detox from the anxieties of modern life. Roisin was housing the leading ladies of the show but by Chloe's calculations, that wouldn't use up all the rooms she had so there should be one space left. Chloe dialled Roisin's number and the phone was answered immediately.

'So I'm guessing you've heard?' said Roisin before Chloe had even said hello.

'Heard what? I was ringing to see if you had a room free.'

'I did have,' replied Roisin. 'Tell you what, why don't you come down and see for yourself.'

Extremely curious, Chloe forgot her impending homelessness and grabbed her bike from the cycle rack outside the pub and whizzed over to the old farmhouse. Roisin met her at the front door and led her through the house festooned with home-made paper chains and lanterns – they weren't filming inside the retreat so it was the only other place with decorations up besides the pub. Chloe caught a glance of a large real tree crammed into the cosy lounge of the farmhouse – way too big for the room and laden with decorations. She smiled as she followed Roisin into the fields at the back.

Chloe had seen that view so many times but it never failed to stop her in her tracks. The sun was an hour past its midday peak now so it was just a faint ethereal glow that highlighted the wispy clouds while seabirds swooped and turned in that endless sky. Chloe wondered why all but hardy walkers tended to desert the coast in winter – it was every bit as beautiful as summer. The farmhouse stood above a small secluded bay with sand that looked and felt like golden velvet below your feet. Right now a soft end-of-year breeze floated in the air and the sea rolled in then out as gently as a breath.

Chloe realised her own breathing had synchronised with the tide and that she was calming down. This was the Serenity effect, pure and simple peace. Down on the beach Chloe noticed one of Roisin's clients taking it all in; a solitary figure sitting cross-legged on a blanket, face and palms raised towards the sky. Chloe had participated in many of Roisin's beach yoga sessions and could imagine how perfectly content this client must be. She watched as the figure stood up; silhouetted she could see it was a woman in a free flowing kaftan and as she stretched, for a moment Chloe felt as if she was intruding on her privacy and turned to look away. As she did, the woman also turned and Chloe caught a glimpse of her profile.

'Hang on a minute'—Chloe looked at Roisin who stood arms folded as if waiting for this moment—'is that my mum?'

Roisin nodded and gestured for Chloe to follow her to the sand.

'Yep, Theresa arrived this morning,' explained Roisin. 'She insisted I didn't tell you but I think you two need to talk.'

'Chloe,' called her mum, pulling a wrap tightly around her shoulders then strolling towards them with a contented glow on her face. 'Isn't it just magnificent?'

She gestured out to the sea and inhaled deeply.

'Doesn't it make you feel glad to be alive?'

'It certainly does but what brings you here, Mum?' asked Chloe.

Her mother said nothing but led her to a large piece of

driftwood that had been washed ashore and made smooth by its journey. Chloe raised her eyebrows as her mother, who at any other time would have been afraid to crumple her clothing, sat down and beckoned her to do the same. Chloe thought back to all those times when her mother had refused to sit on a perfectly clean park bench for fear of ruining some outfit and wondered whether the woman in front of her was actually an imposter. Surely identity thieves weren't this good.

'I've realised life is too short,' Theresa said, 'and too materialistic.'

'*Okaaayyy*,' Chloe really didn't know how to respond. Yes, many people re-evaluated their lifestyles as they got older but as far as she knew, her mother still loved all things materialistic – keeping up with the Joneses had previously been her favourite form of exercise.

'Your father has been promoted and they've given him a new company car.'

'I didn't know that. It sounds like wonderful news,' replied Chloe.

'No, it isn't wonderful at all. It has cream leather seats and lots of safety devices. It beeps when you go over the speed limit or go over lines or get too close to the fence. Sensible, that's what it is – sensible and boring.' Theresa practically spat out the words.

Chloe stayed silent, really not sure how to respond to this.

'Then last week,' continued Theresa, 'I had a health check and they told me everything was working well and I was perfectly healthy.'

'But that's good too – surely?' said Chloe even more confused as to why two pieces of perfectly good news were being so harshly regarded.

'For someone in the "50–70 age category",' exclaimed Theresa before dropping her shoulders and running her fingers along the grain of the wood.

'It shocked me,' she said. 'In my mind I'm nowhere near that age. All I could think about was how soon I'd be in the next category and how, if things didn't change I'd spend all that time doing exactly the same thing.'

'But you've been happy so far haven't you?'

'Is that enough, Chloe? I mean surely there's more to life and it's our duty to seek out and *seize* opportunities. After that health check I was watching a documentary on Kylie Minogue and I realised she would be in that age category too. I thought to myself, look at all she's done with her life. Look at that career and all the gorgeous men she's been out with – I tell you what Chloe I should be so blooming lucky.'

Roisin snorted and Chloe gave her a stern look. It was funny but not the right time to laugh.

'What are you saying, Mum? Are you and Dad okay?' Chloe thought this sounded like a very late midlife crisis and knew that often caused people to divorce or separate. She hoped it wasn't about to happen to her parents, particularly not on account of feeling inferior to Kylie.

'Things need to change and I don't know how but I know I have to start somewhere. In the reality show that was filmed here – the celebrities revitalised themselves and turned back their physical ages through exercise so I thought this was a good place to start. I want to learn some yoga and think things through.'

'Okay, well that doesn't sound too bad,' said Chloe relieved.

'Tell Chloe the rest,' said Roisin nudging Theresa.

'Then,' added Chloe's mum tentatively. 'When I know a

little more, I might go on a desert trek or something and try to be more … spiritual. I'll try and find myself.'

'What does Dad think about all this?' Chloe was trying to keep an even tone in her voice.

'He went off on one of his conferences this week so I haven't told him.'

'You mean he doesn't know you're here?' Chloe was failing at the even tone of voice and that came out as a surprised squeal. She cleared her throat and continued more calmly. 'You haven't told him anything of what you're feeling?'

'We're not joined at the hip any more. We are independent souls,' said Theresa with more than an ounce of petulance. 'I don't have to tell him everything. Now if you'll excuse me, I need to go and do my breathing exercises. You've surrounded me with a lot of negative energy.'

Theresa flounced back to the farmhouse as Chloe watched her, shaking her head in disbelief.

'I've never been so lost for words so many times in one day,' she sighed, turning to Roisin who wrapped her arms around her in a big hug. 'I'm so sorry you're caught up in this Roisin, but at least she came here. Can you cope with this as well as all the TV stars? I'm guessing Mum has booked in for a few days.'

Roisin released Chloe from the hug and looked affectionately at her. 'Yes, don't worry. I can cope and yes, she booked in for the full week. It's all okay but this is why I have no space for you unfortunately – your mum took the last available room.'

'No problem, at least I know where she is. I'll call Dad to let him know what's happened. Keep me updated won't you?'

Her friend assured her that she would and said goodbye. Chloe cycled back to the village slowly and deep in thought. It was just after two o'clock and she guessed that her dad's conference would finish around five and then he'd go back to his room to change for dinner. She decided not to disturb him now but to try and catch him then to gently explain that his wife seemed to be having a midlife crisis brought on by tiny pop-star envy. Her father was a kindly, pragmatic man who always seemed to know what to do but Chloe could picture him sitting on the bed of his business hotel, still in his sensible business suit, trying to comprehend this. Chloe really couldn't guess what he would say but decided that was for later. Right now her most pressing concern was a roof over her head so while still out of Maggie's earshot she called Tony, Charlie, Louise and everyone she knew asking if they had any spare rooms. It was as she'd expected; there was no room at the inn tonight.

Well actually that's the only place there was a vacancy – the inn. Chloe parked her bike back at the pub then walked to her flat and packed a suitcase. Chloe cleared the rooms of as many personal pieces as she could and packed them in boxes which she stored in the back of the gift shop. Now that the flat no longer looked like hers, Chloe closed the door and made her way back to the pub to accept Maggie's offer. The landlady was delighted and dragged her upstairs immediately to show Chloe the room that would be home for the next fortnight.

'I knew you'd take it so I've opened the windows,' said Maggie while Chloe tried to hold her breath. 'I'm sorry but that arome de boy takes a while to go. You'll get used to it. I've also cleared the wardrobe for you.'

Chloe thanked her and waited until she'd closed the

door before plonking herself down on the bed and looking around properly. The dark blue curtains, black ceiling and poster-filled walls made for a very oppressive ambience and yes, there was definitely a whiff of sweaty gym bag in the air. She opened her case and sprayed the room with so much perfume that even she choked on it. Still it was better than before although, having practically emptied the bottle, Nick would probably still be enjoying the remnants of Marc Jacobs when he got back. She looked at the single bed in dread but at least Maggie had replaced whatever bedding her son might have had with something feminine and floral. Chloe perched on the edge for a moment and it creaked beneath her.

A parent behaving like a teenager, a diva of a leading man taking over my home and death metal posters to watch over me when I sleep. Whoever said TV work was glamorous?

Chapter Four

Chloe unpacked her things then took out her phone to call her dad. It was nearly out of juice and she berated herself as, picturing it in the kitchen drawer, she realised she'd left the charger in her flat. She couldn't go back there right now but could probably do one call before it died completely. She dialled her father's number but got no answer so after leaving a slightly cryptic message about needing to talk to him rather urgently, she left her new abode and went back downstairs into the pub where Kareem had the rest of the day's shooting schedule laid out on the table. For the next fortnight they'd be working long days from seven in the morning until ten at night with one day off mid-shoot. However, for this first day, Kareem seemed to be easing everyone in gently and simply using the main man.

'Now that the sun has gone down and we have some naturally spooky darkness, I want to get Dominic Montgomery discovering the first murder. It won't be a long session,' he explained.

'Great.' Chloe nodded along. 'What do you need me to do?'

'Just help manage any fans. The actor who plays the first murder victim isn't terribly well known but every time Dominic comes on set I can guarantee someone will rush up to him for selfies so just keep an eye out and hold them back.'

Chloe looked over at Maggie laughing with some of the crew at another table and wondered for a moment whether she should lock the landlady in a cupboard for the whole of the shoot. It might be illegal but it could be a lot safer for all.

Chloe ran back upstairs to grab what she'd need for the evening. Even when the shoot moved indoors, she'd be stationed with the production team and that always involved standing around outside. It would need tight management to ensure they finished at a decent hour but that's what she'd signed up for and nothing could get in her way. Her hidey-hole for the script was back at the gift shop and she could check that Dominic had everything he needed so that would be her first stop.

'Have you seen what they've done to my shop?'

The voice in her face as she stepped out of the pub to start work was Tony's.

'There are cables all over the place, they've moved out all my equipment and they've re-painted it. You said I'd get extra business after this but no one is going to come looking for chocolate – they'll be looking for a crappy local museum. Can't you get the script changed? Dominic could come in to buy a gift or a treat for himself and still find the body.'

'It wouldn't fit the script for it to stay a chocolate shop,' replied Chloe. 'And it's probably too late to change anything now. Don't worry, it's the village viewers will see and they'll come to look at every shop here; yours is almost the star of the show with the first murder happening there. Tell you what, I'll take pictures of the shop transformed and put the before and after shots on our social media accounts, then they'll know where you are. And I don't think it's giving too much away to tell you that in this first scene about to be filmed, an ancient dagger is used. I'm sure you could make a chocolate version of that – you're an absolute genius with ideas so I know you could do it.'

Chloe guessed that telling Tony something small about the script before the rest of the village found out would pacify him slightly. And it did initially but then as he left her he grumbled that he could probably create something but he'd have to talk to her about his fee if he didn't make up the business. Chloe suspected that she'd just had the first of many similar conversations. By the end of this fortnight she'd probably have earned a degree in placating people. Now what was she supposed to be doing? That was it, the script.

Dodging moving scenery and stepping over cables, she reached the gift shop to find a small crowd of villagers outside watching the filming of the establishing shots – the dark sky and darker sea with white waves foaming onto the shore and in the background the beam of a distant lighthouse. It was something they all saw every day but somehow it was more fascinating watching it through someone else's eyes. In the doorway Louise was taking pictures of everyone watching.

'Just to prove I was here,' she said.

'Any word from our distinguished guest?' asked Chloe gesturing to the flat upstairs.

'Nothing from him but there's been a parade of people up and down taking his dinner then bringing him clothes and people with vanity cases who I presume are make-up. Funny but you don't think of a rugged character like that wearing mascara do you?'

They laughed and it rang out louder than they'd expected because all around, the crowd suddenly went silent. Dominic had emerged behind them and phones started flashing; he held his palms up to his face and Chloe ran around asking people not to take pictures.

'I promise to pose for any photographs later,' said

Dominic, 'but right now I need to get on set and as the ladies have just said – the mascara's barely dry.'

The crowd laughed with him but Chloe caught the sideways glance – that was twice he'd overheard her saying something untoward. It had just been good-natured banter but it might not have sounded like that to him.

'Anyway, I have to get to work,' continued Dominic. 'I will see you good people later.'

Rather bizarrely the actor got a round of applause for that. He gestured to Chloe,

'Would you do me the honour of walking with me to the set?'

Knowing that it wasn't actually an option to say no, Chloe ran quickly to the kitchen area in the back of the shop and opened the vintage metal bread bin where she'd decided to store her copy of the script. She grabbed the pages she needed and got back to Dominic who was signing autographs rather than allowing selfies. He extradited himself on seeing her and they left the shop, heading away from the seafront.

'I'm told your dog will meet us there,' said Chloe.

'Oh yes, Agatha is always on time and in costume.' Dominic laughed. 'The consummate professional – if only I could say that about all the ladies in the cast.'

Sure enough, when they reached the exterior of the chocolate shop, Agatha the chocolate Labrador and her handler were ready and waiting. Although Chloe thought Dominic had been joking about the costume, Agatha was in fact wearing the harness and braided brown leather lead she always had in the show. The dog started wagging her tail when Dominic appeared.

'Who's my girl?' he said stroking her ears. 'Are we going to solve another crime sweetheart?'

As he made a fuss of the dog, Chloe softened towards the actor. This affection didn't seem forced so maybe he actually was just a little bit shy around people and overcompensated. She'd heard some actors started out that way – pretending to be other people as a way of coping with their own awkwardness. It could also be why he preferred being called by his character name; he simply wasn't comfortable letting people get close to him.

The murder victim, Bartholomew, arrived on set. He was a small portly man dressed in corduroy trousers, a mustard coloured shirt and a knitted tank top stretched over his round belly. He certainly looked the part of a studious museum curator.

'Okay everyone let's get this show on the road. Places please,' shouted Riley.

It was starting. Chloe tried to appear as nonchalant as the rest of the crew but inside she was fizzing. A major TV drama was about to be filmed in their little village! She turned to join Riley and Kareem in the director's tent which she'd see a lot of over the next fortnight. Everything that was being filmed was fed back to a screen in the tent so they could all watch it and assess how it looked. After every scene they would check the footage and decide whether they needed another take or not. As she turned to take up her place inside, Andy appeared looking flustered.

'What's happened?' he said. 'I was heading up to your flat to drop off these gloves because I thought you might get cold standing outside all day and some security guy told me to vacate the premises – that no one was allowed near.'

Chloe took him to one side, 'Oh God, I'm sorry and thank you, that was a lovely thought. I had to move

Dominic in so he could have a sea view. I'm in the pub with Maggie now – she's given me Nick's room.'

'Is that why you were both up there earlier? You could have called to let me know.'

'I'm sorry. My phone died and the charger is in the flat but I'm not allowed back either. Look it's been the weirdest day – my mother's gone mad, I can't get in touch with my dad and now I'm about to watch a man get murdered. Come to the pub later and I'll explain?' she pleaded. 'Oh, and if you have a spare charger could I borrow it?'

'One of these days your life is going to be less dramatic than the TV shoots,' replied Andy shaking his head in equal measures of humour and despair. He handed her a pair of knitted gloves with a snowflake design.

Chloe blew him a kiss and ran off to catch up with the crew. They'd finished the exterior shot of Dominic looking into the window of the museum and were setting up the main event of the day – the first murder scene.

Back in the director's tent, Chloe watched as Dominic peered in through the window of the shop which now looked like every small town local history museum. A poster promised daily talks where the secret history of Serenity Bay would be revealed. The sign on the door said the museum was open but when Dominic tried the handle, it was locked. The actor looked down at Agatha and smiled.

'It looks as if they want to keep those local treasures to themselves,' he said.

Then as Dominic started to walk away there was a scream and the director shouted "cut". They ran the footage back and decided it was good so moved onto the next scene.

'So Dom,' Riley was saying. 'You hear the scream and

run into the back of the shop with Agatha following. You see Bartholomew on the floor and turn him over checking his pulse. Then you spot the trail of blood and follow it out the back to the hedges where we do a close up on the dagger. Okay with that?'

Dominic nodded sagely and Chloe thought he looked as serious as if he'd just been given instructions for disarming a ticking bomb; it was a very strange job, this acting lark.

The cameras started rolling and Dominic barged the door open nearly taking it off its hinges. He used his phone as a torch as he and Agatha crept through the dark museum lighting up old smuggling maps on walls and a huge fish skeleton suspended from the ceiling. On the shelves that had once housed chocolate novelties sat a range of bizarre ancient artefacts like creepy wooden masks, rusted metal fishing hooks and carved bone effigies.

Chloe watched as Dominic and Agatha did exactly as they'd been asked with the actor adding the horrified, puzzled, thoughtful and finally determined facial expressions needed for the story. He followed the trail of blood to hedges at the back of the shop and rummaged around where he'd been told to.

'Hold on,' he said as he pushed aside branches and kicked up leaves while Agatha sniffed around the garden. 'It's not here.'

The assistants crowded into the shop and garden looking everywhere for the deadly weapon but it wasn't where it was supposed to be. Even Bartholomew got up from his death bed for the search.

'I put it right there,' said the props woman. 'It was definitely in place before we started shooting.'

Riley threw his arms up in the air.

'Bloody souvenir hunters,' he exclaimed. 'Where on earth are we going to get a replacement jewelled dagger?'

'I could get one sent up in a couple of days,' replied Max looking it up on his phone.

Kareem rubbed his chin looking anxious. He explained to Chloe that Bart was due to go home after his one day of filming and without the dagger they'd have to find accommodation and rearrange the shooting days which would cost them time and money.

'I won't let that happen on your first day,' she said doubting that there'd be anywhere for Bart to stay. 'What did Riley mean about souvenir hunters?'

'It might be a villager,' replied Kareem gently. 'It could have been a kid who simply found something bright and shiny but we have known locals take the props as souvenirs. We don't mind that if it happens at the end of filming but we can't afford for it to happen at the start of shoots.'

Chloe couldn't assure him that it wouldn't be anyone from Serenity as it might very well be one of the fans who simply didn't realise the consequences of their actions. Equally she couldn't ask the villagers because that would sound as if she didn't trust them.

'This dagger,' she said. 'It has to look old, anything else?'

Kareem described some jewelling then Chloe darted off and returned in a few moments breathless from running. She held out a brass coloured dagger with a large blue stone at the hilt – it was actually a plastic toy but looked the part from a distance.

'Will this do?'

Kareem took it to Riley who looked it over and nodded; they hadn't shot any scenes with the original one so there wouldn't be any continuity issues. The props woman put it quickly in place and the shoot restarted.

'Good save,' said Kareem. 'Where did you get it?'

'Louise's gift shop. She has some fake Viking weapons and shields that she keeps for tourists who ask for them; apparently they sell quite well.'

'Well thank the heavens for that,' replied Kareem. 'But I still wonder what happened to the original.'

'Me too.'

Chapter Five

Dominic and Agatha stood outside the local museum as a police car drove off, its blue lights flashing into the distance. The actor rubbed the dog's head affectionately and Agatha wagged her tail.

'Well done girl,' he said to her. 'But alas, it looks as if we've another murder on our hands.'

The dog barked at him.

'Okay, on our paws too.' Dominic smiled as Agatha held up her paw for him to shake. The watching crowd let out a spontaneous *ahhh* then collectively clamped their hands over their mouths remembering that they were supposed to be silent. Chloe couldn't help but smile at how wrapped up in the scene the villagers were. The shot was taken again with strict instructions for quiet on set and this time the residents did as they were told.

'And cut,' shouted Riley. 'That's a wrap for today.'

Immediately, Agatha's trainer came to retrieve her and the crew scurried round to clear the set and store away the equipment; they were a finely-tuned team, each person knowing their role and simply getting on with it. Within the hour, everything that needed to be was packed away and the open book canopy of lights inviting visitors to the festival looked rather incongruous glowing brightly against the now black sky and silent streets. Then finally, the plug was pulled on that too until the following day.

'Thank goodness,' said Dominic, 'I wouldn't have got a wink of sleep with that outside my room all night.'

Chloe widened her eyes in disbelief thinking that he'd have slept perfectly well if he'd stayed in the cosy cottage she'd planned for him. Unfortunately Dominic spotted her look and obviously read her thoughts.

'Sorry,' he said with his palms pressed together pleading forgiveness. 'That sounded incredibly ungrateful and it wasn't meant to. I am extraordinarily happy staying in your flat. I'm afraid I just need the old beauty sleep at my age.'

'I understand.' Chloe smiled, determined not to pander to the actor with another compliment this time.

She felt obliged to ask both Dominic and Kareem if they wanted to join her for a drink at the pub and to her relief they both declined saying they needed to finish up and then get ready for the next day's shoot. Chloe said goodnight and skipped down the road, delighted that she wouldn't be on duty this evening and even more delighted that she was going to be meeting Andy.

In the four hours Chloe had been out at the shoot, Maggie had been working hard in the pub. As well as getting evening meals ready for the crew, she'd been decorating. The exterior of the pub was only being used for that one shot with the creaking sign and it had been captured that afternoon just before Dominic's scene. So now, as long as she had no lights visible during the shoot, Maggie had been given permission to put up her Christmas decorations and boy, had she taken advantage of that. As Chloe stood at the doorway, she saw the pub festooned with every version of Christmas that had ever graced a garden centre. A white contemporary twig tree with tiny white lights twinkled in one corner while in another a frenzy of neon pink and purple was weighed down with sparkly glitter baubles. The red and white Scandinavian look graced the tables in the form of tiny reindeer candles and wooden ornaments while Father Christmas was suspended from the ceiling in many guises

– astride a rocket, in a hot-air balloon and rather boringly, in his sleigh. The bar itself was sporting a more traditional look; boughs of holly that Chloe knew Maggie would have taken from her own garden were tied with ribbons in the red and gold colours of the Northumberland flag alongside bunches of mistletoe – lots and lots of mistletoe. It also hung menacingly over every doorway and above every bar stool. Including the one her boyfriend was sitting at. He blew her a kiss as Maggie walked towards her with another bunch of mistletoe in one hand and a mini step-stool in another.

'You can hold the pins while I climb the ladder,' she said to Chloe, thrusting a tub of drawing pins at her.

'I like what you've done with the place, although this amount of mistletoe might be construed as entrapment,' said Chloe. 'You do know that simply sitting underneath it doesn't count as consent – don't you?'

'Where do you think he'll sit when he comes in?' asked Maggie ignoring her comment.

'Who?'

'Dominic of course,' replied Maggie as if the answer was obvious. She looked around and scratched her chin.

'He looks like a whiskey by fire kind of man doesn't he?' She walked over to the fireplace and stood on the step-stool to fix her mistletoe trap above an armchair.

The juke box was soothing the room with John Lennon's "Happy Xmas (War Is Over)" and its lyrics, "... this is Christmas" and Chloe giggled as she noticed that a few customers were subconsciously swaying from side to side in time with the music. A wafting aroma of something sweet and comforting caught Chloe's attention; she glanced at the specials board and guessed it was the cinnamon spiced apple crumble creating that rumble in her tummy. The extra staff Maggie had hired for Christmas were run off their feet bringing food and drink orders to the film crew but now back behind the bar, Maggie herself stood like a queen in her hive, calm and content. She was talking to Andy, both of them leaned in for a moment and it was evident to Chloe that her boyfriend was telling the landlady something very important as Maggie nodded along listening intently.

'What are you two conspiring about?'

They both jolted from the conversation so quickly that Chloe couldn't help but know something was up. The overly-loud exclamations that they'd been talking about nothing important simply confirmed their guilt. They were saved by the bell when a young woman and an older grey-haired man approached Chloe and she could tell by their approach that they were part of the crew. Andy said he'd get them a table and winking at Maggie he headed off.

'We don't want to disturb your evening,' said the woman. 'We just wanted to introduce ourselves. I'm Lizzie, the associate scriptwriter and I would have had to make so many changes if you hadn't found that replacement dagger today. I just wanted to thank you for stepping in.'

She held out her hand and they shook then the grey-haired man did the same.

'And I'm ex-Detective Sergeant Campbell,' he said. 'Or Kevin to my friends.'

'Kevin is our police consultant,' explained Lizzie. 'He helps to make sure the procedural elements of the show are accurate.'

Kevin snorted. 'Well as accurate as they'll let me. No self-respecting detective would ever have that crime-writer anywhere near one of their crime scenes. Or that blooming dog.'

Lizzie and Chloe laughed but Kevin didn't.

'I can imagine,' replied Chloe. 'It's all a bit of harmless fun isn't it.'

'So they tell me,' murmured Kevin rolling his eyes.

They left to find the table they'd reserved for dinner.

'He was a barrel of laughs,' said Maggie as she stood there polishing a glass that was already spotless.

'I don't even think the crown jewels gleam as much as that glass,' replied Chloe. 'Do you miss any conversation in this pub?'

'It's part of the job description.'

Chloe leaned over conspiratorially. 'Talking of which ... what were you and Andy discussing just then?'

'Can't tell you – Landlady code of honour I'm afraid.'

'Suit yourself,' said Chloe making to go. She knew Maggie wouldn't be able to resist saying something and she was right.

'All I would say,' Maggie added quickly. 'Is that you need to think carefully about what you're getting that man for Christmas. He absolutely adores this time of year.'

Maggie went off to serve a customer leaving Chloe slightly gobsmacked. She looked over at her boyfriend who was chatting and laughing with another of the locals. He seemed very happy and relaxed which is more than she was. There were exactly twenty days to go until the big day, which seemed like a long time but it would go by in a flash – especially as she'd be working for most of that time. Chloe hadn't bought Andy anything yet, not because she didn't want to buy him something wonderful, but because she simply couldn't think of a single thing he would like. She'd seen a nice watch back in November but he had his favourite sports watch which had all kinds of functions she hadn't even heard of so she didn't want to risk buying the wrong thing. He wasn't really a clothes fan and from his kayaking job for the TruNorth advertising campaign, he had enough aftershave and toiletries to last him all of this life and into the next. Men were just impossible to buy for and now she was being told, in a very Maggie kind of way, that she needed to find something very special for him. Did that mean he'd bought her something special?

Chloe walked over to Andy as the local wished them both a Merry Christmas and left. Andy got up and pulled her close in a tight embrace; boy did it feel good. She breathed him in and wrapped her own arms even tighter around his broad body.

'What I wouldn't give for us to be in my flat tonight,' she murmured into his chest.

'Me too.' He lifted her face to his and kissed her softly. 'Still it's not for long and by the time the big day comes it'll be just us and a turkey made for two.'

'I'll drink to that,' replied Chloe sitting down and lifting her glass of wine to him.

They picked up the menus and signalled the waitress to take their orders. As other meals were delivered to tables around them, it took all of Chloe's strength not to grab one and scoff it up. Her stomach rumbled so loudly the people at the next table turned round and laughed. Chloe blushed.

'Sorry, I'm absolutely starving.'

'Didn't they feed you on set today?' asked Andy. 'I thought that's what the big catering bus was for.'

'It is, but cometh the hour I was over at Roisin's sorting out my mother.'

'Which reminds me,' said Andy handing her a phone charger and smiling. 'Now you can call me when actors steal your home. Sorry – bad joke. Tell me all about your mother.'

Chloe explained what had happened, then food arrived and they stopped talking, finally relaxing over dinner. They fell into an amiable rhythm as if they'd been together many years rather than just over one. Andy pinched her chips, she ate half of his spiced apple crumble despite not wanting a pudding and then they both had an Irish coffee to end the day. It was only when someone decided to play Slade's "Merry Christmas Everybody" and sing along loudly that Chloe actually remembered there was anyone else in the room. Andy declared that he loved the song and started to join in the chorus, although he had an absolutely awful voice. Chloe laughed and pressed her hands over her ears.

She looked at the gorgeous guy in front of her and remembered the first time she'd set eyes on him. Anyone would have fallen for him; his tall strong body had been shaped by years of being out on the sea while his wavy dark blonde hair and tanned face bore the touches of summer all year long. His character though was at odds with his looks. He hated being regarded as the beach bum; he thought deeply about things and that made Chloe even more curious about what he'd bought her for Christmas and how on earth she should reciprocate. His great love was the outdoors and she could hardly wrap that up for him – she had to get more information.

'Do you still want it to be just us?' Andy was asking as she tuned back in. 'My folks will be abroad as usual but I don't mind if you want to invite your parents, the more the merrier.' He was talking about Christmas Day.

'I'm absolutely sure,' she replied. 'After this shoot, all I'll want is to wake up slowly with you, have breakfast in bed and spend the whole day snuggled up.'

She reached over and intertwined her fingers in his imagining a whole twenty-four hours undisturbed.

'I know what you mean,' he murmured pulling her hand close and kissing it. 'I love Christmas and I want this day to be perfect for us. We can start a whole new set of traditions and it might even be nice to get out on the waves to work up an appetite before dinner – just the two of us and the sea.'

'I can think of other ways the two of us can work up an appetite.' Chloe smiled up at him.

'Temptress,' he said. 'Not fair when I have to go and sleep on a mate's couch and you're on a death metal fan's single bed.'

Chloe laughed and stretched her arms above her head before getting up from the table.

'Talking of which, it's probably time to turn in. I've been up since dawn and we've another early start tomorrow.'

They kissed slowly then Andy left the pub waving to Maggie as he closed the door. Chloe waited five seconds to be sure he was definitely gone and then hotfooted it over to the bar.

'You have to tell me everything you know,' she begged. 'What does he mean by a perfect Christmas? What has he bought me?'

'I promised,' said Maggie shaking her head regretfully. Chloe slumped onto a bar stool and put her head in her hands. Maggie looked from left to right as if she were in a spy film and then leaned forward.

'But what I can tell you,' she whispered, 'is it's something big.'

Chapter Six

'Good morning gorgeous.'

With just the sound of that sexy, sleepy drawl Chloe would have been able to picture Andy stretching those toned arms above his head but she didn't have to – there he was on video call. Live from his friend's couch, snuggled up in a duvet but revealing one naked shoulder. Chloe's finger lingered over the phone simply aching to touch him.

'Did you sleep well?' he asked.

'I did,' replied Chloe, 'despite the lack of someone to keep me warm.'

'It's not for long and then we have that perfect Christmas Day to look forward to,' he said.

Chloe was now suddenly very keen to end this call. She was feeling rather uneasy at those words "perfect" and "Christmas" appearing in the same sentence yet again and so early in the morning. Fortunately they both had very busy days ahead so exchanged details on their respective agendas for the day and blew each other kisses goodbye. Putting down her phone, Chloe checked to see if there was anything from her dad but there was nothing. She left another message and thought again about the conversation with Andy.

She'd lied to him. In truth she hadn't slept a wink last night; she'd tossed and turned for hours wondering what on earth she could do to make Christmas perfect for him and what this present he'd mentioned to Maggie actually was. *Big* could mean anything. It could mean big as in expensive or it could mean big as in huge. Chloe thought about what he'd said at dinner last night – that they could spend some time on the waves on Christmas Day before lunch. Oh no, what if it was a kayak? She loved being out on the sea with Andy, it was his natural home and his face simply came alive as he paddled the coastline, exploring caves and pointing out all the wildlife that simply couldn't be seen from the shore.

The sex afterwards was always incredible too with his muscles warm from the exercise and his body smelling of the soft, ocean breeze. Oh yes, there were definite advantages to spending the day in a kayak, but she didn't have time to spend every day at sea so was quite happy borrowing one; she didn't really need her own. How would she react if that's what he got her? And fretting over this, she'd spent the whole night practising her reaction just in case. He'd think it was a fabulous gift and she didn't want to sound ungrateful so she'd decided on "Wow, that's amazing" as it sounded positive but she wouldn't have to pretend it was just what she'd always wanted as she knew Andy would very likely see through that.

Although this would be their first Christmas alone, they had been together last year although they'd spent it at the retreat with Roisin, her new boyfriend Lloyd and Chloe's parents. Apart from Chloe and her best friend, no one knew each other particularly well back then, so they'd agreed to only exchange Secret Santa gifts. She'd bought Andy some bright purple flip-flops for pottering around the Surfshack and although they looked completely comical on his huge feet, he'd said he loved them and still wore them. Chloe had received a seashell bracelet from her best friend which was truly lovely and so symbolic of the year they'd spent building the retreat. They'd been small, funny and home-made gifts.

But this year was going to be different; it was their first *real* Christmas and it had to be special. That's why it was proving so darn difficult to think of a gift that showed how much she felt. In her imagination she pictured them both around a gorgeous tree handing each other small beautifully wrapped gift boxes and okay, the one she was unwrapping might just be a turquoise blue colour with a white ribbon. That was probably taking the fantasy too far and besides, what right did she have to dread Andy's gift when she hadn't found anything for him yet? Knowing she had to fix that while also managing this shoot, she stretched and threw back the covers. Outside the seagulls were already calling out and the bright shard of sunlight that had fought valiantly through those dark curtains told her that this was going to be another beautiful December day. She leapt up, got washed and dressed then plodded downstairs putting her game-face on as she went.

And boy did she need it. Even before she'd opened the door to the pub restaurant where everyone was having breakfast, she could hear the pandemonium going on.

'It was just here,' Lizzie was crying out in panic.

'Are you absolutely positive? It can't have walked off by itself,' replied Kevin.

'Of course I'm positive. I know whether I had a bag with me or not.'

Chloe walked in to find Lizzie searching under every table and Kevin standing with his hands on his hips protesting that she had to be mistaken, that it was probably still up in her room.

'I'm a policeman,' he said. 'I would have noticed someone taking it and apprehended them.'

'An ex-policeman,' replied Lizzie frustrated and frantic. 'And if your powers of observation are so good, you should have noticed that I definitely brought it down with me in the first place.'

Maggie arrived on the scene with two plates of eggs and bacon, paused at the chaos, then put the plates down and asked what had happened.

'My bag was under the table,' explained Lizzie. 'I went to the buffet bar to get some juice and cereal and when I came back it was gone.'

'But no one has been in or out of the bar,' replied Maggie leaving her next question unsaid.

'I know that,' replied Lizzie, 'and before you say the same thing he did, I definitely brought it down from my room.'

'Okay, you sit down and eat your breakfast while it's still hot. I'll be the fresh pair of eyes and look for it.' Maggie spoke calmly. 'What does it look like?'

Lizzie described a royal blue leather satchel with all of her notes and her copy of the script in it. When she heard that, Chloe understood instantly why Lizzie was so concerned; she'd have been more worried about losing the script than losing her purse during the shoot. Chloe helped Maggie look around, including places that Lizzie simply couldn't have been – like behind the bar. It was simply nowhere. They were about to give up when a waitress came back into the room from the Ladies.

'Is this it?' she said holding a bulging satchel up in the air.

Lizzie jumped up and grabbed the bag with a huge sigh of relief. The buckles were open and she rifled through the contents, pulling out leaves of paper with the tell-tale font and layout of a TV script.

'It's all here,' she exhaled and Chloe joined her in breathing normally again. Although she'd felt a very bad person for even thinking it, Chloe had been mightily relieved that it hadn't been her who'd mislaid her own copy of the script. Lizzie was looking again at the pages and frowning.

'What's the matter?' asked Chloe.

'There was a bulldog clip at the top,' Lizzie said. 'Marking out today's scenes and it's gone. And the buckles were fastened when I brought it down this morning and now they're open.'

Maggie looked across at the waitress who'd found it; she raised her palms in innocence and promised she'd brought it straight in exactly as she'd found it. Maggie nodded her acceptance.

'Do you think someone's been reading the script?' asked Chloe, fearing that a local hadn't been able to resist the temptation.

'I just hope that's all they've done,' replied Lizzie. 'Kareem will have my guts if it's been photographed and any of the storyline gets out.'

'Can't have him thinking we've lost the plot,' said Maggie obviously trying to lift the mood. Chloe shook her head and frowned at her. Now was not really the time to make jokes.

A whoop of applause distracted everyone in the pub and they turned to the windows to see Dominic and Agatha walking past on their way to the first scenes of the day.

'Come on,' said Chloe leading Lizzie and Kevin towards the door. 'No damage has been done. We have the script and the weather looks fabulous. Let's go and join the team.'

Warily, Lizzie nodded and collected her things together.

Although it was bright outside, it was also bitterly cold giving rise to the most magnificent blue sky. If it weren't for the facts that every conversation happening was marked by a cloud of air and that everyone was wearing thick gloves and hats, you could have thought it was summer. All three reached the director's tent where Riley was standing outside talking through the schedule.

'As per the scripts, the day is about Dominic and this morning we'll be outdoors. We need to film the establishing shots while the weather is looking good: street scenes, shop exterior, coastline etc. Before that we'll have Dominic walking his dog on the beach and later when the light fades, we'll be in his study where he gets the warning letter and then in the museum looking for clues. We'll finish the day with some prop close-ups so let's not lose any more. The other principals arrive this afternoon and the extras for the crowd scenes arrive later this week so we're just using a couple of people for distant background shots – it's mainly Dominic to begin with.'

The crew gave a collective nod and got into position. The make-up lady checked the red glow from the cold on Dominic's nose and then the costume lady corrected the angle of his fedora by a tiny percentage. Chloe looked on amused by the fuss and noting how completely at home Dominic looked, being fussed over like this.

'Okay, clear the set,' called Riley. 'Position please, Dominic.'

Chloe stepped back inside the tent and watched as Dominic walked to a spot marked on the beach while Riley checked the shot with his assistant. When they were happy, they shouted 'action' and Dominic began ambling along the beach with Agatha playing at his feet. The camera followed as he strolled past the grasses of the dunes bowing gently in the wind. Dominic picked up a strategically placed stick and threw it for Agatha – the well-trained dog bounded towards it and dutifully brought it back to drop at her owner's feet. The whole scene looked absolutely idyllic and as she watched it, Chloe made a mental note to seek out some dog-owner websites and magazines to promote Serenity Bay. The beaches really were the most perfect place to walk and exercise a furry friend.

She was pulled from her thoughts by Riley yelling "cut" in an exasperated voice.

'I thought we'd cleared this set,' he shouted at someone while pointing at the beach.

Chloe followed the line of his finger. Further along the beach was a figure that they either hadn't noticed or who hadn't been there when the camera started rolling. Through the zoom lens Chloe could see the figure was now sitting cross-legged, her palms upright on her legs. The figure was completely oblivious to everything going on around her. Chloe gulped, realising it was her own mother ruining the shoot. She was about to offer to go and talk to her when Riley rechecked the scene and mumbled something to Lizzie who ran up to Dominic with some new instructions.

'Okay from the top,' shouted Riley. Dominic repeated his walk along the beach, threw the stick again, but this time continued his walk and as he approached Theresa, lifted his fedora to her and continued on his way.

'I'm afraid that was my mother,' said Chloe to Riley when he had the shot. 'I could have asked her to leave. She probably didn't realise what was going on.'

'No worries,' Riley replied, 'I've decided that it kind of fit in with the whole relaxed theme of the show.'

He went to consult his team while Chloe made her way to her mother just as Dominic was doing the same. He apologised for ruining her meditation and then held out his hand to help her up. She accepted with a gracious smile and said there was no need for an apology.

'It's just as well you weren't doing a downward dog,' said Dominic still holding her hand. 'Agatha would have been very interested.'

Theresa giggled girlishly while Dominic kissed her hand.

'Au revoir,' he said as he walked away.

Chloe was distracted from the nauseating scene by her phone vibrating in her pocket so she took a quick look and saw it was her dad. She spun around so she could take the call without her mother hearing.

'Thank goodness, where have you been?' she asked. 'I called you yesterday.'

Her father explained that he always turned his phone off during conferences and thought that anyone who didn't was extremely ill-mannered.

'Well never mind, I've got you now,' replied Chloe knowing that her father really did hate the mobile era. She stumbled over the right words but somehow managed to explain that his wife was at the retreat and seemed to be a little unhappy.

'She's been like this before,' was his answer. 'She always bounces back eventually.'

He told Chloe that he'd paid for this conference and he was going to stay for the full week. Chloe turned her head to look at her mother who'd wrapped herself up in a shawl and seemed to be caressing the spot on her hand that Dominic had kissed.

'I really don't think that's the best course of action, Dad.

I think you need to come over here and talk to her very soon to find out what's wrong,' urged Chloe.

He wasn't going to be budged though so Chloe was left with no choice other than to beg him to reconsider and let him go back to his conference.

'Men!' she growled angrily at the phone.

Chapter Seven

'Hello handsome, I wasn't expecting to see you at all today. You said that you were training up new instructors until late.'

Chloe and the crew had arrived back in the village and everyone was heading towards the catering truck when she saw Andy walking towards her with a huge smile on his face. Although she smiled back, completely subconsciously anxiety was bubbling up inside her as she anticipated another conversation about that perfect Christmas.

'I got through much more of it than I'd thought I would this morning so now we're all on a break,' replied Andy. 'But anyway for possibly the first time in my life, I'm not actually here to see you.'

Chloe relaxed but was now very curious about the possible reason for his visit. He had an excited look in his eye and although the stars of the show were arriving this afternoon, Chloe couldn't imagine he was here to see any of them – did he have a secret crush she didn't know about?

Agatha was being handed back to her trainer and led towards her own catering bowl as Andy followed eagerly. Chloe's face broke into the broadest smile – so he did have a crush after all!

'Would it be okay to stroke her?' Andy asked the trainer and was told that it was. He held out his hand for the dog to take a sniff and then approach him. Once the two were acquainted, Agatha snuggled into him then rolled over on her back inviting a full belly rub and Andy was only too pleased to oblige.

'I was worried you were here to fanboy one of the

actresses,' laughed Chloe as all of her former anxiety now melted away. 'Now I see it's far more serious – I'll never compete with those puppy eyes or that glossy coat.'

Andy had his photo taken with Agatha and then they left the trainer to prepare the dog for her next scene.

'She always steals the show doesn't she,' said Andy. 'I honestly don't know why they need Dominic.'

'Don't tell him that,' said Chloe. 'And especially don't tell Kevin the policeman – he'd be furious at the suggestion.'

'I promise,' replied Andy. 'Actually, I didn't come down just to see Agatha – I came to see if you wanted lunch as they didn't seem to feed you yesterday.'

Chloe looked over at the catering truck and saw that everyone was still inside eating – she had time.

'Only if the food comes with a side order of handsome boyfriend,' she replied wrapping her arms around his neck and kissing him. He put his arms around her waist, picked her up and swung her around.

'You're in a very good mood,' said Chloe feeling slightly dizzy as he put her back down on the ground.

'Why wouldn't I be? I live in the most glorious place on earth with the most beautiful woman in the world, I've just met my on-screen heroine and though I say so myself, I have completely nailed Christmas already.'

'Wow, really?' asked Chloe trying to suppress that churning feeling which had now reappeared and hoping that if she chatted calmly, some clues might just leak out.

Andy said nothing but took her hand and led her down the promenade to sit on a bench facing the sea. From his rucksack he produced two packs of home-made sandwiches and a flask of coffee. He handed one of the sandwiches to Chloe and poured out cups of coffee into reusable cups.

'It's never too early for a bit of turkey and cranberry,' he said smiling. 'Not quite the standard of your catering truck but made with love.'

'I can taste it,' Chloe said taking a bite out of one of Andy's trademark sandwiches and realising just how hungry she was.

She picked up her coffee and toasted "to us" while trying to think of a subtle way of asking about her present. They sat quietly eating while gazing out to sea as seagulls gathered around them ever hopeful. Andy's sandwich-making style was well known amongst his kayaking clients and extended to enormous crusty rolls filled with huge slices of turkey so it took an awful lot of chewing and Chloe's jaw was aching by the time she got through it. She took another gulp of coffee to wash it down and then politely refused a second sandwich – her break wasn't long enough to tackle two of them.

'So you've bought all your Christmas presents?' she eventually asked. It wasn't subtle but by not looking at Andy while she asked, she hoped it sounded nonchalant. 'Even mine?'

'You were easy to buy for,' replied Andy throwing a piece of roll onto the sand to divert the birds. 'I want our first real Christmas together to be memorable so I've known all along what I wanted to get you for your main present and now I just need something small to put under the tree and I've got a pretty good idea what that's going to be.'

'Ooh, so I have a main present and something under the tree,' continued Chloe. 'Does that mean my main present doesn't fit under a tree?'

'Maybe, maybe not,' teased Andy kissing her on the nose. 'All I will say is that this Christmas will be uniquely us.'

Unique. Memorable. They were very good words, thought Chloe, but they could apply equally to an awful day. The day she was sacked from the advertising agency she worked for before coming to Serenity was still very memorable. Why wasn't he using words like romantic or snugly? Chloe felt a sinking feeling in her heart knowing exactly why he wasn't using those words. She looked at him smiling broadly as he threw more bread to the gulls and laughed at their antics; his strong jawline, that tousle of dark blonde hair and those hazel eyes. He was gorgeous inside and out but rarely conventional and Chloe wondered whether her thoughts on the perfect Christmas might just be a bit too ordinary for her action man. Around her people started stirring so she sighed to herself knowing the crew were finishing their break and it was time to get back to work. She tidied her wrappers and cup back into the rucksack and kissed Andy goodbye.

'What time do you finish tonight?' asked Andy as they both stood up and brushed crumbs off their clothes. He took hold of both her hands and they intertwined fingers as they spoke.

'It'll be around ten,' replied Chloe. 'The extras arrive this afternoon and then the principal actors so the filming begins in earnest and of course, there'll be more murders.'

'*Aaaargh*,' screamed Andy aiming for a menacing tone but sounding more like a seagull with laryngitis. Chloe laughed and promised to call him if the sound effects department were well and truly desperate. They started walking in opposite directions, fingers intertwined until the very last moment. Then Andy blew her a kiss and Chloe reached up into the air to catch it. Corny, but she loved it. It would keep her going for the rest of the day.

Chloe spotted Kareem by the director's tent and jogged

towards him. He had his head down, frowning and was stabbing at a number on his phone.

'Hi there,' said Chloe breezily when she reached him and he didn't look up. 'Is there something wrong?'

'Not sure,' he said. 'I can't get in touch with the extras agency to find out what time they're getting here.'

'They'll be on their way – maybe the reception is just awful. It can be on coaches.'

Kareem nodded and tucked his phone back into his pocket.

'You're probably right,' he replied. 'Let's get this next Dominic scene in the can shall we?'

They walked over to the cottage that Dominic had decided not to stay in and Chloe looked around wondering why anyone would reject this. She had always loved this place. It was usually let out to holiday makers and Chloe would often imagine their delight when they arrived and found somewhere that looked even better in real life than it did in photographs. It was such a cosy place. Right now, set up for the scene, the wood-burning stove was lit and glowing with warmth while Agatha dozed in her basket in front of it. On the desk, an old-fashioned style bankers' lamp with brass base and green glass shade provided exactly the right atmosphere for a crime writing den. Dominic was the type of detective who got results through character analysis and deduction rather than CCTV footage and Google searches and this room reflected that.

Chloe listened as Riley gave his directions to the actor and then retreated back into the tent with Kareem to watch the scene happen. The author walked into the room and poured himself a tumbler of whiskey from the decanter and took a sip, making the cold tea that was actually in the glass look as if it tasted richer and stronger. Then he sat down at his desk in front of the old-fashioned typewriter, rolled up the sheet of paper already lying against the rest and with a focussed frown on his face started typing. From the angle of the shot, viewers couldn't see what he was typing, just that his fingers were flying across the keyboard.

'I can't imagine his publisher is very happy that he still uses a typewriter,' whispered Chloe as they paused the shot to move an ornament in the background.

'Apparently they tried to give him a laptop in one of the Christmas episodes,' replied Kareem. 'The fans went ballistic.'

Chloe smiled and could imagine that Dominic without his fedora or his typewriter or his dog wasn't the Dominic anyone wanted to see.

The cameras started rolling again and the actor pressed a final key particularly hard which was the sign that he'd finished typing. He rolled the page and read it through then sat back in his chair with his hands behind his head, obviously satisfied with his work. Then the actor moved out of the way so the cameras could change angle to get a close up of the title of the novel which was always the title of the episode. Every viewer knew that the theme music would start playing as the camera zoomed in and they saw the words "The Hanged Man" at the top in a large bold manuscript and the few lines of Dominic's next masterpiece. They'd only be on the screen for a few seconds but they'd set the mood for the show. Chloe could imagine the scriptwriters having great fun playing with the fictional author's elaborate style.

'Okay everyone,' said Riley after the close-up. 'I think we have this one.'

'Erm, just a minute,' said one of the assistants quietly from the back of the tent. 'I'd just like to check something.'

She was a very junior member of the team and looked flustered as she searched for something on her phone. Riley stood with his hands on his hips, waiting. Chloe watched the assistant wipe her brow and nervously tuck her hair behind her ears and guessed that Riley's impatient stance wasn't helping the poor assistant at all. Eventually she looked up at everyone staring back at her.

'I thought something was wrong,' she said handing the phone over to Riley who read the screen and then checked the first page of the manuscript still in the typewriter.

'What is it?' asked Chloe.

'Those first few lines,' replied the assistant. 'The ones that are in shot – they're not the ones that are in the script. They're from a rather more famous author – Agatha Christie. They're the first lines of *The Unexpected Guest*. I've just been reading it and I thought I recognised them.'

'Wow,' replied Chloe. 'That was lucky. I would never have known the lines were wrong but I guess loads of viewers would be Christie fans so they'd have spotted that straight away.'

'They certainly would and how stupid would we have looked then,' said Kareem. 'How on earth did they get there?'

He called for Max who appeared with the set instructions.

'My guys say that when they came to set up the scene, the piece of paper was already in the typewriter wrapped around the roller waiting to be scrolled up so they assumed it was all okay and left it like that.'

Riley threw his hands up in the air.

'So a dagger that should be there isn't and a page that shouldn't be there is? Would someone like to tell me what is going on with this shoot?'

Chloe thought back to the morning at the pub and the

script going missing for a short while. She desperately hoped it wouldn't result in anything more untoward happening and decided it was probably best not to say anything right now, just in case it got Lizzie into trouble. Riley demanded a new typewritten page and the scene was re-shot. This time as Dominic placed the title page down with a flourish, Agatha opened her mouth in a huge yawn and the actor spontaneously said, 'It's not that boring a book is it old girl?'

It lightened the mood as everyone on set smiled and Riley admitted that the second take had been much better and perhaps the error had been a blessing in disguise. Chloe knew he was simply being the calm professional but it worked and everyone seemed to breathe a little easier.

'Okay,' continued Riley. 'Let's get the sets shifted then we'll have exterior with other authors arriving – can you let the extras know we'll be ready for them this evening?'

Everyone moved out of the tent and as Kareem walked off to check his phone, Chloe saw some local journalists waving her over so trotted off to answer their questions and arrange interview times with the stars of the show. This episode featured a couple of very famous co-stars and they were all happy to talk about their role on the show but Chloe also wanted to be sure the media mentioned the forthcoming Serenity Bay Midwinter Festival and encourage people to visit. As she was saying goodbye to the last journalist, she caught sight of Kareem out of the corner of her eye. He was half-jogging towards her as if trying to hide the urgency and panic he really felt. His wide eyes gave the game away.

'What's the matter,' whispered Chloe as he got close.

'We've got another problem,' he gasped. 'The extras aren't coming.'

Chapter Eight

'What do you mean?' asked Chloe.

'I've just had a call from the casting executive travelling up with them.' Kareem started to bite his fingernails ferociously. 'The coach has had to stop so many times because some of the extras have been sick and it seems to be affecting more of them as time goes on. They can't say whether it's just coincidental food poisoning or whether there's some gastroenteritis thing going round. A lot of them were together doing a football crowd scene yesterday so they might have caught something. Whatever it is, we can't take the risk of bringing any of them up here now.'

'But we need them tonight,' she said starting to mirror the producer and bite her own fingernails. 'I'm sorry, I should have called the agency before they left, I should have ...'

'It's not your responsibility,' replied Kareem. 'The agent didn't take any of my calls and didn't highlight any problems until it was too late. But that doesn't help us. I can tweak the schedule a little but Riley will not be happy and we've got to film all the crowds arriving soon. There's no way I can do that without an actual crowd.'

'What can I do?' Chloe gulped and calmed herself.

Kareem checked his watch.

'I guess we can call all the other local extras agencies – see if they have anyone who can get here today. It's only three o'clock so if they can get people up by six or seven then we may still be able to film something tonight and will only need a half-day extension which we could make up somewhere. I'll go back to the script and schedule before talking to Riley – I need to present him with an easy option.'

They retreated to the gift shop where Chloe's office was housed; sitting at opposite ends of the table they began their work. Chloe had a database of local agencies and rang each of them. They could offer one or two people at such short notice but not enough to create a crowd scene. All of them said that if they could have had forty-eight hours' notice then there'd be no problem.

If I'd been given two days' notice, I wouldn't have a problem either, thought Chloe as she thanked the final one, put down her phone and looked across at Kareem.

'Any leeway?' she asked but he shook his head.

'Nope, the actors can't move their shooting dates. It's looking like we'll have to do crowd scenes later in the week and that means an extension. Riley will be furious – he hates going over.'

Chloe flicked through a mental calendar and knew any extension would eat into the time the village needed to prepare for the Midwinter Festival. The residents would not be happy either. She thought about telling them they needed to disrupt the village for a little longer and it wasn't a happy conversation. Some might have Christmas holidaymakers or family arriving to stay so wouldn't be able to house the crew anyway. Nope, they had to act now and avoid any delay whatsoever.

'Well let's try everything we can to make sure that doesn't happen,' she replied standing up with her hands pressed down on the table. Now was no time to fall apart. It was time to put on her big girl pants. 'Tell me exactly what we need to keep this show on track.'

Kareem went through the brief as Chloe nodded along, her mind whizzing through each and every household in the village. Basically, they needed a crowd that looked as if it was attending the Book Festival to support one of the shortlisted authors. That meant young and old, men, women and children. If the entire village got on board then they might have the people they needed right here. Who would know the villagers well enough to be able to persuade them? Then the light bulb flashed on. Of course – Lloyd. Since arriving in Serenity and moving in with Roisin, her old friend Lloyd had been building his personal training business and helping out with lots of local community initiatives. He would definitely know people who'd meet the brief and he'd very likely have their details in a WhatsApp group. Chloe dialled his number immediately and held on until she got a breathless answer from the man himself.

'Where are you right now, Lloyd?' she asked on hearing the wind and lots of shouting in the background. It certainly didn't sound as if he was still at the retreat.

'Over at the cricket ground,' he replied. 'I've just finished off refereeing the end of term match and now it's the carol concert. It's kids v. parents and I tell you, the parents had their butts kicked today on the pitch so they'd better be in good voice.'

On hearing this, Chloe pictured the crowd and could have reached out and hugged him. She explained the situation and asked if he'd tell everyone what had happened and ask if they'd like to audition to be an extra and to tell them that they would be paid. Anyone who was keen to take part should meet them after the concert for casting.

'I think they'll go for it even without the money,' said Lloyd. 'See you when you get here.'

As Kareem and Chloe approached the picture-perfect

pavilion the spotlights were on and shining over the white wooden terrace and lush green pitch. The dark indigo sky of the December afternoon provided a perfect backdrop to the setting, somehow making all the colours more surreal – as if they were in a 1950s movie. Chloe couldn't help but hope that this was a sign all would be well. The scene seemed to be saying that if ever salvation were going to be found, it surely would be in a place like this. They crept up the stairs into the clubhouse – being particularly quiet as they heard children's voices softly singing the opening line of "Away In A Manger".

Chloe opened the door to the clubroom and with Kareem slid into the background. The warmth of the room gave rosy cheeks to the children and adults although their costumes – Christmas jumpers and pom-pom hats – probably helped with that. The song ended and the whole room broke into applause and gleeful smiles. It really did seem a magical moment. Chloe spotted Lloyd and the club chairman walking into the middle of the crowd with a trophy. The chairman congratulated the children on winning their match and presented the huge trophy to a tiny child. Then Lloyd asked for quiet and waited until a hush settled on the room. He beckoned Chloe over to join him and when she was standing alongside him he said in a loud and excited whisper, 'So who wants to be on TV?'

The room erupted with children raising their hands and shouting, 'Me, Me!' The adults were slightly more reserved although there was some laughter and ribbing among the teenagers and their parents.

'Do you need someone for a horror film? My dad would be perfect.'

'As long as there's no singing or dancing – my sister is truly awful.'

The jibes were good-hearted and excited but Chloe knew that being a background artist wasn't something to joke about. The children could be kept happy by appearing in background shots but the other people they chose had to take it seriously and do exactly what they were told – they really didn't have any more time to lose. Chloe had some willing volunteers but now just wanted to get on with the casting and get everything back on schedule.

Kareem had the profiles of every extra that had originally been employed and together their plan was to try and recruit people who looked vaguely similar. They needed young guys who looked as if they read the works of Harry Marrs the Science Fiction writer; women who loved the romances penned by Tegan Wavertree, Ewan's historical fiction fans and spiritual-looking followers of Lucinda who crafted Fortune Telling books, crime lovers and of course a range of visitors who would simply be interested in the food and drink of the festival. Lloyd suggested that she and Kareem base themselves in the pavilion and he'd organise anyone keen to be involved. They'd be sent in to see them according to the role they were needed for. First in, were some rugged blokes wearing alien masks; they were the Harry Marrs fans and as no one would see their faces, they were extremely easy to recruit. One of the masks featured was an ET mask.

'Why would a Harry fan wear an ET mask?' Chloe asked Kareem after they'd signed up the first six extras. 'It's not exactly hard-core sci-fi.'

'It's an in-joke,' was the response. 'Riley loves that film.'

'Well we all want to keep him happy.' Chloe sighed, signalling Lloyd to send in more people.

Next up they needed a wise woman who would be reading Nordic runes as part of Lucinda's entourage. The door opened and someone bent over in a ragged cloak and hood, using a walking stick, hobbled in. Both Chloe and Kareem smiled to see the villager so keen that they'd already come in costume – apart from the shoes. As Chloe looked at the woman from head to toe, she spotted a pair of distinctly modern animal print wedges peeping out from the robe; in fact she not only spotted them but she recognised them.

'Maggie what are you doing here?'

The woman stood upright, threw back the hood and blew out her cheeks.

'Lord it's hot in all that stuff. How did you know it was me?'

Chloe pointed at her feet.

'You can't be in this Maggie you need to keep things going at the pub. It'll wreck the schedule just as much if there's no one to look after the crew when we need them.'

'But it's only a small part and Dominic has his runes read doesn't he?'

The part was non-speaking but the main man did in fact sit opposite the rune-reading extra for a millisecond just before the next body was found. Apart from needing Maggie to keep the pub running smoothly, Chloe dreaded to think what she'd do to the shooting schedule if she were placed opposite her hero for any length of time.

'I'm sorry Maggie but you already have such an important role.'

The landlady stomped off complaining of discrimination against publicans. As the next hopeful for the role walked in, Maggie shouted behind her, 'And you can't pick this one for a crime fan. She couldn't detect to save her own life.'

Chloe stood up and firmly pointed towards the door; if

she'd had a red card, she'd have sent her off the pitch or whatever umpires did, given they were at a cricket ground.

Next in were the romance readers, the guy who hosted the hog roast, the crime fans, children who would sit in circles hearing fairy tales and a team who would be demonstrating a battle re-enactment from one of the books by the historical fiction writer Ewan. So far so good, they were pretty much managing to match the extras, person for person. There were just a few more roles to cast and they'd be set up for the shoot.

'So all we have is the owner of the beer tent to cast now,' said Kareem, the relief on what they'd achieved written all over his face.

'Why did you make this character a woman?' asked Chloe imagining the stereotypical big bellied man in charge of a brewhouse.

'It came from the history of this place actually. Apparently Viking women were trusted with important things like the mead and beer while the men went off to war,' replied Kareem. 'So in honour of Serenity, we need someone who looks as if she can handle herself.'

A few promising-looking members of the women's cricket team paraded by and then at the end, someone emerged in what looked like a Heidi fancy-dress outfit; long blonde pigtails, a dirndl skirt and corset carrying drinking horns filled with beer. She handed them over to Chloe and Kareem.

'Lloyd, Lloyd – can you come in here?' shouted Chloe.

He came dashing into the pavilion looking half terrified.

'We did say that Maggie was ineligible for any parts,' continued Chloe. 'She was supposed to tell you that.'

Lloyd gave Maggie a stern look but she just shrugged and brushed back her plaits defiantly.

'Maggie told me that you couldn't use her as the wise woman but definitely wanted to cast her as something and I had to send her in for as many parts as possible.'

'Fortune favours the brave,' said Maggie nonchalantly. 'But persistence guarantees results that are inevitable – I mean who better to run the beer tent than someone who does it for real?'

'Maggie,' sighed Chloe exasperated but still accepting the horn and with a little sip realising that a beer was actually exactly what she fancied right now. 'We've already told you. You can't be an extra when you're already a member of the crew. It would be like me or Kareem being an extra – it just can't happen.'

'Now that's where you're wrong,' replied Maggie, 'because I have looked at the schedule and I'm just needed for the beginning when the festival opens. I could do my scene and be back at the bar within the hour – it's not as if I'd have to change. The punters would have a right laugh at this get up. I can hire my bar-hand for the extra time and you wouldn't even know I was gone. You know how much I love this show – you've just got to put me in it.'

She stood there hands on hips defying Kareem and Chloe to turn her down for the part. They looked at each other and at their shots of the other candidates – they had to admit, with a few tweaks to the fancy dress, Maggie did look the part. And if she were on board then she'd most certainly badger everyone else in the village to rally round should they need anything else over the next few days. It was pretty much unavoidable and so Kareem buckled.

'Okay, you're hired,' he told an ecstatic Maggie and was rapidly buried under an avalanche of hugs and kisses.

Chapter Nine

It was a race to get everyone into costume but they somehow managed it. And as the final villager was fastened into his costume both Kareem and Chloe looked at each other and let out a snort of relief. It was time to get back to the set and Chloe didn't need to be told that the other principal actors were already arriving as she reached the village hall. She could hear the laughter and applause from visitors and onlookers before she'd even turned the corner. The actors had all come straight from make-up and were already in character and as the residents-cum-extras appeared just at the same time, it was almost as if it had been carefully orchestrated. The village hall was actually going to appear as itself so coloured lights were strewn over the door arch; a big, elaborately scripted poster advertised the Book Festival opening ceremony and a red carpet was rolled out from the edge of the pavement to the entrance. The extras took their places behind the roped off area ready to play visitors to the festival and fans of these authors.

The cameras rolled and filming of the episode began. Twins Poppy and Portia – the characters who owned the bookshop – were the first to walk the red carpet; they stopped and waved to the crowd but as directed, the extras just stood with their arms folded. After all, they were simply playing Serenity Bay shopkeepers so wouldn't have got a round of applause in real life. Chloe was relieved that the hastily recruited extras were following orders; in the script, the store owners were identical twins but had very different personalities and Chloe could see that their costumes reflected this. Both had long dark hair but while Poppy had hers tied back in a sensible bun, Portia's hair bobbed jauntily on her shoulders. Poppy wore a sensible A-line skirt, a cardigan and court shoes while Portia rocked cut-off jeans, a T-shirt and trainers and looked a decade younger than her twin.

Next up was the character Harry Marrs – he was dressed in black from head to toe and he raised both his hands in a sign of the horns like a rock star on stage. The similarly dressed extras playing his fans rushed to the front of the rope and all raised their hands in the same gesture.

'Live hard, die young,' he yelled to the spectators getting a massive cheer from his fans.

Lucinda arrived next with Jeremy, the organiser of the festival. The response from the crowd was gentle and dignified very much like the duo themselves. Lucinda glided along the red carpet with her long crimson hair and flowing ankle length dress while Jeremy gave a regal wave, dapper in his three piece suit complete with pocket watch and cravat. Chloe mentally checked off the main characters – they were nearly all here.

Just then, as scripted, an open topped Porsche screeched round the corner and pulled up sharply. A buxom woman with most of her assets on show, stepped out as if she knew she had been born for stardom. The crowd went wild and all the romance fans hollered and held out copies of Tegan Wavertree's latest novel for autographs. Tottering on her stilettos towards the crowd, Tegan peered over rose-tinted glasses and smoothed back her long blonde hair as she posed for selfies and signed autographs. Dominic joined her on the red carpet and took her arm to escort her into the hall. Like a wild animal sensing an enemy approaching on her territory, as soon as the characters linked arms,

Maggie suddenly appeared standing behind Chloe. Fortunately she was no longer wearing her Heidi outfit.

'Hmm, the clothes are a bit too obvious for my liking but I can't deny that she'd be quite attractive to certain types of men,' said Maggie surreptitiously taking a picture of the actress. 'This is the character who writes those bonk-busters isn't she?'

'She is and her character is always gorgeously glamorous,' replied Chloe. Deciding to wind the landlady up a little more she added, 'I think she spends quite a lot of time with Dominic in this episode.'

Maggie harrumphed as next a four-wheel drive car pulled up and from it emerged an exceptionally tall man with thick red hair and a long beard. Although she'd read his character description in the script, Chloe's jaw dropped on seeing him; she guessed he must have been at least six foot six. He was enormous and in his leather trousers with green tartan wool shirt covering bulging muscles he looked more like a huge oak tree than a man.

'And that's Ewan. He's supposed to be descended from Robert the Bruce and he writes historical fiction,' she croaked to Maggie.

'I can believe it,' Maggie whispered in reply.

Ewan walked into the hall and with that, Riley had the shot he needed of all the authors arriving at the book festival.

As the crew set up the interior shot, all the actors re-emerged to pose for photographs as a group. This was the chance for the local press to ask a few questions and inevitably someone asked Dominic how he was enjoying his stay. The leading man said some wonderful things about Serenity and the welcome he'd received since arriving and Chloe could have hugged him as he namechecked some of the villagers he'd met – the man was a true professional. Then another member of the press asked Ewan if they could have a shot of him without the shirt, with Tegan standing next to him admiring his muscles. It was a cheeky request and while the actress was very happy to oblige, the enormous man looked a little perturbed on hearing it.

'I really don't think so, it's awfully chilly up here,' he said in a completely unexpected high pitched voice. The crowd laughed on hearing it and Ewan just looked puzzled. 'No, I mean it, I'm not acclimatised yet and it really is rather cold. I might need another vest.'

Poppy and Portia looked as if they were about to burst out laughing but held it back. The laughter of the crowd turned into confused murmuring as Kareem whispered to Chloe, 'I think they've realised he wasn't kidding. He has layers of thermal under that shirt – a bit of a softie is our Ewan.'

Chloe discreetly giggled at the thought of the enormous man-mountain in his thermal vest and slippers.

With the media satisfied, it was actually time for everyone, extras included, to move inside the hall and shoot the opening of the festival. Everyone piled through the door and Maggie looked puzzled as Bartholomew joined the other stars.

'I thought he was already dead,' she said.

'This scene takes place before he dies,' explained Chloe. 'It'll all come together when it's on TV.'

'I should hope so. There's no crime to solve if the dead people don't stay murdered,' replied Maggie. 'Now if you'll excuse me I need to take my place. It can't start without me.'

And with that the landlady pushed her nose in the air and strode past Chloe into the village hall.

Chloe moved back to the director's tent as the filming began. It was entertaining to watch as the camera panned across the seated audience as each group of fans was very easy to identify by their outfits. Harry Marrs fans were mainly geeky looking guys in black T-shirts bearing the names of prominent TV shows like *Star Trek* or *Battlestar Galactica*.

Every bit as lively but very different in appearance were Tegan's fans. The noise levels from the romance readers were far higher than any other group in the room as they chatted and laughed with each other. In complete contrast followers of both Ewan and Lucinda were quite quiet, sitting calmly and very upright waiting for the proceedings to begin. Jeremy, the organiser of the festival stood up and the audience fell silent apart from a few wolf whistles from the romance fans.

'I see Tegan's fans have started on the Prosecco already,' said Jeremy smiling and getting a collective giggle in response.

'I'd like to welcome you all to the annual Serenity Bay Festival of Writing and awards ceremony. As most of you know, I established this event in memory of my great-great grandfather who was born here and wrote many of his masterpieces overlooking this shoreline.'

Jeremy paused to encourage the audience to give a round of applause which they enthusiastically did. He then continued, 'Over the course of this week we will have some wonderful workshops and lectures for you to take part in, a literary brunch with our shortlisted authors and of course, the cherry on the cake – the award ceremony itself.'

There was more prompted applause as the assistant director raised his hand for the audience to start clapping and lowered it when he wanted them to stop. Jeremy went on to introduce each author and the work nominated for the award.

'Harry Marrs for the graphic novel – *Lost in a Time Warp*, Lucinda Duvall for *The Paranormal*, Ewan McFawden for *Highland Souls*, Dominic Montgomery for *A Perfect Revenge* and Tegan Wavertree for *Take Me As I Am*.'

The relevant fans cheered at the mention of their favourite author and Chloe noticed that when his name was mentioned, Dominic stood and waved politely to the audience just like every other nominee but then when he sat back down out of shot, he nodded very discreetly to someone. Chloe followed the line of his gesture and saw her mother in the audience smiling at him and waving back like a star-struck teenager. He had to have invited her in as she wasn't on the extras list.

A mild panic ran through her body but there was nothing she could do about it at the moment; the scene was going well and there was only Bartholomew's speech to film before the crowd and her mother would be streaming back out of the hall. Bartholomew was introduced as the curator of the newly opened Serenity Bay Museum and in his speech he promised to reveal some incredible new findings on the history of the area at his forthcoming lecture. After this, Jeremy invited the audience outside for the final part of the ceremony, the official ribbon cutting.

The crowd flowed out and with a quick change to the camera setting, all the actors and extras were standing under the book canopy at the top of the promenade. In homage to the historical fiction novel written by Ewan, the ribbon cutting had become a little more swashbuckling. The ribbon had been replaced by a huge tartan sash which was stretched tightly over a large piece of wood. Jeremy invited Ewan to stand beside him and handed the big guy a battleaxe that looked very authentic. The actor took it and walked up to the sash, standing, legs astride in front of it. There was a collective intake of breath as Ewan raised the axe above his head, then paused dramatically and brought it thudding down, severing the sash and wedging the axe into the wooden block.

'I declare this Festival open,' he shouted as the audience cheered and strode under the canopy.

Maggie rushed up to Ewan and to Chloe's horror took a selfie with him.

'And cut,' said Riley. 'What was that?'

'That is what you call impro-vis-ation,' replied Maggie. 'Someone would have done it at a real festival and you didn't have it in your script. No need to thank me.'

She flounced off leaving the director shaking his head.

Kareem and Chloe had to confess to the director that there'd been a problem with the extras but the villagers had stepped in. They'd all been absolute stars doing exactly what was required except Maggie but Riley reviewed the footage and said although he was happy that it did look completely natural it would still in all likelihood end up on the cutting-room floor. They moved on to the final scene. All that was needed to complete the day was a shot of Agatha lying down and putting her big paws over her eyes as the axe was raised. The dog trainer uttered some instructions and the clever pup did exactly what she was asked. Riley said he was happy. As soon as he was gone, Kareem turned to Chloe and high-fived her. They'd survived the day.

Chapter Ten

The extras were yawning as everyone gathered before dawn the next day. Chloe knew the shoot hours had been explained before they signed up but she also knew that for some, being told you had to be *ready* for a 7 a.m. start and doing it were very different things. The crew had been up even earlier erecting a pergola not far from the farmhouse. It had been another clear night and the morning air, though still, was fresh and cold. Today they'd be filming one of the writing workshops and it would be an exterior scene featuring the four fiction writers – Lucinda wasn't part of this scene. It began with the authors standing in front of their fans/the extras to explain the workshop.

'As writers,' said Dominic, 'we have to take our readers to wherever we want them to be. We have to feed all their imaginations so that they are with us, in the moment. To do this we have to use every sense we have.'

'This session today is designed to help you do that in your own writing,' added Ewan. 'We are going to watch the dawn thinking about how it makes you feel and how it might have felt in times gone by, when the science of the world wasn't known and it would have felt like a mystical experience.'

'Or perhaps you'll wonder what else might be out there,' said Harry. 'Does sitting beneath this vast expanse make you feel tiny and insignificant or maybe strong and part of this huge universe?'

'And we'll be talking about colour,' continued Tegan. 'We'll work on descriptions that aren't so clichéd. The sky isn't always cornflower blue and the sunset isn't always an orange glow, there are so many ways to describe it. In fact I like to call this workshop *50 Shades of Sky*.'

The audience giggled and were then asked by Dominic to walk slowly and notice how the darkness made them feel. Everyone was given a torchlight in case they felt uneasy but they were asked not to use it if they could help it.

'I know the sky is dark,' Dominic whispered to them. 'But the moon and stars lying within it are so bright, they'll light our way.' He turned to leave and Agatha, who'd been lying by his side while he spoke, got up and trotted behind him.

'And cut,' said Riley. 'Perfect. Love it. Now can everyone walk carefully towards the camera over by the pergola, not too close together and gazing up at the sky.'

'So,' said Harry as the filming continued. 'Who'd like to tell me how that walk here made them feel?'

'It's like there's this big black blanket over the earth – it's not infinite at all. This is all there is,' said one sci-fi fan.

'That's certainly how some early travellers might have felt,' replied Ewan. 'And we writers of historical fiction might use that notion. How could a prehistoric man ever comprehend infinity?'

'Well my prehistoric boyfriend can't comprehend my need for infinite handbags,' said Tegan getting a laugh from her followers. 'So I guess this would definitely be beyond him.'

Chloe watched as the actors and extras chatted between scenes. She felt a warm tingle of admiration for the villagers who were taking everything in their stride. No one would have been able to separate the professionals from the residents if they didn't know the famous faces. Chloe looked up at the sky which was definitely lightening in a rather beautiful way and she decided it made her feel that they were all in this together. They were a team.

'You'll like this next piece, Maggie,' she heard Riley saying. She looked over at the director who was accepting a cup of coffee from one of his assistants.

'It was inspired by you,' he continued giving her a wink then asking everyone to get into position.

'That would have made her day,' whispered Chloe to Kareem. 'We'll be hearing about it forever more. By the way, how is she still on set?'

'She begged me last night,' replied Kareem. 'Apparently she's hired anyone coming back from uni for the holidays to take shifts at the pub. Honestly, after yesterday I didn't have the energy to say no.'

'It takes a lot to say no to Maggie.' Chloe shrugged.

The first slither of light started to appear on the horizon and the cameras took up position to capture it. Riley stood in front of the extras.

'Okay guys, so in this scene the authors are going to be asking you to describe the colours that you see and I'd like this to look as fun and lively as possible. The featured artists have lines to deliver but if any of you extras think of a description, I'd like you to raise your hand and we'll zoom in on you while you say it. You might just get a close-up in the show.

The extras shuffled excitedly and Maggie sat upright holding her head high so that Riley would spot her.

'And if you do get that close-up, you'll have Maggie to thank,' said the director. 'I was very much inspired to do this by her impro-vi-sation skills.'

Maggie nodded her acknowledgment of his compliment and smiled beatifically at the other extras who were now staring at her.

'Okay, let's get going,' said Riley.

Tegan stood alongside the attendees of the workshop as each of them picked up a notepad and paper.

'Let's watch the colours of the morning sky unfurl before our eyes and try to describe them without using any expression that we've ever heard before,' she said.

A silence fell over the group and the crew as everyone watched the sky turn from the indigo of the night through the pinks and lilacs dappling the dawn clouds until the winter sun itself rose and sat above the horizon like ...

'The golden yolk of an egg – sunny side up,' called out one scripted extra on cue.

Chloe was completely engrossed in the scene and grimaced thinking this looked nothing like a runny, wobbly yolk.

'If you were writing something very folksy like *Forrest Gump*, that might be quite a nice cheery description,' said Tegan. 'I can't imagine it appearing in a romance.'

The workshop attendees laughed and a sci-fi fan put his hand up to speak.

'It was like the Jupiter 2 approaching from space with it's titanium hull catching the moonlight to warn us all of the apocalypse coming,' he said. 'Then as it approaches the earth getting closer and bigger, the lights from the hull trick us all into thinking the sun is rising but it's not. Those beams are the scorching flames of rocket flares and they'll rip up the earth in less than a minute.'

'Wow,' said Dominic. 'I doubt Tegan could put that in a romance either but I love that the light isn't getting brighter, it's getting closer and the idea of us thinking it's the sun and welcoming it but really it's something far more ominous.'

All four actors gave the two speakers a round of applause and next moved onto colour descriptions asking everyone to call out ideas for the oranges, lilacs, greens and blues that were gracing the sky right now.

'It's a bit like caramelised peaches,' murmured one of the residents slightly wary of speaking up. 'You know, when they go all soft and warm.'

'I love that,' replied Tegan getting a shy smile from the extra. 'Any other thoughts?'

'Like a tie-dyed shirt,' called out another brave soul.

'Gold like the heraldic flag soon to be raised as the army heads into battle,' said one of the scripted artists from the group of Ewan's fans. 'With telltale smears of vermillion foretelling the future to come.'

'You see how the description of each colour tells you the genre too,' said Harry. 'So we're gonna have a mash-up now. We're all going to describe a shade of sky but Tegan's fans will describe it from a sci-fi perspective, Ewan's as if they were in a crime book, mine as if they were romance and Dom's as if they were appearing in an historical fiction novel. Everyone okay with that?'

Harry waited for the extras to follow the script and start shuffling around but no one moved. Even the crew were transfixed on the horizon behind him. He turned to see the dawn sky now in it's full splendour as the rising sun turned the entire sky a fiery tangerine and highlighted the foaming tops of waves as if the sea could bring those flames to the shore. A light breeze blew the remaining darkness away and seagulls called out to each other as if saying it was time they began their day. The beauty stopped everyone in their tracks for a moment as the entire cast and crew simply watched the dawn. Eventually Riley clapped his hands together.

'That was stunning,' he said, 'but shall we get back to work now?'

Harry did his line again inviting the extras to describe the scene from a different perspective.

'I'll start us off,' said one of the extras. 'The sky was as blue as the forget-me-not she gave him at the station as he left.'

'Hmm, bit clichéd,' jibed a romance fan. 'How about – it was as red as Captain Kirk's sweater.'

The sci-fi fans laughed out loud.

'His sweater was mustard I'm afraid,' shouted someone from the sci-fi fans. 'Unless you're referring to one of the later films?'

The romance fan shrugged good-naturedly and a fan of Dominic's crime novels stood up.

'The sky was grey like the smoky quartz of the ancient wizard.'

He got a whoop of appreciation for that and even Ewan shook his hand. Then one of the extras from the village raised his hand. He was representing the historical fiction team and was obviously going to try some improvisation as requested. Riley nodded for him to continue.

'Well romance could be historical romance couldn't it,' said the man. 'So why not – the sky was a steely grey like the brave knight's mighty weapon.'

There was an explosion of laughter from the romance fans which spread throughout the cast and then into the crew. The poor guy who'd spoken sat down still completely oblivious to what he'd said.

'Well,' said Tegan wiping tears from her eyes. 'I don't think I'll be using that in one of my novels, as much as I'd really like to.'

The scene finished shortly afterwards and the teams made their way back to the village still talking about that final description.

'It's such a shame we don't have an outtakes programme,' said Kareem as he and Chloe walked back to the pub. 'That was a classic.'

'Yes I think he'll be dining out for a while on that one,' said Chloe.

Maggie was walking quietly beside them.

'I was surprised that you didn't say anything,' continued Kareem. 'The improvisation was your idea after all.'

The landlady smiled in an uncharacteristically meek way.

'Oh that wasn't proper improvisation, what he did,' she replied before sighing softly. 'Besides, my heart wasn't really in it.'

'What's the matter?' asked Chloe concerned having never seen Maggie look so sad.

'I just looked up at that sky and thought, as blue as my Nick's eyes, as green as his favourite boxer shorts, the red and blue clouds like when I put his jeans in with some designer T-shirt and it all ran. But that's all over now and like a fledgling seagull, he's flown the nest.'

Chloe linked arms with Maggie and pulled her close.

'I'm sure he'll be home from his travels soon,' she said, adding in a jokey tone, 'though hopefully not until I have my flat back.'

'You're probably right,' replied Maggie straightening up and putting on a fake smile. 'Although if I were you I'd be looking for somewhere else to live. I can't see his nibs looking to move out of Serenity any time soon.'

She nudged Chloe to look to the left where the star of the show was now standing at the edge of the bay taking off his long coat and placing it gently round the shoulders of her mother.

'I don't like to spread rumours,' continued Maggie. 'And if it were me he was interested in, the gossip wouldn't bother me but I thought you'd want to know that Dominic was seen over at the farmhouse last night.'

Chapter Eleven

Now on the fourth day of the shoot, the villagers seemed to be taking everything in their stride. As Chloe watched the people she'd come to know as butchers, bakers and teachers, arrive in costume, on time ready to walk on to set, she was delighted that they seemed to have settled in quickly. They were doing a good job and enjoying themselves at the same time. They looked and acted like professionals; perhaps this could one day be another string to Serenity's bow – extras on site. The fact that both Kareem and Riley were no longer giving the villagers extra coaching before each scene was a good sign. Riley simply ordered everyone to their places and then asked for the set to be cleared; they had a run through of the action to be shot and then it was time for the real thing. Riley shouted, 'Action,' and the day began.

Today they were filming the village fayre part of the festival where stallholders would be selling various books and souvenirs as well as food and drink to the visitors. The extras walked under the book canopy and along the high street festooned with bunting. They were still dressed in the style of one of the authors and so throughout the crowd Chloe could see that the villagers had also started to take on some characteristics of the authors they were supposed to admire. Charlie, who used to run the tourist information desk before Chloe arrived, was one of the crime fans and was wearing a fake moustache and a monocle like his hero Poirot. Mrs Robertson, who normally worked as a freelance bookkeeper was sitting on the steps of the deep crimson gypsy caravan that stood on the front; she wore a headscarf and hooped gold earrings as she gazed into a crystal ball.

Chloe could picture the scene when this episode aired. They would hold a big screening of it where the whole village could watch it together; probably in the village hall or the cricket pavilion and they'd spend more time trying to spot each other than following the story. She really hoped that every single person got at least some air time after the editing but there was absolutely no way to guarantee that. Chloe continued to watch as the crowd of villagers strode into the fayre and pretended to engage with the exhibitors. Along the promenade and on the beach, stallholders sold all the food and drink anyone would expect to find at a fete and some were more specific to the festival like books and writing materials, sci-fi memorabilia and psychic paraphernalia. It all looked perfect and Riley checked it confirming that, yes, he was happy with it.

Onto the next scene; Tegan Wavertree had been getting tipsy with some of her fans and she staggered out of the cocktail tent with a few other women clutching their high heels in their hands and propping each other up. Chloe watched as Tegan swayed from one tent to the other ridiculing the contents.

'Dummies Guide To Detective Work?' slurred Tegan. 'Well good old Dominic certainly wrote that one – the dummy part anyway.'

'Cocktails to match your star sign? Don't mind if I do – I'm a Gemini which means I need two of them,' she continued, picking up two plastic cocktail glasses from the stallholder and downing the drinks in quick succession. Her entourage did the same then tossed the empty glasses over their shoulders before tottering on.

Next the romance writer came face to face with Lucinda who was strolling peacefully through the festival chatting with her fans. Tegan wobbled a bit in front of her then prodded her in the chest with a finely manicured pink fingernail.

'How on earth did you get nominated for a *non*-fiction prize? It's all fiction – just look at it.'

She swerved round flailing her arms at the stalls. 'Star signs, crystal ball reading – next you'll be telling me you can interpret my dreams.'

'I could probably try,' replied Lucinda gently holding Tegan by the elbow to keep her upright.

'Well interpret *thiszz*,' slurred Tegan. 'I was on a big stage getting a fabulous award while a sad woman who looked like a hobo sat crying in the audience. And we had a huge magnum of champagne which exploded and showered everyone in bubbly.'

Tegan was throwing herself into this insult, rubbing her eyes when she talked about the crying and flinging her arms out wide when she mentioned the stage and throwing her head back to look up into the air for the champagne. It was this last move that finally toppled her over and she fell flat on her back in the middle of the field. Rather than panic, Tegan's fans burst out laughing and all plonked down beside her and lay on the grass like a hen party at the end of an exhausting night.

'And cut,' shouted Riley. So far the shoot was going according to plan. Chloe crossed her fingers and prayed silently for the rest of the day to go as smoothly but she knew there was a major risk to proceedings just up ahead. The next scene involved Dominic mingling with the locals and buying some produce from the stallholders – that in itself wasn't the problem. The danger zone lay in the part where he had to buy ale from Maggie and she had to stay in character rather than quiz him about what he seemed to be up to. Chloe kept every finger crossed as the actors took their places again and Riley moved the cameras to track Dominic's approach.

The lead character walked up to Maggie, Agatha the Labrador trotting alongside him sniffing the air which must now be filled with so many tempting smells. Dominic pretended to exchange pleasantries with Maggie then smiled and began to walk away with a bottle of ale; suddenly the landlady put her hand on his arm – Chloe gasped dreading what would happen next. Maggie bent down to give the dog a biscuit and stroke her ears. It wasn't in the script but Dominic – and Agatha for that matter – took it all in their stride. Chloe could have murdered the landlady but Riley let the cameras roll so Chloe exhaled. She only realised she'd been holding her breath for the whole scene as she near exploded now. She looked skyward and mouthed a silent little thank you.

'Let me see, let me see.' Maggie pushed her way into the tent as the crew moved the cameras ready for the final scene.

'You're not supposed to be in this tent and you weren't supposed to improvise in this scene,' said Chloe as Maggie elbowed past the director and producer.

'No you weren't but it's okay, it was very natural and you looked great,' said Riley generously. 'But you have to promise not to do it again – ever.'

Maggie curtsied to the director – which Chloe thought didn't look like either an agreement or an apology – then watched herself and the famous actor on the playback.

'I do look natural don't I?' Maggie said. 'Now that's how you do proper impro-vis-ation. And if the camera does add ten pounds then I must be very skinny in real life – can I have a copy of it?'

Chloe tried staring daggers but Maggie was steadfastly refusing to look in her direction.

'We don't normally do that,' said Kareem, 'but it would be a bit stupid not to keep a landlady happy wouldn't it? I'll try to get you a still at the end of the shoot.'

Chloe then firmly took hold of the landlady by the arm and marched a floating Maggie out of the tent and sent her on her way. As she watched her go, she noticed Dominic and Agatha still having selfies taken with some of the villagers. She wasn't sure what to think about this guy; she'd initially thought him a real diva, and let's face it, it was rather bold to ask someone to give up their apartment – she wouldn't have dared. But he was well known and he evidently lived away from home most of the time so perhaps he really did just want to be part of the hubbub while he was here. He'd been very polite to the landlady and was being simply charming to her mother and Chloe hoped that was at the root of the rumour Maggie had heard. He was a famous actor and maybe everyone thought he was up to no good wherever he went because here he was simply keeping the villagers happy during his break – it might be exciting for the villagers but to him it was a job. How many other people would be happy to give up their free time talking to strangers?

'Is it all going to plan?'

Chloe turned to see Roisin and her mother arriving on the promenade.

'Yes – fingers crossed. What have you two been up to?' asked Chloe.

'We've had a quite intense yoga session this morning so thought we'd have a walk,' said her mother, Theresa. 'I have to say I feel ten feet tall now. My spine has never felt so ... liberated.'

Chloe looked at her mum and did think she looked enormously well, even in such a short space of time. Theresa was walking taller and certainly seemed less anxious about life. Chloe told her mum this.

'Thank you,' she replied. 'I honestly believe that just making the decision to do something new has helped. Never in a million years did I think I'd ever appear in a TV show and besides all of that – this woman is an absolute miracle worker.'

Roisin smiled in response. 'What scene is next?' she asked.

'It's the final one for today and involves Dominic overhearing Poppy and Portia from the bookshop,' replied Chloe. 'They have a meeting to think of ways to unseat Jeremy from the festival of writing.'

'Why would they want to do that when they own a bookshop?'

'I'm allowed to say that in the plot there's another writer from the area who's very famous but Jeremy never shortlists them for an award. Jeremy wants to keep the festival in honour of his ancestor so he can keep earning royalties from the books he wrote through his publishing company.'

They all smiled. It was a typical *Montgomery Mysteries* plotline; villagers up in arms over something completely irrelevant to the whole world outside. It was complete escapism.

'He's so patient isn't he?' Theresa was watching Dominic as he continued to pose for everyone who asked him.

Chloe looked over at Theresa and a wave of concern ran through her brain as she watched her mother smiling at the actor. Maybe Dominic's nice guy act was fooling her mother. Maybe Theresa's revitalisation wasn't entirely due to yoga after all. Chloe noticed Roisin raising her eyebrows at the scene so guessed she was thinking exactly the same and knew she had to find time to ask her friend about the supposed farmhouse visits. At that moment, Dominic turned and spotted them; he waved and then apologised to the crowd saying he had to go. He approached Theresa with his arms outstretched, hugging her and kissing her on both cheeks as if they'd been friends for years.

'Have you come to watch more of the filming?' he asked.

'Oh I think the next scene is a closed set,' said Chloe hurriedly checking her notes.

'Oh yes, you're right and not even I can get guests in, not even *very special* ones, but you could walk me there,' said Dominic and Chloe could have sworn that her mum blushed at the word "special". The actor held out his arm and Theresa linked in as if she were on the set of a period drama.

'If I weren't being totally professional, I think I'd have gagged at all that schmaltz,' said Roisin quietly as they followed slowly behind the couple.

'Me too,' whispered Chloe. 'It's not real is it? She's just playing up to him isn't she? Please Roisin – tell me my mother hasn't been talking about Dominic? I've heard a rumour that he visits the farmhouse.'

'I've never seen him there Chlo, but if your mum wanted to talk about him, I'd have to respect her confidentiality,' Roisin said. 'However, I don't think you have to worry but this is her time to confide safely. I have to let her release any stresses she has.'

'Sorry, I know you do.' Chloe sighed. 'But I'd appreciate a signal of some sort if and when you can.'

Roisin nodded and squeezed her hand.

'Right now she's just really getting into all the exercise,' said Roisin. 'I know she's done yoga before and is pretty flexible but I think she's surprised herself by how much she loves being outdoors.'

'I can see that. She's glowing. I honestly don't think I've seen her look as happy for a very long time,' said Chloe.

'Which is more than you can say for good old Tegan.'

Roisin pointed towards the actress who having finished her scene stood hands on hips glaring at Dominic and Theresa who had stopped just outside the set. She called out for him but he just tipped his hat. Then he kissed Chloe's mum on the hand and walked towards Tegan who very firmly took hold of his arm and dragged him away.

'Oops,' said Roisin. 'Dominic's in trouble for flirting. Wasn't there a rumour that he's actually seeing the actress who plays Tegan?'

'I think there are millions of rumours about him – but Tegan didn't look happy did she?' Chloe laughed, relieved that someone else would be trying to break up her mum and the lead actor. They reached Theresa who had a mischievous smile on her face.

'I tell you something,' said Theresa, 'I bet Tegan isn't the victim because with that look she's just given me, she's the one holding all the daggers around here.'

Chapter Twelve

The next scene went smoothly and the team managed to capture the majority of the daylight action shots in the first take.

'Well done team,' Riley shouted to everyone as they finished. 'That's a good morning's work. Now let's get out of this freezing cold shall we?'

The team cheered and laughed. The temperature had really dropped since the festival scene. The north east thermals might create the most stunning sky and cloud formations but sometimes you could barely see them as your eyes were watering so much from the accompanying biting cold. What was the saying? Ah yes, "The north wind doth blow and we shall have snow".

Chloe was used to it by now but the members of the crew whose job it was to stand around beside equipment looked extremely pleased to be taking a break and were soon hugging mugs of hot drinks as if they'd found a new best buddy. Kareem brought Chloe a cup and as they sipped he told her that he probably didn't need her for the rest of the day.

'I can't foresee any issues with what we have left today,' he said. 'It's going to be a long slow afternoon as we need to get all the slow-mo shots like that deadly drop of poison falling perfectly into the tea. I'm sure that you have things you'd like to be getting on with so close to Christmas day.'

Chloe was mightily relieved to be excused from the afternoon's shoot. Viewers had no idea just how much time and painstaking detail was put into the simplest of shots. They'd see one single droplet falling from a phial into some herbal tea and rippling out. It would be a couple of seconds on screen at the very most but getting that single drop and the perfect ripples was quite often hours of work and it was so dull. She didn't need to hear the offer twice.

'If you're absolutely sure,' replied Chloe quickly grabbing her jacket from the back of the chair. 'I haven't even started Christmas shopping and I could do with going into town. It might be on the same date every year but I never seem ready for it.'

'I know that feeling.' Kareem smiled, waving her off.

Chloe left the director's tent and on the way back to the pub called Roisin.

'I don't suppose you fancy coming into town with me do you?' she asked. 'I could really do with some help in finding Andy a pressie and we could do the Christmas markets too, maybe get a glass of mulled wine while we're out?'

'Sounds good but you'll have to help me find something for Lloyd,' replied Roisin. 'He's leading the guests in a fitness and nutrition session all afternoon and won't notice I'm missing so it's perfect timing.'

They agreed to meet at the pub, get a taxi to the station and then a train into town. Cheered by the thought of an afternoon off with her best friend, Chloe skipped the rest of the way to the pub and took the stairs two at a time up to her room. She changed into smart black jeans, her favourite ankle boots and a deep red wool jacket that showed off her dark wavy hair to best effect. She looked at herself in the mirror and nodded, thinking she almost looked like one of those women in a Christmas movie – the type who absolutely adore gift buying and always get it just right. Maybe it was a sign that she'd find some inspiration for Andy after all. With a little lipstick and a spray of perfume, Chloe was in the well and truly mood for some retail therapy.

Back in the bar, the juke box was on full volume and Maggie was taking advantage of the fact that the crew were still out working. As she swept the floor, she belted out the chorus of "Rockin Around the Christmas Tree" using the broom as her microphone and making up some of her own lyrics when it came to the verses. Chloe tapped her toe along to the tune despite Maggie's singing and poured herself a cup of coffee while she waited for Roisin. She was desperate to ask Maggie if she'd heard any more about the Christmas present that Andy was buying for her but it would be wrong. Maggie couldn't keep secrets so it wasn't fair on her boyfriend if he really wanted to surprise her. And yet Chloe just couldn't stop herself.

'You know when you said *big*,' she said as the song – and the landlady, finished.

Maggie nodded and obviously guessing what Chloe was asking, held her hands out wide like a fisherman with a prize catch. Chloe nodded her understanding. So it meant big as in large not as in expensive then.

'I think it's going to be huge,' continued the landlady. 'He's asked if he can hide it in my garage. And you know me, I wouldn't betray a confidence but he did say it's something that'll help you spend more time together.'

Chloe's heart sank a little. It seemed as if her guesses were on the right track. She opened her mouth to ask another question but Maggie held her palm out.

'I've said enough,' she said sternly. 'There will be no further clues from these lips.'

Maggie left to put the broom away and then started laying out the tables for lunches. Chloe sat gazing into her coffee thinking about the gift enabling them to spend more time together and being so huge it needed a garage to hide it. She was sure she'd guessed correctly – what else could it be?

'You look as if Santa has already told you he isn't going to leave you anything under the tree,' said Roisin.

'Just the opposite,' said Chloe not looking up. 'I'm worried about what he is going to leave. I don't suppose you know what Andy's getting me for Christmas? Maggie says it's ...'

Chloe looked up at her friend and stopped mid-sentence. Once again Roisin had surpassed herself in a sparkly Christmas jumper and on top of her wild red hair, a bobble hat with a huge snowball pom-pom.

'Sorry I don't,' replied Roisin. 'What do you think?' She pushed down the bobble on the hat making the whole thing start flashing with little hidden lights.

'Well I certainly won't lose you in the crowds,' laughed Chloe. 'Come on let's get going.'

The train into Newcastle city centre would take an hour and was filled with lively, boisterous groups going to enjoy the Christmas markets. With the number of novelty jumpers and hats on display, Chloe thought that Roisin was actually managing to blend in somewhere for once in her life.

'Any update on my mum?' asked Chloe.

'She still seems quite happy,' replied Roisin. 'A book she'd ordered arrived this morning so she took herself off to the quiet room. She's been completely absorbed in it all day.'

'What book is it?'

'I didn't ask but she seems mesmerised,' replied Roisin shrugging then pointing out of the window with a big smile on her face.

The train had pulled up at a station and a man dressed in a full Santa Claus suit was getting on to huge whoops of delight from the other passengers. The whole carriage, including Roisin, rushed up to him to take selfies.

'Do you have any idea what you're getting Lloyd?' asked Chloe as Roisin returned delighted with her photo.

Roisin shook her head and grimaced. 'I have absolutely no idea.'

Like Chloe and Andy, Roisin and Lloyd had met just over a year ago. He was a personal trainer who'd come up to help her out at the retreat but the chemistry was instant and he never left.

'You can't really get a guy who spends his whole life keeping fit a box of chocolates or a bottle of whiskey can you,' said Roisin. 'And he has all the fitness gear he could possibly want.'

'What about clothes? He'd look really good in one of those merino wool crew necks. That would really show off his muscles,' suggested Chloe.

'Not a bad idea. And the sight of him in one would make my Christmas morning at the very least.' Roisin smiled.

They reached the city centre and stepped out into the beautiful Victorian architecture of the central station. Outside the streets were buzzing with life; although Chloe loved the peace and space of Serenity Bay, every now and then she yearned for a trip to the city with all its bustle and noise. In the main atrium of the station beneath a magnificent Christmas tree, a soloist in a group of carol singers began to sing that first haunting line of "Silent Night" so the girls waited and listened to the whole song before dropping some coins in their collection box and heading up through streets lit with bright lights draped from one side to the other. The city sky was now the deepest blue but cloudless and bright stars competed with the scenes below.

'It's going to be a cold night,' said Roisin looking up. 'We might even get snow.'

The very thought of snow at Christmas gave Chloe goosebumps. This little trip was turning out to be exactly what she needed to get into the spirit of things. She linked arms with Roisin, humming the only line she knew of "White Christmas" and continued up to the market.

They soon reached Grey's Monument; this hundred foot statue stood at the centre of the city at the top of a magnificent Georgian terrace and at this time of year it was surrounded by Christmas stalls. It seemed as if every nation was represented here – lebkuchen biscuits from Germany were sold next to nougat from France, cheeses from Holland and wooden toys from Sweden. The aroma of roast chestnuts on the little cart mixed with a cornucopia of smells from other stalls – mulled wine, mince pies and a hundred home-made fudge flavours mingled together in a sugar fusion that was at first glorious and then a moment later was a sensory overload.

'Where first?' asked Chloe. 'We have to promise ourselves not to be distracted by mulled wine until we've actually bought some gifts.'

'Definitely, or our men will be gift-less on the big day.' Roisin laughed. 'Look, there's a stall over there with bespoke men's jewellery. Shall we try that?'

They battled through the crowds to the stall and took a look at the items for sale. It was all beautifully made and there were some very interesting pieces including rings, cufflinks and armlets for men. Chloe picked up a plaited leather bracelet with a silver clasp. The stallholder told her it was handmade and that everything could be personalised. Chloe nodded and then put the bracelet down – it was very smart but she wasn't at all sure that Andy would wear anything like this.

'Let's go and look at those jumpers I mentioned,' she said turning to Roisin. 'I honestly don't know where to start for Andy.'

They left the market stalls behind and headed towards the city's biggest department store. It was famous for its Christmas window display and as they approached it, there were crowds of parents with children peering at the animated scenes with expressions of delight shining from their little faces. This year the store had chosen *Aladdin* as the theme and a magic carpet swooped from one side of the store, pulled on invisible wires through each of the windows across to the other. Chloe smiled on seeing it. *Aladdin* had always been one of her favourite stories as a child and she remembered longing for a magic carpet as a Christmas present.

'If one of those were for sale,' she said pointing to the carpet with its rich Persian pattern. 'Then I would definitely snap it up. Imagine floating above the sea waving down at all the boats.'

'And Andy in his kayak,' said Roisin.

Chloe pictured him bobbing on the ocean looking up at her. In her imagination he was dragging another kayak alongside him, but it was empty and he looked alone and very sad. For a moment she felt quite guilty about wanting the flying carpet instead. They walked from the cold evening air of the street into the sudden heat of the store and looked around.

'Knitwear,' declared Roisin pointing up at a sign and marching in the direction indicated. Chloe followed the pom-pom through the shoppers until they'd reached menswear. This section was much quieter than the rest of the store but it was still very warm so Roisin pulled her hat off and stuffed it in her pocket. The merino wool sweaters were folded neatly on a central island, the colours like the foil wrappers in a chocolate box – deep gold, forest green, sapphire blue and ruby red.

'Oh they're beautiful,' said Roisin picking up one and holding it next to her cheek. 'And feel this, it's so soft.'

Chloe picked one up and stroked the luxurious softness.

'I can certainly imagine Lloyd's magnificent muscles doing justice to one of these,' said Roisin. 'I might never want him to take it off.'

She surprised Chloe by not opting for the brightest colour on the shelf, instead choosing the blue which Chloe knew would really suit Lloyd.

'The green would work on Andy,' said Roisin. Chloe knew it would but her gorgeous boyfriend lived in his favourite fleece and jeans so there was a very good chance that a smart sweater might simply lie unworn at the back of the wardrobe. However, she had no other ideas and at least it would be something to unwrap. Right now that would be a hundred per cent improvement on her Christmas shopping efforts so Chloe picked up a green sweater, reasoning that she could bring it back if she actually ever thought of something better. They paid for the sweaters and took the escalator upstairs to womenswear having decided that they should treat themselves to something to wear on Christmas Day as they were in town. When the escalator reached the top, Roisin suddenly grabbed Chloe and pulled her behind a mannequin.

'What are we doing here?' asked Chloe cowering behind a rather gorgeous jumpsuit.

'It's Andy,' whispered Roisin. 'He's over there – did you know he was in town?'

Chloe's eyes widened but she shook her head. She had no idea he was coming into town today. She knew he was going to be busy but he hadn't said any more when they spoke this morning and she hadn't asked. Chloe peered under the mannequin's arm and there indeed was her boyfriend at the cash desk of the lingerie department. Roisin dragged her back into hiding, giggling.

'It's like we're top secret spies.' Roisin laughed.

A few minutes later, when Roisin had recovered from her bout of giggles, she took a peek and declared the coast clear.

'Well I don't think he'll be wearing that sweater much on Christmas Day.' She gave Chloe a nudge. 'Not if he's buying you some gorgeous lingerie. Who'd have thought it the naughty boy.'

Chloe gave a weak smile in return. Unfortunately she'd had time to see exactly what Andy was buying and it was no laughing matter. It most certainly wasn't gorgeous lingerie. Chloe sighed quietly, her shoulders slumped. Christmas Day was just getting better and better – waking up to a kayak and a pair of novelty, brushed cotton pyjamas.

Chapter Thirteen

Chloe rubbed her eyes, switched off the alarm by her bed and lay there exhausted. She'd had yet another sleepless night thinking about those awful pyjamas. She couldn't imagine Andy buying her anything like that but she hadn't been mistaken. Even from the hidey-hole behind the mannequin she could clearly make out the bright pink nightwear with its novelty reindeer motive. She'd never, ever worn anything like that in front of her gorgeous boyfriend so why did he think she wanted to start now? Was he thinking about the day snuggled up on the sofa in front of old movies? Had he bought himself something similar as a joke? At least they'd be warm after the morning out at sea. Chloe sighed in despair. She knew Andy adored Christmas but at this rate, his version of the festive season would be her worst nightmare.

The scenes being shot today would create suspicion around every character. First of all they filmed Tegan getting up after her hangover and opening her bag to get a paracetamol. Inside the bag, the viewers would clearly see that the author had other prescription drugs in there. Then they went to Ewan's room and saw that he kept an arsenal of antique weapons. Jeremy was seen putting an eviction notice in an envelope and posting it through a letterbox and finally they shot Lucinda with some dried purple flowers that were clearly deadly nightshade. Despite remaining weary throughout the day, Chloe found herself smiling at the thought of all these scoundrels gathered together in one place.

At the end of the shoot she left the crew clearing up

and grabbed her bike from the rack outside the pub. Although each day seemed to be colder than the last, Chloe was wrapped up in the thick fleece and gloves she'd specifically bought for standing around at shoots and she felt extremely cosy. She lifted her face to the cool sea air, looking forward to the peace of the short journey. As she pushed the pedals harder, she started to feel completely invigorated and found herself soaring all the way to the retreat. By the time she arrived, Chloe felt ready for anything. She opened the gate to the house and knocked on the door before opening it and popping her head round.

'Yoo-hoo, only me,' she called out into the kitchen where Roisin was prepping for dinner. 'It's a lovely afternoon out there,' said Chloe, her skin tingling from the exercise and fresh air.

'I know.' Roisin wiped her hands dry on a cloth then flicked the kettle on. 'Lloyd has taken everyone out for a jog. You should have seen them as they left – all wrapped up like Rocky Balboa.'

'My mum went jogging?' Chloe was trying to reconcile the person that seemed to be staying here with her mother who only played tennis for the G&T afterwards, believed women should always glow rather than sweat and swore that jogging caused wrinkles with all that grimacing.

'Yep,' replied Roisin making two cups of coffee and handing one to Chloe. 'She emerged this morning and declared that she was going to start saying yes more often and that she would be trying everything and anything from now on. She didn't even flinch when Lloyd suggested the run.'

Chloe shook her head in disbelief and took a sip.

'I wonder if it's because of that book you said she bought,' she said. 'It could be some self-help book. There are some that just encourage you to say yes to anything aren't there?'

Roisin nodded. 'Most of them encourage you to try new things to see life from a different perspective but she might also have just come to that conclusion herself. She has been meditating and mindfulness encourages us to live for the moment and not worry about the future or what people think. I know Theresa has spent a lot of her life concerned about social conventions and fitting in so this could be a very positive fresh start, Chloe.'

Chloe nodded and hoped her friend was right, that her mother was discovering what she really wanted from life – Serenity Bay had that effect on people. Chloe also hoped that whatever her mother discovered, it still included her father.

'Oh, I very nearly gave Lloyd that jumper last night,' said Roisin. 'I'm just dying to see him in it. Do you think Andy's going to like his?' In one sentence Chloe was dragged from one of her problems to another. She shook her head.

'I don't know. I know he'll look good in it but I wish I knew what he really wanted. You're lucky – Lloyd is really into his fashion but Andy just isn't. I keep going through all the things men are usually bought – watches, jewellery, smellies, music, books, gadgets and gizmos – none of it inspires me. There's probably a sporty gadget out there that he'd like but I have no clue what it would be.'

'It's a tough one,' Roisin said. 'Sorry I don't have any ideas – why don't you just ask him?'

'It feels wrong. He hasn't asked me and seems to have no problem in thinking of something even if I'm dreading it. Asking him would be like saying that I don't know him well enough to know what would really delight him.'

'You do know. It's a day out on the sea with you.'

'I guess so.' Chloe sighed, thinking that the best gift she could give Andy would be an expression of complete and utter delight when he presented her with her very own kayak.

Half an hour later the retreat guests started to arrive back from their jog with Lloyd and the girls went outside to welcome them. He led them through a stretch and cool down in the courtyard then they went back to their rooms for hot showers. Chloe waved at her mother who stood out in the peaked cap she usually wore for tennis. Theresa jogged over and put in a few more stretches for good measure.

'I've never seen you jog before,' said Chloe as her mother did side stretches then touched her toes.

'You're going to see me do a lot more things I've never done before,' Theresa said. 'It's time for a new me.'

'Good job there Terri,' said Lloyd patting her on the back then heading inside with Roisin. 'I'll jot down some brands of running shoes you might want to look at.'

'Thanks coach,' replied Theresa.

'Terri? Coach?' asked Chloe frowning.

'Really darling, if you're going to question everything I say or do next, especially with that look on your face, you're going to get a very deep furrow here on your forehead.' Theresa pressed a finger between Chloe's eyes. 'It would be far better to relax and go with the flow like I am. Now, I really must have a shower.'

Chloe followed her mother to her room and sat on the bed while she took a shower and changed. Chloe took a quick look around the room but there was no sign of any inspirational reading lying around. Chloe didn't want her mother to think that Roisin reported back on what she was buying so decided to wait and coax it out of her gently. Her mother emerged from the bathroom wearing an oriental style kimono with her head wrapped in a towel.

'That's nice,' said Chloe nodding at the kimono. 'I don't think I've seen it before.'

'You haven't,' replied Theresa. 'I've been doing some internet shopping and I thought it seemed more like the new me than my usual housecoat.'

'It really suits you, Mum,' said Chloe and it did. Her mum had only been here a few days and already looked younger.

Theresa took off the towel and rubbed her hair then combed it through with a wide toothed comb. Chloe and her mother were both blessed with the same wavy chestnut hair although Theresa's was now softened with caramel highlights.

'Remember when you used to say we had movie-star hair?' said Chloe watching her mother. Theresa turned and smiled at her.

'We still do darling – although I'd be getting the mother of the bride parts now.'

Wondering whether that was a hint, Chloe quickly changed the subject.

'So, internet shopping eh?' she said trying to make it sound like small talk. 'That sounds sensible. Roisin and I went into town last night and it was lovely but quite crowded. Have you bought anything besides the kimono?'

Theresa stood up, opened the wardrobe and pulled out some brightly coloured outfits. The kaftans and flowing tunics were nothing like the clothes her mother would normally have worn but they looked exactly like outfits Roisin would choose.

'I'd like to look the part while I'm here,' said Theresa as

Chloe struggled to hide the bewilderment on her face. 'And besides, they are very comfortable after a yoga session.'

'O-kay,' said Chloe. 'Well I am pleased you're enjoying yourself here and you do look great. I found the place inspirational too.'

'It's not just the exercise and the fresh air,' continued Theresa enthusiastically. 'It's the mental space too – I've had a lot of to think and to read.'

'What have you been reading?' asked Chloe leaping at the invitation to ask but hoping not to sound too suspicious.

Theresa reached into her bedside table and pulled out a hardback clutching it close to her chest.

'Don't laugh at me,' she said, 'but this has been a revelation.'

Chloe expected to see the works of Susan Jeffers or Paulo Coelho being revealed so her jaw dropped when her mother held out the cover.

'A biography of Kylie Minogue?'

'Do not mock it until you've read just how much this woman has been through,' scolded Theresa. 'Until you realise just how many times she has reinvented herself.'

Chloe held back an exasperated sigh as it seemed that this obsession with the pop star was here to stay. Kylie was evidently guiding her mother through her midlife crisis.

'She was on her way out until "Spinning Around",' said Theresa, 'and I didn't realise what that song was actually about, do you?'

Chloe shook her head. She hadn't thought about the lyrics ever in her life – there really hadn't been any need to.

'You should really listen to them,' said her mother gazing upwards as if contemplating some great wisdom. '*I'm not the same*. It's about reinvention, forgetting the past and moving on, becoming who you want to be. Ever since I read those lyrics, they spoke to me and I just can't stop thinking about them. They're my new anthem.'

Chloe held back a bewildered sigh and sat quietly. There really wasn't anything she could say to that but could imagine her mother strutting along the beach belting out the chorus. She hadn't a clue how on earth she was going to explain any of this to her father.

'Kylie has battled several career troubles, relationship failures and cancer but you'd never know it. Every time someone knocks *her* down, she just gets back up and dusts herself off. Well actually she does more than that – she never waits for anyone to feel sorry for her, she just comes straight back looking fabulous so the critics are the ones who look stupid.'

'Has someone knocked you down, Mum?' asked Chloe wondering whether it was just the check-up she'd had that had triggered this crisis or whether it was something else.

Theresa mumbled something incomprehensible then put the book safely back and placed her hands on her lap.

'Don't you have to be somewhere?' she said in a way that told Chloe she was being asked to leave. 'I usually do some meditation around now.'

Chloe checked her watch; Maggie would be serving food soon and besides which, she wasn't sure how much further she'd get with her mother if she stayed. The situation seemed completely bizarre and she could imagine them laughing about it at some time in the future – but that time certainly hadn't arrived. Chloe had to support her mother through this and trust the Serenity magic would work.

'You're right, I do need to get going,' said Chloe. 'And I'm glad you've found something that inspires you. She sounds like a remarkable person.'

Theresa nodded her acknowledgement.

'I'll let you borrow it when I've finished,' she murmured.

Chloe thanked her, then stood up and together they walked down the stairs and into the kitchen interrupting Roisin and Lloyd who were laughing and dancing around to a song on the radio.

'We think we should add salsa to the programme,' said Roisin breathlessly, 'although we'll have to find a much better teacher than Lloyd.' Her boyfriend launched a full tickle attack on her at these words and Roisin exploded into laughter. Chloe couldn't help but laugh along with them – it was a very different scene to the surreal but sombre discussion in the bedroom.

'That sounds brilliant doesn't it, Mum? You and dad were thinking of taking dance classes weren't you?'

Theresa snorted. 'That was before he decided we were too old for that kind of thing. Well he might be, but I'm certainly not.'

She turned and walked out of the room, humming the chorus to her new theme tune.

'What was that all about?' asked Roisin.

'Your guess is as good as mine,' Chloe said. 'All I know is that I have to get my dad down here as soon as possible.'

Chapter Fourteen

'There she is.' Andy's voice called out over the hubbub of The Fiddler's Arms. The wide smiles on everyone's faces and the roars of laughter created an air of great frivolity and Chloe felt for a moment as if she'd walked into a party uninvited. Through the twinkle of Christmas lights reflecting on the tinsel, Andy strode up to her and wrapped his arms around her before turning and walking back into the centre of the room towards the production team.

'Your other half has just been telling us the forfeits we'll have to do if we don't wrap up this shoot on time.' Kareem laughed. He was sitting next to Riley and although the director was attempting a smile which matched the mood of the room, the expression in his eyes was not in the slightest bit light-hearted. Chloe caught his look and wondered what on earth had been going on.

'Forfeits? What have you been up to?' she asked Andy giving him a light-hearted prod which she hoped hid her mild anxiousness.

'Yep,' he replied with a big grin on his face. 'Just to make sure we have the village up and running for the Midwinter Festival, I've been suggesting that the crew be forced to do some forfeits if they overrun.'

'Such as?' said Chloe.

'I have to swim in the North Sea wearing novelty boxer shorts,' said Kareem. The producer actually seemed to be on the same page as Andy – enjoying the banter, unlike his colleague. 'And Riley has to sing "Good King Wenceslas" on the promenade in a Christmas jumper of the crew's choosing.'

'And it will definitely have flashing lights.' Andy laughed. Chloe shot a glance at Riley who certainly wasn't laughing.

Chloe shook her head as if joining in the camaraderie then, just to be sure Riley knew how she felt added with a very serious tone, 'Don't worry. It certainly won't come to that. This crew are top-notch and Serenity Bay will do everything in its power to make sure the guys are back at home with their families on time.'

She had managed to take the mood down a notch or two but the slight nod from the director told her she'd done the right thing. She led Andy to a table for two rather than join everyone else and sat down.

'So how come you're dishing out forfeits?' she asked.

'Just a bit of a joke,' Andy replied. 'The Midwinter committee have asked me to help out with a few things and as I know you, they thought I might be the person to chivvy things along if they look like overrunning.'

'Do they think we actually *want* to go over schedule? It's the very last thing any of us want,' exclaimed Chloe.

'I know – but letting the crew know that I'm keeping tabs can't do any harm.'

Chloe sighed to herself. It could do harm. It could say that they didn't trust the crew, that they weren't welcome or respected. It had already annoyed the director.

'I understand why you're doing it,' said Chloe reaching out and holding Andy's hand. 'It's just that the crew will already be under pressure and I wouldn't want them to think the village is trying to put them under even more. It sounds as if we can't wait to throw them out.'

'They know that's not the case. Look how much we've already rallied round with the extras,' Andy said. His voice had lost a little of its former joviality and he was sounding rather official now.

Maggie saved the moment by appearing with their usual drinks and a menu but Chloe couldn't focus on it so asked Maggie to surprise her. Andy added that he'd have the surprise too.

'Brussel sprouts with brandy butter and stilton it is then,' cackled Maggie as she left them.

Neither Chloe nor Andy could keep serious faces after that. They both laughed and Andy reached out to take Chloe's other hand, caressing them both gently with his thumbs. It was like getting a massage on a pressure point and relaxed her almost instantly.

'I think we're going to regret asking for the surprise,' he said smiling.

They squeezed each other's hands to say all was well and then picked up their drinks.

'So what else are you helping out with?' asked Chloe after taking a sip of wine.

'Mainly the charity boxes. You know – the shoe boxes that go to the children's hospital over in Northwick. I'm going to be promoting them, collecting them and gift wrapping any that aren't already wrapped then I'll be driving the van down to the hospital with my elf helpers and distributing them – in the full Santa Claus suit of course.'

Chloe knew this was something the village did every year and last year Charlie had played the role of Santa. It usually went to a much older man with a natural beard of his own but she could imagine Andy's delight when he'd been asked to do it.

'I cannot imagine anyone more suited to the role – or the suit,' she replied clinking glasses. 'I tell you what, why don't I ask the actors if they'll do autographed photos for you to hand out too? They may not mean anything to the children but perhaps the parents might appreciate them.'

'That would be brilliant,' Andy said with a big smile on his face.

Maggie appeared with the surprise meal and it looked incredible.

'As you're my two favourite people, I decided not to feed you the scraps after all,' she said. 'This is a trial recipe. I'm thinking of serving it for the wrap-up meal – let me know what you think.'

To cater for the widest possible dietary requirements, Maggie had created the most delicious smelling vegetarian wellington. Chloe sliced through the golden flaky pastry savouring the mushrooms, chestnuts, rosemary and thyme; it tasted both naughty and healthy at the same time.

'It's absolutely fabulous,' said Andy pausing between shovelfuls and leaving no doubt on how he felt about the food.

Maggie looked extremely happy to see each mouthful being so thoroughly enjoyed. She took out a small notebook from her apron pocket and scribbled a big tick before leaving them to it. They ate quietly, apart from the appreciative murmurs and across the pub, as the crew were served their meals, the previously buoyant atmosphere calmed. She stole a glance across at Riley. Chloe could see that the food seemed to have put him in a better mood too as he ate while laughing and joking with Kareem between mouthfuls.

'Do you fancy getting away somewhere next year?' asked Chloe wanting to steer the conversation away from anything related to Christmas. 'Just the two of us?'

'Well the business is always quiet in January so we could head for some sunshine,' Andy said. 'As much as I love the wildness of the sea in winter, I wouldn't say no to getting a bit of a tan.'

'And I wouldn't say no to you getting a bit of a tan either,' added Chloe. 'I'd even help you with the suntan lotion.'

She closed her eyes and leant across the table expecting a soft sultry kiss but instead got a quick peck which made her look up. Andy had turned sharply just as the noise level across the whole room started to rise. Dominic and Tegan had walked in with Agatha and her handler. Andy bolted from his seat and went to pet the dog.

'You don't mind if we join you all do you?' Dominic asked Chloe. It was obviously a rhetorical question as he pulled up some chairs and sat down with his entourage without waiting for an answer.

Chloe looked across at Maggie who was discreetly checking her hair and refreshing her lipstick in the mirror behind the bar before she approached the table to take their orders. Chloe turned to say something to Andy but he was still engrossed. It was as if the incomers were somehow magnetic as so many of the room were now gathered around them. Chloe guessed that's what celebrity meant. She decided to give the actors a little space so picked up her glass and walked over to the bar. When Maggie came back, her cheeks blushing with whatever compliment Dominic had bestowed upon her, Chloe smiled.

'You see him every day on set,' she said to the landlady. 'How come he still has this effect on you?'

Maggie leant over with her elbows on the bar and her chin cupped in her hands. She gazed adoringly at the actor like a love-struck teenager.

'Out there he's just working,' she said. 'He has to be there and anyway, he's just the character he plays on the set. He doesn't have to come in here but he does and when he does, it's the star, the actor who's here. He knows who I am and he does say some wonderful things even though I know he probably says them to everyone. I can't help myself and you have to admit, he has presence.'

Chloe followed her gaze and looked across at the entourage. Dominic did have presence; he seemed to glow in the crowd but Chloe wondered whether that was because he was the star or did he become a star because he had that quality? She guessed she would never know.

'I see Andy is also very attracted to one of the ladies in the cast,' continued Maggie.

Chloe had noticed her boyfriend deep in conversation with Agatha's handler. He was sitting cross-legged on the floor letting the dog lie beside him. The two seemed extremely comfortable in each other's company.

'And how am I ever going to compete with that?' said Chloe. 'Big brown eyes, soft chocolate hair ...'

'Big floppy ears and a belly that always needs rubbing,' continued Maggie making Chloe almost choke on the sip of wine she'd just taken.

'You're right, I've no chance,' she replied.

Andy stood up and gave Agatha a kiss on the head before practically skipping his way to the bar.

'I'd like you to know that we witnessed your infidelity with a TV star and we will be telling the tabloids,' said Maggie.

'She's gorgeous isn't she?' said Andy. 'I had an idea and I thought I'd have a word with the handler.'

'What idea?' asked Chloe.

'Well it was kind of related to yours – you know about getting the stars to sign photos for the hospital? I was going to ask if we could get photos of Agatha with a paw print but the handler came up with an even better suggestion.'

Andy paused as if expecting a drum roll. He was obviously waiting for Chloe and Maggie to guess this great idea – they just shook their heads and signalled for him to continue.

'Agatha is going to do the rounds with me,' he exclaimed. 'She's also a trained therapy dog so is comfortable in hospitals. I can put those little antlers on her head and decorate her harness – she'll kind of look like Rudolph.'

He held his hands out wide as if the most amazing thing had happened and Chloe wondered where on earth the outdoor action man she'd fallen in love with had gone. He seemed to have vanished under a mountain of Christmas chintz.

'That sounds brilliant,' Maggie was saying. 'The kids will love it.'

'Won't they just? Right, I'm going to see what I can scrounge off the rest of the cast while they're here. Strike while the iron is hot – isn't that what they say?'

He made his way back into the throng and the women watched him mingling like a professional. Chloe finished her wine and ordered another.

'Aren't you working tomorrow?' asked Maggie as she poured it.

Chloe nodded. 'It's to help get through tonight. I'll have a big glass of water after this and deal with tomorrow in the morning.'

She took a large sip and looked down into the glass.

'You still haven't thought of anything for him have you?' asked Maggie. Chloe shook her head without looking up.

'Well you know when I couldn't think of anything to get my ex,' Maggie continued. 'I used to wear something a bit saucy and put a big bow on my forehead. I'd tell him that I was his present and distract him long enough to make him forget he didn't actually have a proper gift.'

'Is that the ex who left for the woman who bought him a Rolex one year?'

'I take your point,' replied Maggie.

They stood together in silence watching Andy as he went round each table introducing himself and explaining his project. He seemed to be getting nods, smiles and handshakes from everyone he spoke to. He was rosy-cheeked and flushed with success by the time he came back to the bar.

'I take it you got what you wanted?' asked Chloe.

'More than I'd hoped for,' Andy said. 'Tegan and Dominic are going to donate some big toys for the playroom, the catering team are going to make trays of mince pies for us to give out on the day and Riley's offered to get some stills from the shoot framed for the waiting rooms.'

He propped himself up on a bar stool and shouted for quiet across the bar.

'I'd just like to say thank you,' he said when the room hushed. 'Thank you from the absolute bottom of my heart. You have all been so generous and it will make such a difference to the kids and their parents.'

He raised his hands and applauded everyone as Maggie and Chloe stood to join in.

'But don't let this make you think you're getting away from the forfeits,' he added mischievously getting a knitted decoration thrown at him.

The mood of the room was high yet again and when someone started singing along to the juke box, everyone joined in until Riley stood and scraped his chair back. The effect was like opening the swing doors of a saloon and a gunslinger walking in – the place went quiet and turned to him.

'It's been a great evening,' he said. 'But we have work in the morning and I for one am not keen on those forfeits.'

Riley had the smile of a head teacher so one by one the room emptied as people took the hint and went back to their accommodation or headed upstairs to their room. Within a few moments, there were only three people left in the bar and Andy was still beaming.

'This really meant a lot to you didn't it?' said Chloe wrapping her arms around her gorgeous man. She should never have wondered where the old Andy had gone – that huge heart was still right there in front of her.

'Honestly Chlo, I really never expected all of that generosity – especially after the forfeits. It shows they took it in good spirits.' He kissed her lips softly. 'I really do think this is going to be the most perfect Christmas I have ever had.'

Chapter Fifteen

'Oh I thought you must have gone out before breakfast,' said Maggie. 'I tried your phone and calling up the stairs but there was no answer so I told him you'd already left – Andy that is, you've just missed him.'

Maggie was putting out fresh coffee on the buffet table and Chloe was grateful that her back was turned as she was sure the landlady would notice the exhausted look on her face.

'He popped in to see if I knew the schedule for today,' Maggie continued. 'He was still beaming from last night. He was quite overwhelmed wasn't he? It's going to be quite an occasion with all those donations from the stars. Then there's your first Christmas together and that perfect present he keeps going on about. He still won't tell me a thing though which is very frustrating, I mean to say, he knows I wouldn't say a thing to you. Have you thought of anything for him yet?'

Chloe sat down at a table and managed to ignore the question by immediately leafing through the pages she needed for the day and pretending to focus although, in truth, the words on the pages were all a blur.

'There's a murder being filmed today,' she said aloud trying desperately to change the subject.

Chloe hadn't just "missed" Andy, she'd heard his voice as she was walking down the stairs and had hidden in the broom cupboard until he'd left. She loved her boyfriend deeply but his enthusiasm for creating that absolute perfection was starting to cause her real anxiety.

The hot breakfasts were finished and the tables cleared

but Maggie popped into the kitchen and brought over a croissant for Chloe and coffees for each of them then plonked herself down. Maggie slipped off her shoes, sighed with relief and started rubbing her bright pink varnished toes in their beige pop socks.

'Talking of murder, I tell you these feet are killing me at the moment,' she continued oblivious to Chloe's grimace at the sight of feet alongside her pastry. 'And that can only mean one thing – there's trouble ahead.'

Chloe looked up half expecting a flash of thunder and lightning to tear across the room with those words – she'd spent far too long around the special effects people.

'The last time they felt this bad,' said Maggie, 'I found a wasp nest under the eaves outside one of the guest rooms. And the time before that, a mouse chomped through the pipes in the cellar. Never mind that dog, my feet should be starring in this show as the harbingers of doom. They always know what's coming.'

Chloe was tired from having spent another night worrying and didn't really have the time or energy for this. First of all she'd worried about her mother who seemed a great deal happier without her father in tow, then about her boyfriend who she was surely going to disappoint on Christmas Day and finally about the shoot that seemed to have had a couple of lucky escapes already. She hoped that being busy all day would keep her from fretting over things but as she sat there, Chloe realised she'd tuned out of Maggie's bizarre conversation and drifted back into her worries. She felt Maggie shaking her arm brusquely.

'Do you?' she was asking.

'Do I what?' asked Chloe.

'Do you think I should ask Riley if my feet could feature in the show somehow?'

Chloe buried her head in her hands and sighed. Then she opened her fingers to peer through them.

'Are you seriously asking me that question?' she said exasperated. Maggie shrugged. Chloe stood up, swigged a mouthful of coffee and then gathered up her papers and stuffed them in her bag. 'No, I don't think you should ask Riley. No, I don't think your feet should get a starring role and no, I haven't thought of anything for Andy. Now if you'll excuse me, I have work to get on with.'

Chloe turned to stride away but instead of the dramatic exit she planned, she bashed into the corner of the table as she left and it really stabbed into her thigh – she'd have a bruise there for sure.

'Ow,' she yelled rubbing her leg and sighing.

'I told you something would go wrong,' murmured Maggie slipping her feet back into her shoes and standing to clear away the cups.

Chloe reached the door without any further mishaps, but as she left heard the voice.

'These feet don't lie.'

It was going to be a big day and the key scene for the morning was the next murder. Each episode of this series usually served up at least three dead bodies which would have been quite horrific in any normal small town but for some reason the residents of anywhere Dominic visited chose to take it in their stride. Chloe had no preparation to do for this morning so arrived on set as they were ready to start.

'Is everything good to go?' she asked Kareem. She knew that Maggie's feet were not actually real harbingers of doom but was desperate not to tempt fate. She touched the back of a wooden chair just to be sure.

'Yep, all good,' replied Kareem holding the shoot notes. 'No changes needed so everything is per schedule today. First we have Poppy from the bookshop touring the stalls of the festival. She takes a cup of herbal tea that she's offered and later we find her lying dead by a rock pool.'

'Poisoned,' says Chloe nodding along and reading the scenes for today. 'They seem fairly straight forward and after Poppy is found, Dominic and Agatha come along to investigate.'

'Places please,' called Riley and everyone took up their spots for the first take. From the tent, Chloe watched Poppy make her way through all the stalls nodding at a couple of stall holders and taking an interest in what they were selling. She picked up a candle and bought it then walked on to a herbal remedies stall run by one of Lucinda's fans. There was no dialogue but Poppy and the stallholder made it look as if they were in conversation about a sore throat. The stallholder poured a drink from a thermos jug and handed Poppy a paper cup, Poppy paid her and walked away. Then she visited another stall trying on a hat and for a moment put her cup down while she looked at herself in the mirror. After a couple of takes, Riley declared it all good and ordered they move on.

In the next scene, a young woman screamed out and dragged her child, who was carrying a small fishing net and crying, away from the rocks. The villagers ran from their positions down to the rocks to see what had happened and within seconds, Dominic appeared, parting the crowds. Poppy was dead and the crowd gasped. The actress was lying across the rocks facing upwards and the make-up team had done a fabulous job creating her deathly pallor and blue lips. For her sake, Riley demanded that they do the shot in one take so everything was set up and double checked before Poppy was asked to lie down in a very shallow pool of sea water. One of the crew arranged her hair so that it fanned out across the rocks with seaweed intertwined like the oil painting of Ophelia and the cameras rolled. As soon as the director had the shot he was looking for, the production assistant wrapped the actress up in a big blanket and handed her a hot drink. She would be needed later to film some of her back story but for a day or two Poppy could now relax.

'Dom and Aggie please,' shouted Riley as the actor and his trusty chocolate Labrador moved into position.

Chloe felt her phone vibrate so walked out of the tent to check it – a text from Andy asking if she wanted to meet for lunch again. Chloe pictured his handsome smiling face last night, overwhelmed to get so much support from the crew. Then the scene in her head changed and she imagined him unveiling a kayak on Christmas day thinking she'd adore it while waiting to see what she'd bought him. In this scene, she was handing over a gift-wrapped box which Andy excitedly opened only to find it empty. Chloe shook the images away. Although she'd felt incredibly guilty for hiding on the staircase, she knew she simply couldn't face another session of her boyfriend's Christmas cheer until she had something to be cheerful about. Chloe sent a reply saying she was really sorry but she'd have to work through lunch and would check in later. She ended with a big heart emoji so at least the text didn't look the way she was actually feeling. On set everyone was ready so she put her phone back in her pocket.

'This is what I find annoying,' said a voice behind Chloe as she moved to go back into the tent. She turned to see the police script consultant, Kevin Campbell, with his nostrils flared looking slightly more than just annoyed.

'They hire me, an ex-detective, to try and get some of the procedures right and then go ahead and do this.' He waved his hand dismissively at the scene about to be shot. 'A bloody big slobbering dog all over an already precarious crime scene – it just wouldn't happen, ever.'

'I don't think anyone expects it to be completely accurate,' said Chloe, smiling and trying to appease him.

'It's not even vaguely accurate,' replied Kevin. 'What is the point of me even being here?'

Chloe left him muttering to himself and found Lizzie in the tent.

'Your police consultant doesn't seem very happy,' she said to the scriptwriter. 'Surely he knew what he was getting into when he signed up?'

'I think his ex-colleagues have been ribbing him,' whispered Lizzie in reply just as Riley called for quiet on set.

Dominic and Agatha walked onto the rock pools as the glorious Northumberland sky silhouetted them in a steely winter blue. Agatha wandered off and then barked at her fictional owner who came bounding across the rocks asking her what she'd found – it was the cup that had held the tea. Dominic pulled out some gloves and a plastic bag from his pocket as Chloe thought that Kevin would be at least happy with that little attention to detail. But then, Dominic let the dog sniff the cup before bagging it. Chloe had to stifle a giggle at what she heard in the background.

'Well that just takes the biscuit.'

After a couple more pieces where the local police force turned up and were extremely grateful for Dominic's find, the crew took a break for lunch. As she'd turned Andy down using work as the excuse, Chloe decided to use the time to follow up on some media leads back at her office.

The production company had been happy for her to tell local journalists that the village had been recruited to work as extras and yesterday she'd had a request through for photos of locals in their day job and in costume. She had some great shots of the butcher in his apron and then as a sci-fi character and of course she would have to feature Maggie – although the publican turned brewer wasn't much of a leap. As Chloe walked along the promenade to her office at the gift shop, she was surprised to see her mother waiting at the door holding a Tupperware box.

'Oh hello,' said Chloe. 'This is a nice surprise, is that for me?'

'Hello darling,' replied her mother fidgeting awkwardly and trying to cover the box. 'Err, no. I've brought Dominic a quiche and mixed grain salad. We're having lunch together.'

'In my flat?' asked Chloe feeling just a little put out but knowing that Dominic could ask whoever he wanted back to lunch.

'Yes, if that's okay with you,' said the deep voice of Dominic arriving on the scene and giving her mother a peck on both cheeks. 'Did you want to join us? Although the quiche looks so delicious, you'll have to forgive me if I keep it all to myself.'

On the one hand, she could keep an eye on these two. On the other hand, she couldn't stomach the idea of witnessing any more of these awful flirtations. Also on the other hand – and Chloe knew that meant she was now using three hands – her mother was glaring in such a way that told her very clearly that she wasn't really welcome. Chloe politely turned down the offer saying once again that she had paperwork to catch up on. Dominic and Theresa went giggling up the stairs leaving Chloe feeling very slightly nauseous. She dug out her phone and called her dad. Obviously he didn't answer so now he would find both a voicemail and text message begging him to get his backside over to Serenity as soon as he possibly could.

Sighing, Chloe sat down at her laptop and sent out the photos she'd been asked for. With each request she answered, she also asked the journalist if they'd feature the forthcoming Midwinter Festival which would launch the village into Christmas after the film crew had gone. Everyone hoped the shoot would attract visitors and of course the fabulous tree would be up by then so Serenity would finally feel magical rather than murderous. Chloe was just putting the final touches to a press release when out of the corner of her eye she spotted Andy, standing on the promenade, hands on hips, looking up at her flat. Her phone pinged to say she'd received a message and hoping it would be her dad, she took her eyes off Andy to read it. It was just a journalist with a quick query so she answered the question and then popped out to ask Andy what he was looking at. Too late – he was already storming off down the street. Puzzled, Chloe stood in the exact spot Andy had and looked up to her living room window. There, a table for two had been set up, overlooking the sea. Dominic was in full view, smiling and holding out his hand to someone across the table but his dining partner was hidden by the curtain, with only a smidgen of dark chestnut hair visible.

'Give me strength,' said Chloe. 'You surely didn't think that was me did you?'

Chapter Sixteen

Chloe was about to chase after her boyfriend but could see that he was marching away at top speed. She'd never catch up with him at that pace and besides which, there was really no point as they had to be back on set very soon. She felt exasperated. It was bad enough that her mother seemed to have disregarded her own relationship with her father but for her midlife crisis to unknowingly put her daughter's in jeopardy was quite another. Chloe was wondering whether she had enough time to go up to the flat and knock on the door when she heard the door clunking shut followed by laughter on her staircase. Dominic and her mother emerged from the flat with huge smiles on their faces.

'Good lunch?' asked Chloe looking pointedly at her mother. 'You seem to be enjoying yourselves.'

Theresa returned the glare then turned and directed a broad and very genuine smile up at Dominic.

'It was lovely thank you,' she replied while still looking at the actor. 'This man is fabulous company.'

'And your mum is an absolute hoot. I don't think I've laughed as much in ages,' added Dominic. 'She's the one who should be on stage.'

'I bet you say that to all the girls.' Theresa gave him a coquettish little push.

Chloe resisted shaking her head in complete dismay but that's exactly what she felt like doing. On the one hand her mother was looking better than she had in a long time and she was suddenly the life and soul of the lunch party. Perhaps it was only a little harmless flirtation between the two of them and who didn't need that once in a while? This shoot would be over soon and then her mother could go back to her normal life with a great story to tell her friends. On the other hand, what if her mum decided that she wanted more stories like this? What if she became star-struck and didn't want her old life back? It was all just speculation. Thank heavens for work to keep her distracted. Chloe suggested to Dominic that they'd better be going so they headed along the promenade and Theresa walked with them until they reached the set, then she said goodbye and continued on to the retreat.

'This is turning into one of my very favourite shoots,' said Dominic smiling at Chloe as he waved Theresa off. 'It's so much more relaxed when it isn't all work, work, work, isn't it?'

'Yes, relaxed,' murmured Chloe under her breath. 'That's exactly how I feel right now.'

Chloe found Kareem while Dominic took hold of Agatha and got into position for the next scene. He was about to have a very short conversation with Lucinda.

'As I'm sure you realise,' said Dominic when the cameras started rolling. 'The woman who died here drank a herbal remedy that featured in one of your books.'

'You're not suggesting that I had anything to do with her murder are you?' replied an outraged Lucinda with her palm pressed against her chest in a very melodramatic *Montgomery Mystery* way.

'Not at all, but what I am suggesting is that there could be a connection. I have heard that you are able to make contact with those who have passed over. If that's the case then perhaps we should try to contact Bart and Poppy to see if they can help us find out who did this to them.'

'I'm not sure.' Tears formed in Lucinda's eyes. 'Souls do

need time to adjust to what has happened to them and they may still be traumatised from their experience. Also, I personally could become possessed by their spirits and if they relive their moment of death it could be extremely draining for me.'

Dominic took hold of Lucinda's shoulders with his strong manly hands as if he were transferring some of his own steeliness to her.

'You have to be strong, Lucinda. I'll be right there with you every step of the way. Bart and Poppy need your help and the police have no leads – they need your help too, don't they Aggie?'

The dog barked and wagged her tail. Lucinda had red blood shot eyes and began to weep as she looked up at Dominic.

'I'll do it.' She nodded bravely through the tears now streaming down her cheeks. 'I'll hold a séance.'

'And cut,' shouted Riley. He checked the footage and declared it a take. It was time for all the main actors to move indoors for the séance scene so the whole crew got to work making that happen.

'I was really impressed by the tears,' said Chloe to Kareem. 'I assumed someone would come and put some droplets on her face.'

'Not everything in this show is fake you know.' Kareem laughed. 'We do occasionally offer viewers some reality.'

'Though just a smidgeon,' replied Chloe light-heartedly. 'I can't imagine our police consultant will be very happy with where the plot is going. We have a dog and a psychic solving the crimes now.'

'Even he knows it all just harmless fun,' Kareem said as they walked towards the set. Chloe wasn't so sure.

Inside the set, there was a commotion going on. The

main actors were sitting at a round table waiting to get started. On the table, a perfect circle of letters had been set up on a green felt cloth, to the right of the circle was a "YES" card and to the left a "NO" card. An upturned glass was in the centre. It looked like any séance setting in a TV show except that when Chloe looked, she could see that some of the letters had been removed and the circle just nudged closer together to try and hide the fact. She scanned the circle and saw that A and R were definitely missing.

'We're not going to spell out "Bart" with that board,' said Dominic.

'Which other letters are missing?' asked Chloe straining to see.

'Erm, it looks like D, U and F,' replied Harry. 'So we'll be okay if it's the ghost of Poppy we hear.'

Chloe mentally put the letters together and re-arranged them. She'd always loved anagrams and this one was hardly difficult.

'Fraud,' she spurted out startling everyone. 'The letters that have gone missing spell the word *fraud*.'

'Wow, you're right,' Dominic said. 'I don't remember this in the script – Riley, has there been a change?'

Riley and Kareem walked up and looked at the table.

'There most certainly hasn't.' Kareem sighed. 'What on earth is going on?'

'Can someone sort this out quickly,' shouted Riley. Looking up at the ceiling he added, 'And if we've got a poltergeist out there moving all these props, would you kindly stop?'

The set designers hurriedly pulled together some materials to make a new set of cards rather than waste more time looking for the originals. Then they checked the set instructions and tidied up the candles and incense burners that had been scattered on the mantelpiece behind the table. With everything where it should have been in the first place, the actors sat down in their places.

Lucinda asked for some personal items belonging to the deceased. Jeremy handed her a pair of spectacles that had belonged to Bart and Portia passed her a book that had belonged to Poppy. Lucinda placed them both down on the table then lit the candle and the incense. Then all the participants – Portia, Lucinda, Jeremy, Harry and Dominic put a hand on an upturned glass at the centre of the circle.

'I light this candle to welcome you to the warmth and light,' said Lucinda. 'Poppy, Bart – this is a safe place and we are your friends, please join us if you can. If you're here let us know.'

The actors jumped as three loud knocks sounded and the book flipped open to a page listing poisonous mushrooms.

'Poppy,' Lucinda called out. 'Poppy is that you?'

The knocks sounded again.

'Poppy, we are here to help,' said Lucinda. 'If you saw the person who sent you to your death, please let us know.

The glass started moving, swirling around to begin with and then it shot towards the E, then the R ...

'Jeremy,' gasped Lucinda looking up at the festival organiser. His face bore a look of astonishment as he held his palms outwards as if to say he hadn't a clue what this was all about and that he was completely innocent. At that moment, Agatha bounded around to the other side of the table and sniffed at Jeremy's jacket as it hung on the back of his chair. Dominic leapt up to see what she'd found and despite Jeremy's protestations, Dominic plunged his hand into the jacket pocket and pulled out a sachet of something that looked like dried herbs or mushrooms. Jeremy pushed back his chair and went to run but Agatha leapt up and grabbed hold of his arm refusing to let go as the man tried to shake her off. Dominic and Harry then wrestled Jeremy to the ground as Lucinda shouted out that she'd call the police.

'And cut,' called Riley. 'Good work and good recovery crew although if anyone can exorcise that poltergeist, I'd be eternally grateful.'

As the team cleared everything Riley had a quiet word with Kareem.

'I'm guessing he wasn't as relaxed about the situation as his jokey comment seemed,' said Chloe when Kareem rejoined her.

'Nope,' said the producer. 'We've got to double down on every scene from now on. He's a huge name in the TV world but this is my first big drama show so I can't afford to have him think I don't know what I'm doing. So from now on, after we set it up, I'm going to ask someone I can personally vouch for to stay in situ until the moment the cameras roll.'

'That's going to slow things down.' Chloe knew the set designers moved from scene to scene getting everything prepared in multiple locations wherever they could.

'It's either that or hire some extra security people to guard the set,' Kareem said. 'And we just can't go over budget.'

'I'll help however I can,' said Chloe seeing the concern on Kareem's face.

'Thanks,' he said gratefully. 'The next scene is Dominic perusing the shelves of the bookshop looking for clues. The team are setting it up now but then they have to create a morgue scene in the school so I could do with a guard on the shop.'

'No problem,' replied Chloe saluting Kareem and heading out towards the grocery store aka *Serenity Books*.

The designers were finishing up as she arrived. It really was quite wonderful to see this old style shop with ancient leather-bound volumes set up where baked beans and bags of sugar once stood. Of course most of it was simply a fake backdrop but there were a couple of shelves with real books that Dominic could pull out and read. Chloe thought that if she were trying to disrupt the filming, these would be the props she'd aim for as without them, the scene simply wouldn't work. There was a table and chair set up in the middle of the room so she took a seat directly facing the books and vowed not to take her eyes off them. Which Chloe found, was actually pretty difficult to do. She realised fairly quickly that staring at anything for long periods made her feel very sleepy so she was extremely relieved when Dominic walked in and asked if she wanted any company.

'Oh thank goodness for you. I'm not sure how good a security guard I could ever be. It's too quiet in here and I'm in danger of falling asleep.'

'Then let's keep ourselves entertained,' said the actor. 'I'm guessing that a woman who likes anagrams also likes Scrabble?'

'I love it,' replied Chloe as Dominic reached into a bag and pulled out a travel-sized version of the game. 'I just don't really have anyone to play it with,' she added. 'Roisin and Andy get bored with it and Maggie – well let's just say that the words she makes up aren't often found in the dictionary.'

Dominic laughed as he set up the board and letters. 'I can definitely imagine that.'

They passed the time amiably and Chloe found Dominic

a worthy opponent. It had been years since she'd played with someone who'd really challenged her. The last person had been her dad. Chloe felt a pang of guilt – Dominic seemed to have replaced her father in rather too many scenes today. He'd entertained her mother over lunch and now here he was giving her a run for her money at Scrabble. The guilt was illogical but she knew she had to keep pestering her dad until he started to see the urgency of the situation. She studied the board and added the letters to create the word FOXGLOVE on a triple word score.

'Outstanding,' said Dominic. 'I think that's me well and truly beaten.'

When Chloe smiled weakly he asked her what the matter was.

'Oh it's nothing.' She sighed. Not wanting to tell him what she was really thinking about, she added, 'I'm just struggling to come up with ideas for Christmas presents – Andy's in particular.'

'The man who has everything eh?' said Dominic.

'More like the man who really wants nothing,' corrected Chloe. She looked around the fake bookshop they were sitting in. 'I've wracked my brain but I still can't think of anything.'

'A fine whiskey and a good book always do the job for me,' Dominic said. 'You can have too many possessions in life but I always see books as friends rather than possessions.'

Chloe thought this sounded like something he'd say in an interview and anyway it wasn't much help.

'He downloads books and hates whiskey.'

'So much for my advice then eh?' Dominic laughed.

Andy chose the moment they were both laughing to

peer into the set. Chloe turned to see him with a big smile on her face.

'Hi there,' she said, getting up to give him a kiss on the cheek.

'The very man we were just talking about,' added Dominic.

'Talking?' said Andy and Chloe noted he was gripping the handshake rather tightly. 'It sounded an awful lot like laughter to me.'

Chloe knew Andy had a tendency to get a little jealous and led him off the set as the rest of the crew arrived to begin filming.

'Stop being so petulant,' she told her boyfriend hopping onto her tiptoes and giving him a kiss. 'Especially after everything the cast and crew offered you last night – it doesn't suit you.'

'I know – he's been great but I just can't help it when you spend so much time around movie stars.' He gave a small reluctant smile. 'And anyway I thought you found the petulant look adorable.' He stuck out a pet lip.

'You have better looks. Look, I'm sorry but I have to get back to work.'

'I know, I know.' Andy sighed. 'Drinks later? I've put together a playlist for Christmas day that I want to show you.'

Chloe pulled an apologetic face and groaned, 'I wish I could but the shoot doesn't finish until ten and I'm going to be exhausted by then.'

'I promise I'll make it worth your while.' Andy pulled her to him for a kiss that would linger for quite some time. Chloe touched a finger to her lips as he walked away – how could she turn down an offer like that? Her man certainly knew how to tempt a girl.

Chapter Seventeen

As all of the characters came pouring out of the bookshop from the shoot, Chloe spotted Roisin and her mum standing by the balustrade on the promenade stretching their legs and sipping from water bottles. She checked that Kareem didn't need her to guard anywhere over the break and then skipped over to the ladies who were both flushed a healthy shade of pink.

'We've been power walking this afternoon.' Theresa was breathing heavily but beaming from ear-to-ear. 'And now I feel absolutely marvellous.'

'We were wondering whether we could drag you back to the retreat in your break,' added Roisin looking equally rosy. 'I have a wonderful spiced fruit loaf I baked this morning and I think we've earned a slice.'

'I'm told it's one of Heather's old recipes,' continued Theresa. 'And if it tastes anywhere near as good as it smells then we're in for a real treat.'

'That's certainly the best offer I've had all day,' Chloe said as her mouth began watering in anticipation of some of Roisin's baking. Heather was Roisin's gran and she was a fabulous cook with bread recipes being her speciality. Heather was currently enjoying a late-life adventure seeing the world, and she frequently sent old-fashioned postcards from the countries she visited. Chloe wondered for a moment whether this was what her own mother needed and hoped that if it was, she would want to have that adventure with her father rather than her lunch companion. She linked arms with Theresa and Roisin and added, 'It would be good to have a bit of a catch-up.'

Now that the shoot was in full swing, everyone in the village seemed to be permanently dressed up as something else. They strolled along now taking the efforts of the film crew completely in their strides and barely batting an eyelid at many of the things that greeted them. Historical warlord having coffee with a gypsy palm reader? No problem. Crowds of children fighting with light sabres? Seen it all before. Landladies signing autographs ...? What?

'What on earth are you doing?' Chloe asked as Maggie posed for a selfie then signed a beer mat.

'They think I'm an actress,' said Maggie delightedly as Chloe pulled her to one side. 'And who am I to argue with them? Honestly, I think this is almost the best week of my life – the village is busy, the pub is full, my hero is on first name terms with me and I'm going to be on telly! The only thing missing is my son but at least I'll have loads to tell him when we Skype – it might even have him rushing back home.'

Maggie looked as if she was floating on a cloud as a group of women approached her. She signed three more beer mats and handed them to the ladies. 'Here you go – now you can tell people you knew me before I made it big.'

'I don't think I've ever seen her happier,' Chloe said to Roisin and Theresa. 'Though I'm not sure how she'll cope when her fifteen minutes are up.' They watched Maggie heading back towards the pub raising her hand in a royal wave at the visitors looking around for the main actors.

'Oh it's all just harmless fun,' her mother said. 'And why shouldn't she enjoy the moment? We don't get out of this alive you know.' She didn't look at Chloe, just dipped her head and continued walking.

Chloe didn't know how to respond. She looked across at Roisin who simply raised her eyebrows. They strode on and reached the farm without having said another word to each other. Walking inside felt gloomy and Chloe knew they needed to lift the mood if they were going to have any sort of conversation. She suggested filling a flask instead so they could have the fruit loaf and coffee on the beach under the early evening sky.

'I've been inside all day,' Chloe explained. 'And it isn't that cold.'

'If we wrap up it'll be lovely,' agreed Roisin. 'The air is always so invigorating at this time of day. You two grab the camping chairs and choose a spot – I'll be down in a jiffy.' She pushed big blankets onto Chloe and Theresa then shooed them out of the door.

As they walked, Chloe took hold of her mum's hand and gave it a squeeze. Her mum looked at her, smiled and squeezed back. It was a tiny gesture but Chloe took it as a good sign. They reached the sand and agreed a spot slightly sheltered by the dune grasses. Theresa opened the folding chairs and they sat down wrapping themselves in the blankets and then gazing up at the sky where the pale crescent moon was already visible in the fading light. Chloe wasn't sure how to start the conversation she wanted to have but fortunately Roisin arrived very shortly after with a flask and a cake tin so she could think about it for a few moments longer. Chloe really didn't want to upset her mum so had to get this right.

The three women avoided meaningful conversation and instead focussed on the fruit loaf which was indeed delicious.

'The secret to making it moist,' said Roisin, 'is to soak

137

the fruit for a short while before you bake it. Not too long or it'll go soggy.'

'And none of us want a soggy bottom.' Theresa laughed.

They fell silent again until the last cup of coffee was drained and the lid of the tin firmly closed. Chloe started to feel slightly awkward; she didn't have a great deal of time until she had to be back on set but had really wanted to talk to her mother about lunchtime. As if knowing that an awkward conversation was on the verge of happening, Theresa kept her gaze downwards, paying a great deal of attention to the border of the blanket. Roisin broke the tension.

'So who thinks Maggie will be the surprise BAFTA nomination this year for her stand-out performance?' she asked.

It did the job as shoulders dropped and genuine smiles broke out from everyone.

'Would she be happy with the award for an actress in a *supporting* role though?' asked Theresa. 'After all, she's not quite the star.'

'Definitely not – it's leading lady or nothing,' said Chloe laughing. 'In fact if Dominic isn't careful, he'll be ousted from his part and there'll be a new female detective solving the crimes of rural Britain.'

After a few more giggles, there was a brief moment of quiet again until Theresa bent down and started combing her fingers through the soft sand, lifting handfuls and letting it fall gently back to the ground – like a human hourglass.

'There's nothing actually happening you know,' she said without looking up. 'With Dominic – he's great fun to be around but I'm just the decoy. He doesn't want people to know that he and Tegan are dating. She's great fun and we've been getting on like a house on fire and besides, although he's handsome, I don't think I would ever actually fancy *him*.'

This statement was both a relief and a watch-out. Chloe was delighted to hear that the only shenanigans taking place were between Tegan and Dominic but her mum's last few words caused alarm bells. Was there someone else her mum fancied?

'Just as well,' said Chloe. 'I'd hate you to be in the middle of the bun fight that's bound to erupt when Maggie finds out that the rumours about Tegan are true.'

Theresa smiled absent-mindedly then stopped what she was doing and sat cross-legged looking out to the sea as it ebbed and flowed.

'The problem is,' she said, 'I don't think I fancy anyone any more.' As she finished the sentence Theresa looked across at her daughter for a sign that what she'd said had been understood. Chloe felt a tiny squeeze on her heart but pushed it away and smiled gently at her mum.

'What's happened, Mum?' She tried to keep her voice steady.

'Nothing has happened. But it's just not worth it is it? You get close to people and build your life around them but they can be gone in a flash can't they? Far better to stay independent, travel, keep moving and have lots of loose connections so if one goes then you have plenty of others to fall back on.'

'Wow, that doesn't sound like you, Mum – what is it?' asked Chloe quite shocked by her mother's words. 'Dad isn't gone – he's at a conference and probably on his way back soon. I've spoken to him very recently.'

'That's not what I mean – oh you wouldn't understand.'

With that, Theresa stood up and walked back to the farmhouse. Chloe went to follow but Roisin pulled her back.

'Give her space,' she said. 'Your mum needs to process some things.'

'What kind of things?'

'She's been through a bit of a tough time. And she's dealing with it in her own way. She'll get there, I'm sure she will.'

'You can't leave it there, Roisin,' pleaded Chloe. 'What's wrong? Is she ill?'

'No.' Roisin sighed. 'I'm breaking Theresa's confidentiality here but it's the only way to stop you worrying.

'Your dad had a twinge in his chest and they thought it might be his heart.'

'They never told me.' Chloe was horrified by what she'd just heard.

'They didn't want to worry anyone and when the tests came back, they were completely clear.'

'I don't understand.'

'Your mum told me that for a moment she thought she was going to lose him. She said she steeled herself against getting bad news and mentally worked through every possible scenario – how she'd tell you and how she'd cope without him.'

'She'd have to learn how to work the smart TV,' said Chloe trying to give herself some light relief in what she was hearing.

'That's what she said. And the satnav – she told me she can't work the new satnav.'

'That's why she really hates the new car.'

Roisin nodded. 'When he got the all clear, Theresa said

she was so relieved that she decided they weren't going to waste a single minute of their lives together. They were going to do everything they'd ever wanted to,' continued Roisin. 'To see the Taj Mahal, visit the Galapagos Islands, get a sports car, that kind of thing.'

'And then Dad came home with that sensible saloon and to her it felt like a symbol of what they weren't doing.'

'Yep.'

'So she's realised that none of us are immortal and one day, she'll lose Dad.' Chloe could picture the scene playing out in her parents' home and could easily finish the story she was being told. 'So now she's really looking after her health but also wants to have adventures with him and he's still quite happy in his armchair watching the sport.'

Roisin nodded. 'You got it. She's wondering what the point of it all is.'

Chloe sighed and thanked her friend for letting her know what was going on. She knew that many people evaluated their lives again after a health scare – suddenly they see that the big house and fancy car are far less important than low blood pressure and a good cholesterol score. She knew that a significant number of people also looked at their relationships and while for some, it reignited passion and togetherness, others found something wanting. At least her mum hadn't looked at her dad and decided that divorce was the only way to go; instead she'd decided she needed to make every moment with him precious and memorable. But Chloe knew her mum far too well and guessed that her planning and fussing was, in her dad's eyes, making each moment annoying and monstrous instead. She had to get her parents together and talking before the situation got any worse. Chloe took her phone out and started stabbing numbers.

'Dad? Dad? For goodness sake, pick up,' she shouted then waited to see if he did. When there was no response at all she threw the phone down on the beach where fortunately it landed face side up.

'I wish he'd just get here,' she said bending down to pick it up. 'I'm sure he'd be able to sort this out.'

'Honestly Chloe, leave them to it. This is one issue that you can't just fix,' Roisin said.

Chloe checked her phone, wiping the sand from the face and it suddenly burst into life – her dad, thank goodness for that.

'Dad, I know you said you were staying until the end of the conference but I think you should be here. No, she's not ill. In fact she looks fabulous – just come and see. Is there nothing I can say to change your mind?'

Chloe sighed, finished the call and had to use every inch of willpower not to throw it back on the sand.

'He says he's paid for it so unless Mum is ill he's staying. He says he'll be here when his wife stops being so ridiculous.'

When Chloe had calmed down a little from the talk with her dad, she thought about the parallels with her own situation. She was the one being ridiculous by not simply talking to Andy about her concerns. Chloe grimaced at the thought that she might be turning into her mother. She was nothing like her – she would find the time and have a grown-up conversation with her boyfriend. She'd explain why she felt under so much pressure and he'd understand.

But right now Chloe had to get back on set so Roisin left her to it, telling her not to worry too much. They had a few hours of filming to complete today. Tegan would be seen sneaking out of the bookshop at night having obviously stuffed something in her jacket and there'd be a hint of someone watching her doing it. She'd walk onto the beach, rip out some pages and then set fire to the book. Tegan would be disturbed by a noise and run off. Then when she was gone, a hand would reach into the scene, throw sand on the flames and then take the charred tome.

Even with the potential issue of a fire, the scene went smoothly and before long, everyone was packing up for the day. Chloe waited in the tent going over the footage from the day with Riley and Kareem and despite the hiccups, it looked good so everyone was happy with it. The lighting in the bookshop had been great and even the cobbled together séance cards looked the part. All in all, they'd had a good day's filming.

'Fancy a quick drink to celebrate the day?' asked Kareem.

'Just the one,' replied Chloe knowing she should really call Andy but thinking that Kareem and Riley were the people paying her wages. 'Then I've got to go and meet someone.'

They walked into the pub and ordered a glass of wine and a pint of local ale. Maggie served them at their tables and asked if she'd be needed for the next day's shoot. Kareem thanked her but politely told her no, they didn't need her tomorrow. Maggie left them grumbling something about it being their loss.

'Well done you,' said Chloe raising her glass to him. 'Not many people manage to stop Maggie doing anything.'

'Not sure we could cope with any more impro-vi-sa-tion,' said Riley clinking glasses with her.

Chloe laughed as they lowered their heads together and joked surreptitiously about how much worse it could have been. The three were locked in their secret joke as the pub door opened and Andy walked in.

'No time for a drink?' he said. 'Not with me anyway.'

Chloe knew how it must look and as Andy turned to walk back out, she apologised to Kareem and Riley then ran after him.

Chapter Eighteen

'Stop right there – do not move an inch!' Chloe shouted down the street and to her surprise, that's immediately what Andy did. He stopped dead in his tracks then turned to face her with his hands on hips looking very annoyed.

'I ask you to lunch and you can't come because you're with Dominic.'

Chloe walked towards him.

'Then I come down to try and find you on your break but you've gone somewhere. I ask to meet you for one drink and you haven't got time but you manage to find time for your new best buddies. Should I be sending out meeting requests to see my girlfriend?'

'Have you quite finished?' asked Chloe having caught up with him. She held out her hands and having calmed down a little, he took hold of them. Chloe pulled him closer and could see he was still breathing rapidly but keeping it under control.

'First of all,' she said. 'I wasn't with Dominic at lunch time. The woman in his apartment, well my apartment obviously but you know what I mean, anyway – that woman with the chestnut hair was my mother.'

'Your mother? What was she …?'

Chloe let go of his hand and raised her palm to stop the question.

'I'll explain later but that's where I was during the break when you couldn't find me – seeing her,' she said. 'And as for tonight, well, I was truly exhausted and I would have loved to go straight to bed then Kareem asked for one drink and I didn't think I could say no. They sometimes decide on changes to the next day's shoot in the evening so I feel obliged to meet with them and – well, I'm sorry if you feel left out but it's just my job.'

Andy's shoulders dropped and he nodded slightly to reluctantly show he understood.

'I'm sorry. Don't get me wrong, I know you have to work and I get that you do crazy hours but I really wanted to see you tonight and sometimes lately, I just get this feeling that it's not just the job. I sometimes think that you're avoiding me.' He wrapped his arms around her and kissed her gently on the top of the head.

Chloe dropped her gaze and started studying the pavement. It was her turn to have a racing pulse but she knew it was time to tell the truth. She took a breath and looked up at Andy as he squeezed her more tightly.

'You're right. I sort of have been avoiding you. And I'm sorry this time.'

'But why?'

At that precise moment, his phone in his pocket rang out with his new ringtone – "Jingle Bells". Andy let go of Chloe and switched it off immediately then turned his attention back to her.

'It was only Lloyd – we're meeting up tomorrow but I can call him in the morning ...' He'd seen she was wiping tears from her eyes. 'What's happened, are you okay?'

She looked up with a big smile on her face so he could see that they were tears of laughter. Chloe took a tight hold of his hand and led him to the bench where they'd eaten their enormous turkey sandwiches then sat down.

'I was laughing at your ringtone,' she said. 'It kind of embodies the reason I've been avoiding you.'

Chloe explained that while she found his love of Christmas completely adorable, she also felt intimidated by the need to make their first Christmas alone together absolutely perfect. Andy took hold of her hands and kissed them before pulling her back into a tight hug. Chloe nestled into his chest as the warmth and strength of his body against hers relaxed her into believing that things would be absolutely fine. Then her gorgeous boyfriend ruined the moment by saying completely the wrong thing.

'Of course it'll be perfect. How could it not be? You and I being together is all we need to make it perfect.'

Chloe tensed up again and pulled away from him.

'You see, people say that but what does it actually mean?' she exclaimed. 'Why does anyone think they can make a day *perfect*? How do you know that the things you like to do will be perfect for me? And how can I make sure your day is perfect? Take breakfast for example, are you a smoked salmon and bucks fizz kind of guy or freshly ground coffee and croissant? What traditions did you have as a boy? Did you open presents first thing in the morning or later just before lunch? Or maybe you do that Scandinavian thing of opening them on Christmas Eve? And when do you like to eat lunch? Before or after the Queen's speech? Do you even listen to the Queen's speech?'

'Whoa,' replied Andy smiling at her. 'I never realised there were so many planning decisions.'

'That's not even the half of it,' continued Chloe ignoring his smile and turning to face the sea which was black dark except for the white tops of waves which rolled in and out without a care in the world. That certainly wasn't how Chloe felt and now that she'd started, she seemed unable to stop her mouth spurting out every thought that had been doing battle in her brain for the past few weeks.

'Take snuggling up on the sofa with a movie,' she said.

'What's your idea of a classic? Are you a *It's A Wonderful Life* kind of guy or *The Muppet Christmas Carol*? Tears or laughter? Real tree or fake? Get dressed up or spend all day in pyjamas? Mince pies or stollen? "Mary's Boy Child" or "Fairytale of New York"? There are just *so* many options.'

Chloe paused to take a breath and then opened her mouth to begin the rest of her list. Andy pressed his finger to her lips and then kissed her. Chloe tried to resist and get back to her list but Andy wasn't having that and kept kissing her until she felt her body surrender.

'That's better,' he said when she finally stopped talking. 'Who was that crazy demon Christmas lady who replaced my girlfriend? Is she gone now?'

'She is,' replied Chloe. 'But I can't guarantee she won't return.'

Andy suggested that they walk for a while and as they did, he asked her to explain why she was so anxious about the day. Chloe hesitated, wondering whether to be completely honest and then decided that Andy would be able to tell if she wasn't.

'My ex,' she started quietly. 'He had very particular views on what made a perfect Christmas. Everything had to be very tasteful, as if we were about to be photographed for a celebrity magazine. Because of that, everything was co-ordinated – the wines carefully chosen and even our clothes had to be complementary to make sure our social media posts looked fabulous. I tell you I was terrified in case I did something wrong and ruined his moment just by wearing the wrong shade of lipstick.'

Chloe looked at Andy who was strolling along with his eyebrows raised and mouth wide open as if he simply couldn't believe any of this.

'I don't blame you,' said Chloe. 'It sounds insane now and it was. But the same pressure was on gifts – they had to be perfect, expensive and tasteful. The cashmere gloves that you're too scared to wear in case you lose them, the mountain biking gear that he used once – it was all for show. I know you're not like that but I want to get you something special, something that you'll love and I just haven't a clue. That seems so wrong – I should know what you want. I know how much you love Christmas and I feel as if I'm letting you down.'

Andy clamped his mouth shut as the words stopped tumbling from her mouth. He sighed and looked up, pointed at the sky and she followed his lead. He was pointing at the North Star shining brightly in the blackness.

'Whenever I look up at that,' he said. 'I always relax because it reminds me how utterly insignificant we all are. It will shine whether we have salmon or chocolate for breakfast, whether we have turkey or cornflakes for lunch. What matters is that we're together and able to gaze up at that star at the end of the day.'

Andy probably intended his words to relax her but they had the exact opposite effect. Chloe slammed her hand down on the bench and quietly screamed.

'You see – that's exactly what I'm talking about,' she exclaimed. 'Those hopelessly romantic moments which are impossible to achieve! In Christmas movies they look up at stars and say nothing else matters but being together and then snowflakes fall and choirs sing, they exchange the most perfect gifts wrapped in huge bows and it's magical. I know it's not real but I want to give you that if that's your dream.'

Another soft but firm kiss stopped her in her tracks.

'I'm sorry – I can get a bit overexcited.' Andy was

looking into her eyes and brushed his hand down her cheek. 'But I don't want to cause you any more stress so that stops now. You have an extremely important job to do making this village a fabulous place for film companies so you need to focus on that. I don't want you to worry about anyone else's ideal day for a moment longer. Do you trust me?'

'Of course I do.'

'Trust me enough to organise Christmas?' continued Andy.

Chloe felt a tiny bit of tension take hold of her and she clenched her jaw; she knew she was a bit of a control freak, well not just a *bit* of a control freak. A total and utter, unable to leave things to chance type of woman and she'd been like that for as long as she could remember. She was the type of person who always had a to-do list and loved ticking things off. And if she did something that wasn't on the list, she wrote it down at the bottom just so she could tick it off and feel satisfied. It wasn't a bad thing to be per se, after all, it had helped her build her career and secure these film shoots for the village. You couldn't afford to be lackadaisical when you had a crew on a schedule. But hand over complete control for the biggest day of the year? Even to someone she utterly adored? Chloe felt twitchy even contemplating it but what other choice was there? To tell Andy that she didn't trust him?

She knew she'd been weighing up his question for far too long now but when she looked up at Andy, he had a very entertained look on his face as if every thought she'd just had was appearing in a thought bubble above her head.

'Okay,' she said, forcing the word out on a big exhale. 'I do.'

'Fabulous, then it's sorted,' he said. 'You concentrate on the shoot, keeping that crew happy and getting them out of here on time so the whole village can start the Midwinter celebrations. Meanwhile I will do all that needs to be done to give you the most wonderful Christmas day of your entire life and I promise you – it will not involve matching outfits.'

He asked if she had her notepad with her. She shrugged an *of course* and rummaged around in her bag to find it. She always preferred being able to physically scribble something off her to-do lists so never used the notes function on her phone. The pen pushed firmly onto the paper until it almost poked through to the other side felt altogether more satisfying than deleting it on a screen.

'Great,' said Andy. 'So here's the plan. If you think of something that you would like me to exclude or include in our fabulous first Christmas, I'd like you to jot it down on a piece of paper, hand it to me and then forget about it completely. Consider it ticked off.'

Chloe laughed – this man knew her too well. With that one sentence she felt her shoulders relax just a smidgeon. She snuggled back into his chest.

'You are too good,' she said. 'I wish this night didn't have to end with me going back to my sad single bed and you heading for your friend's sofa.'

'I'm very glad you said that,' replied Andy with a twinkle in his eyes. 'I have something to show you.'

He took her hand and gripping it as if he were afraid she'd try to escape, he started walking briskly along the promenade and down the slipway. Chloe knew they had to be heading for the Surfshack but couldn't imagine why at this time of night.

The Surfshack was an old stone building around the

size of a double garage and stood at the end of the beach. It had once been a boat storage unit but had fallen into disrepair until Andy bought the derelict remains and rebuilt it himself, working to create his own personal haven. Inside, Chloe knew it was fairly sparse as Andy used this space to give safety briefings and show customers the routes they'd be taking out on the sea. There were maps of the coastline on the walls and the building housed the changing rooms plus a small office that Andy used to schedule classes and do his invoicing. The equipment – the kayaks, surfboards and wetsuits were all stored on racking which ran lengthways down the walls. As they approached it, Chloe felt, as she always did, that this little corner of the earth said everything you would ever need to know about the man she loved. The building was strong but not flashy, his belongings were lovingly cared for and the sound of the ocean outside was his absolute favourite soundtrack.

Andy unlocked the door and asked her to wait while he stepped inside and flicked a switch. As he did, a hundred tiny lights twinkled – draped across the roof beams and around the door frames.

'I know the rule is no Christmas lights until the shoot is over,' he said. 'But I figured that if I only put these on when the crew were finished then it wouldn't matter.'

Chloe stepped into the fairy grotto he'd created and felt her heart melt. As well as the lights, there was the tiniest silver tree in the corner with a little star on top. This man really did love Christmas.

'I'll forgive you breaking my curfew.' She smiled. 'Just don't tell the rest of the village.'

'There's more. Follow me.'

He walked into his office and tentatively, Chloe followed him.

'This is why I really wanted to see you tonight.'

Again the room was decorated with fairy lights along each wall but they weren't the main feature. The office had been cleared of the old desk and swivel chair normally housed here and instead, right there on the floor in the centre of this room, was a bed. A bed piled with cosy blankets and plump pillows. Chloe looked at Andy and saw that mischievous grin light up his face. He pointed at some mistletoe he'd hung from the ceiling then pulled her towards him and kissed her.

'It's only an inflatable camp bed so I know you can't stay here every night and get a decent sleep but I thought that once in a while, when the job threatens to get too much, a night of cuddles might be just what you need,' he told her.

Chloe pulled him down onto the bed which wobbled slightly under their weight. She giggled and jiggled around a little to make it wobble again before lying back and pulling Andy with her. She lay in his arms looking around at the sanctuary he'd created.

'It's perfect,' she said. 'Thank you for doing this.'

Chloe slipped her hand under Andy's jumper and stroked the soft hairs on his stomach.

'How strong do you think this camp bed is?' she asked leaning over him, placing tender kisses all over his face.

Andy pulled Chloe on top of him and began unbuttoning her shirt slowly then easing it over her shoulders.

'Let's see shall we?'

Chapter Nineteen

Chloe snuck out of the Surfshack before the dawn had even thought about showing it's rose-gold glow across the bay. She had to stop herself skipping the whole way back to the pub and instead delighted in a slow stroll along the promenade in the invigorating freshness of the early morning. She couldn't hold back the huge smile on her face and as she crept along the glistening pavement, she felt like a cat burglar who'd just pulled off the biggest jewellery heist ever. She was still grinning when she quietly unlocked the door of the pub and stepped inside.

'So what time do you call this?' growled a voice from the corner making Chloe gasp with fright.

'Maggie!' Chloe gasped when she'd recovered from the shock. 'What on earth are you doing up at this hour?'

'I could ask you the same thing. And don't go telling me you've been out for a jog – no matter how rosy your cheeks might be. I wasn't born yesterday.'

Chloe blushed a little more.

'I thought as much.' Maggie kept her gaze fixed on a rather embarrassed Chloe. 'So did you two work it out then? Whatever it is that's been bothering you?'

Having decided to give up asking how she seemed to know everything, Chloe told her that they had sorted things out and Maggie nodded back replying, 'Good. Life is way too short to fret over small things.' Chloe thought that was rapidly becoming the lesson of the week.

The filter coffee machine wasn't on yet but Maggie had a pot of tea made and poured her a cup. Chloe had planned on perhaps getting an hour's sleep before the crew got up but as that didn't look as if it was going to happen now, she accepted the tea and sat down with Maggie. She took one sip of that strong, hot drink and sighed – it was very good and she probably needed this more than the extra hour.

'So why are you up at this time of day?' Chloe asked again when she remembered that she hadn't had a response to her question.

'I've been awake for hours. I just can't sleep,' Maggie said.

'Why?' asked Chloe with genuine concern. 'Has something happened?'

'I just need to know whodunit. I won't rest until I do.'

Chloe shook her head at Maggie. 'I hope you're not going to ask me, you know I can't tell you.'

'I don't want you to.' Maggie harrumphed. 'I'm good at detective novels. I always guess the ending. In fact I'm so good at guessing the murderer I once thought I should join the police. The problem is that I work on intuition and courts tend to want evidence these days.'

The landlady was deadly earnest and Chloe had to hold back a smile imagining her standing up in front of a jury telling them that the defendant simply looked dodgy and her fortune-telling feet were throbbing so that should be enough to convict him.

'You're right,' she said playing along with Maggie. 'And it's damned inconvenient if you ask me, all that evidence stuff.'

'You may scoff, but sometimes you look at a person and you just know. In this case, they all look dodgy though so let's go over the evidence. We started with nine main characters but that includes Dominic who I think we can dismiss.'

She looked up at Chloe for confirmation or otherwise. Chloe folded her arms and sat perfectly still waiting to hear the great detective speak.

'Bart's dead,' continued Maggie. 'And so is Poppy so they're out. Different murder weapons were used so it could be two different people but is that what they want us to think? You see women tend to poison people and Lucinda knows about herbs and things which could mean it's her doing the killing but then would she have the strength or stomach to thrust a dagger into a grown man?'

Maggie suddenly stabbed an imaginary dagger hard into the table and then rather inexplicably, wiped the invisible weapon across her thigh as if cleaning the blood on her breeches. Chloe grimaced but could see that she was now really getting into the part. Maggie stood up and started striding across the pub floor with her hands clasped behind her back. Chloe watched and thought that all she needed was a pipe and a deerstalker hat to complete the image.

'What if Bart was Lucinda's lover but Poppy wanted him for herself. Poppy killed Bart and then Lucinda killed Poppy in revenge,' Maggie declared with a finger raised in the air. 'Now that would work.'

'You still have a woman stabbing someone,' Chloe said. 'And you said that was unusual. Also, why have you discounted Jeremy when the letters at the séance would spell his name and they found the mushrooms on him?'

'It's a red herring.' Maggie sucked on her thumb as if it were a pipe. 'The first one arrested on these shows is never the murderer. No, I need to study the remaining characters a bit more. One of them will slip up eventually.'

'Have you considered that the letters E and R also feature in Wavertree?'

The voice came from the doorway. It was Kareem who

had an amused smile on his face and had evidently been watching Maggie's machinations. Maggie looked up at him as if a light bulb had gone on behind her eyes.

'Oh that's a very good point,' she exclaimed. 'You know what? I think the rest of the village might want to get in on the act of solving this case. I think I'm going to set up a sweepstake. You two are excluded obviously.'

She marched up to the specials board, rubbed out all the menu options and started writing up the character names and their odds: Tegan 5/1, Dominic 500/1, Agatha 5000/1 ... Chloe shrugged at Kareem and invited him to sit at her table, pouring him out a cup of tea while Maggie scribbled away.

After an early breakfast the fifth long day of filming began in earnest. Today would be all about Ewan and his backstory. It began with a wide shot of the festival with all the stalls busy being attended by crowds of visitors so most of the residents of Serenity Bay were out there again as extras. As Chloe approached with Riley and Kareem, a few of them – all dressed in their costumes, smiled and waved at her. Since they'd been recruited, she'd had several messages telling her this was the most exciting thing to happen to them all year and the fact that they were being paid, even if it was only the background day rate, was an added bonus. As she'd read them, Chloe had smiled at the thought of all those Christmas lunch conversations about the filming and the actors. The non-appearance of the original extras had really turned out to be a blessing in disguise.

Filming began with Tegan; her band of cynical romcom warriors started marching down the centre of the fayre as the actress once again mocked Lucinda's books and the stallholders who were selling spiritual or paranormal goods.

'These are supposed to be divining rods aren't they?' Tegan said to one of them, picking up a pair of metal sticks and holding them aloft. The stallholder nodded at her.

'Then why aren't they pointing at the sea?' Tegan laughed. 'I mean, there's a huge big ocean of water just over there and your magical mystery sticks are pointing at the freaking sand.'

Her entourage jeered and messed up the stallholder's merchandise before barrelling on to the next.

'Crystals?' said Tegan. 'Oh they certainly work don't they? What's this one for? Success and prosperity? Well I guess that's why you're standing behind a stall selling rocks for a living. And this one? Health? Is that why you have the walking stick?'

Tegan held a beautiful bright blue coloured crystal up to the sun and then slammed it back down on the table declaring Lucinda and the stallholder a charlatan before walking off.

Riley continued to film the stallholders all watching her leaving then called cut. He asked to watch the footage and seemed quite happy until a voice behind Chloe spoke up.

'Chloe, I don't want to disturb the scene and I'm not sure if this is important,' said Roisin. 'But the crystals are wrong.'

Chloe hadn't noticed her friend appear on set but was really happy to see her and introduced Roisin to Riley. He asked her to explain what she meant.

'For success and prosperity she should really have picked up the malachite. It's the bright green one. For health, especially if it's to do with something painful, you'd probably pick red jasper. I don't use crystals at the retreat but a lot of my clients believe in them and the one she picked up is so distinctly lapiz lazuli; that's supposed to enhance creativity so it's completely wrong.'

Roisin sheepishly took a step backwards as if she'd been discovered at a party she wasn't invited to. Riley thanked her then sighed and stood with his hands on his hips.

'Kareem, can your guys get this checked out quickly?' He called a break while the producer rang the set designer and met her over by the crystal stall. Roisin looked at Chloe and mouthed an apology.

'No need to apologise,' said Chloe standing beside her friend. 'Someone would have noticed at some point and at least now we have the chance to fix it. You can imagine all the fan forums getting agitated over the wrong crystals being used – this may be complete fiction but they do hate inaccuracies in their cosy mysteries.'

The friends laughed and took a stroll while the scene was being investigated.

'I actually came over because I have news,' said Roisin. 'Your dad finishes his conference the day after tomorrow and he's coming straight to the retreat.'

'Oh thank goodness for that! Why didn't he call me?'

'I think he tried,' Rosin said.

Chloe took out her phone and saw that he'd attempted to call at what would have been his mid-morning break but it was also during filming when her phone was switched off. Typically her dad hadn't left a message but that didn't matter – he was finally coming and soon the world would be right.

'He doesn't want us to tell your mum he's arriving,' continued Roisin. 'He wants to surprise her, be spontaneous.'

'That's a good idea. Mum doesn't think he's capable of surprising her any more so this might change her mind.

Where is he staying?' asked Chloe remembering that the rooms had been full. 'I can't imagine my mum wanting to share her space at the moment.'

'That's what we thought,' Roisin said. 'So Lloyd called around and apparently Andy has a camp bed which is quite comfy.'

'So I hear,' murmured Chloe realising that was most probably the end of their secret love nest.

Roisin waved her goodbye as Kareem and the set designer approached. He didn't look at all happy.

'What's the matter?' asked Chloe.

The set designer held out her phone which showed a photograph of the crystal stall.

'This is how the stall was set up this morning,' said Kareem. 'All the crystals have labels on them and they're all in the right place. The next picture is the stall as we found it – honestly, I didn't think we'd need to guard this set as we're out here all day.'

Chloe swiped on to another picture of a stall with crystals. Swiping back and forwards between the two, even with no knowledge of crystals, she could see that the ones at the front were originally bright green and red and they had been switched to the back with the bright blue ones taking their place.

'Did the extra move them around? They probably wouldn't have known they had to be in a particular place,' said Chloe. It seemed the obvious explanation.

'She says she didn't touch them but I have no idea how else it could have happened,' said Kareem. 'I want to gather everyone together and reiterate the importance of not moving anything on the set after it's been set up. Will you help?'

Chloe nodded that she would. The villager who was

playing the stallholder was an ex-lollipop lady and she definitely wouldn't have lied to Kareem so Chloe completely believed what she'd said. Perhaps someone else had accidentally knocked them out of place not knowing how important the layout was? There had to be a simple explanation.

Together with Kareem, they called all the extras to gather round on the sand and from the promenade, the producer addressed them. He stressed the importance of the schedule, the need to leave sets exactly as they were and said unfortunately the incident had cost them a morning of filming. The scene needed bright daylight so they couldn't just shoot it again now. They'd all be needed again in the morning but they would still only receive one day's fee due to the issue. When he'd finished and left them, Chloe could hear the extras mumbling and tutting.

'It's like being told off by the headmaster for something you haven't done,' said one in a purposefully loud voice as they disbanded.

The ex-lollipop lady came up to Chloe and profusely apologised telling her that she hadn't touched anything and didn't want others to suffer because she hadn't noticed the stall was wrong. Chloe looked into her face which was wracked with angst and knew this old lady hadn't caused the delay at all. Someone else had.

Maggie chose that moment to walk up with her sweepstake notes.

'After those shenanigans, I can't decide whether to lower the odds on it being Tegan or raise them,' she said seemingly oblivious to Chloe taking absolutely no notice of her. 'She's either the murderer because she hates all this stuff or she's going to get bumped off next because someone hates her. Either way she's a nasty piece of work.'

Maggie seemed triumphant in her analysis of the situation but Chloe wouldn't be drawn into the conversation.

'What's the matter?' asked Maggie. 'You're not worried about this crystal lark are you? One of the lads most likely bumped into the stall and made a mess of tidying up, that's all.'

Chloe tuned in and looked at Maggie.

'If that had happened, it would just have been an accident and the person would have owned up, I'm sure of it,' she said. 'I don't know what your feet are telling you but my spidey senses are saying something's up. The dagger, the cards, the extras and now the crystals; they're all small things but together they're starting to add up to a real delay and none of us want that.'

'Don't these things happen all the time on shoots?' asked Maggie. 'They have to build in contingency for things going wrong don't they? And no one here could have given the extras food poisoning.'

'I don't know Maggie. It just doesn't feel right.'

'And you know what they say, if it doesn't feel right then it probably isn't,' Maggie said, pulling her shoulders back and standing tall. 'So it's a good job you've got me on the case.'

'What case?

'The curse of the Montgomery mysteries,' cackled Maggie. 'I told you, I have a sixth sense when it comes to investigating. I'll find out what's going on here.'

The landlady tapped the side of her nose and strode off leaving Chloe watching her go, shaking her head in despair and thinking, *What on earth have I unleashed on the world?*

Chapter Twenty

During the next stage of filming, Dominic began interviewing the suspects. Everyone who watched the show knew that the author's trademark style was very subtle and while he asked the questions, his trusty companion Agatha was usually off somewhere sniffing around and getting the real results. Sure enough, as Dominic asked Ewan how he felt about the writing festival and the quality of the competition he was up against, Agatha stole the show by finding an empty phial of poison in the pocket of a jacket that had been pushed into the bottom of a dustbin. The jacket was enormous and could only have fit Ewan so he too was carted off in a police car. As all true followers of *The Montgomery Mysteries* would guess, this did not mean Ewan was guilty. There were always multiple arrests before the real one and Jeremy had already been released following questioning as the herbs he was carrying had turned out to be medicinal. With Ewan and Jeremy arrested early on, Maggie changed the odds on her sweepstake board accordingly so that Tegan was now the odds-on favourite.

As the light dimmed, the crew began preparations for a large set change. They were about to film the story of Ewan's ancestry, as discovered by Dominic in his investigations. He'd already narrated it to the detective who arrested the giant man and the visuals filmed now would be broadcast alongside the narration when it was shown on TV. As the actors got into position, Kevin and Lizzie walked up and stood alongside Chloe.

'The detective sounds very authentic,' Chloe said to Kevin as action began. 'I'm guessing that's your work?'

He gave a harrumph in response and Chloe noted Lizzie shrugging her shoulders at him.

'So what does this writing event have to do with the village?' asked the fictional police detective pointing up at the festival banner.

'Jeremy's ancestor lived here,' replied Dominic. 'He was the great writer Walter Kingsley but his books were considered blasphemous back in the day so the authorities burnt them and he was banished to a penal colony. Jeremy has now resurrected the old manuscripts through the Serenity Publishing Company and holds the festival to honour Walter and to celebrate writing of all genres.'

The next scene to be filmed was a flashback to the days of Walter Kingsley.

The villagers were now all dressed in tattered looking medieval tunics with fake dirt smudged across faces and a new actor with a featured part turned up on set. He'd only be needed for the day and was playing the book burner. In a corner of the beach, a fire was being lit and the villagers marched towards it, an angry throng with pitchforks and torches in their hands. A wheelbarrow full of books and parchments was pushed towards the fire while a man, bound in chains was dragged along behind it. The book burner declared Walter Kingsley blasphemous and the writing unholy; the crowd cheered then each of them grabbed books from the wheelbarrow and started ripping pages out, throwing them on the fire as the bound man fell to his knees and wept. Chloe felt a heaviness in her chest as she watched the destruction of these fake books – it certainly looked very real and very disturbing.

'That looked really good,' said Riley as they reviewed the footage. 'The cliff edges in the background and the eerie long call of the seagull crying out at that precise moment – it gave us a much more fearsome atmosphere than I'd hoped for. It was fabulous – I could almost have forgotten we were filming cosy crime.'

Chloe felt exactly the same and moreover, was relieved to hear something positive.

'I'm just glad there were no hiccups this time,' she said.

'Well there wouldn't be would there? No one would dare now I'm on the case.'

Chloe and Riley turned to see Maggie wearing spectacles on a long gold chain and carrying a notepad and pencil which she chewed like a cigar.

'I didn't know you wore glasses,' commented Chloe.

'I don't usually but I couldn't find a magnifying glass at such short notice,' she replied. 'These will do the job just as well.'

'What job is that?' asked Riley as Chloe braced herself for Maggie's answer.

'I'm not going to have anyone ruin this shoot. So fortunately for you, I have made it my mission to establish exactly what has been going on here,' declared Maggie in such a loud voice that Kareem came over to see what was happening. Maggie started to comically pace back and forwards in front of her audience, twisting round dramatically after every three steps.

'Now as a connoisseur of every detective show on TV,' continued Maggie with a mischievous smile on her face. 'I can tell you that there is always a motive, a method and a means.'

She punctuated each word by waving the pencil at Chloe, then Riley then Kareem like she was conducting an orchestra.

'Whether we're talking Miss Marple, Poirot or Inspector Morse, they all look for these three things.'

'You do realise they're not real detectives don't you?' said Kareem getting a stern look from Maggie. She pressed her fingers to her lips and he shrunk back silently and obediently. Chloe bit her lip, holding back a snort of laughter at the look of fear on Kareem's face as he did this. He looked like a naughty schoolboy being scolded by the headmistress.

'So if all these events are not simply accidents or coincidences, I started wondering what the motive could possibly be. Why would anyone want to disrupt the filming? What, as they say, is the motive?'

In fairness to Maggie, Chloe realised that she hadn't considered this and she had no ideas either. Most people involved wanted the filming to finish on time and well within budget. She said as much to the landlady-cum-sleuth.

'Precisely,' declared Maggie triumphantly. 'Which is why I have concluded that the person we are looking for is not acting in the interests of Serenity Bay. Or persons of course. It might be more than one. Instead, they have something against one of you three people.'

Riley had stood quietly, probably out of bewilderment rather than any real interest until now but at this point he rubbed the back of his neck.

'Okay. I don't have time for this I'm afraid. As far as I'm concerned there's only one mystery going on here and that's the one I'm filming. Thanks for your interest, Maggie but it's all down to the set guys needing to take a bit more care. See you tonight for supper.'

He strode off shaking his head.

'I'd better get on too,' said Kareem. 'But I do stand by the crew – they had everything in place and just before filming, things were moved or taken. Talk later.'

Kareem jogged up to Riley who said something and started laughing as the producer reached him.

'Hmm,' said Maggie. 'They won't be laughing when I reveal the criminal and save the day.'

Chloe had to prepare one of the villager's houses for the next day's shoot and invited Maggie to walk with her.

'The question of motive is a tricky one,' said Chloe as they strolled. 'A delay wouldn't be beneficial to any of the actors because they'll want to get home on time as well as all of the crew.'

'And the villagers are having a brilliant time but they want it to go smoothly and get this lot out so they can put their decorations up,' continued Maggie.

'Maybe it's about the money,' said Chloe. 'If it goes over time then it costs more. The production company get a fixed fee per episode from the TV broadcaster so if their costs go up then they make a smaller profit.'

'So it could be someone with a grudge against the production company? What about a grudge against the producer? Do all of these shenanigans make Kareem look bad?' asked Maggie.

'I guess so,' replied Chloe.

'The problem is, they're not just making him look bad, they're risking the future of Serenity as a place to film and we can't allow either to happen.'

'You're right. This is one of his first big jobs in drama and if he can't control the costs or the schedule I guess he won't be given other assignments.'

'Bingo,' said Maggie. 'We have our motive. You know, you're quite good at this and every great detective has a sidekick so if you ever want to be my Watson, then I'd be prepared to seriously consider you.'

'Gee thanks,' Chloe said as they reached the house. 'I'll certainly bear that in mind.'

Chloe left Maggie on the doorstep and promising to keep a very close eye on Kareem from now on. Chloe couldn't help but pity the poor man. However, if it did transpire that anyone was trying to jeopardise his career by ruining the show then she imagined that Maggie would certainly be the one to put a stop to it.

Chloe put those thoughts to the back of her mind and joined a set designer inside the house. The kitchen was going to be used in one shot and it simply had to be cleared of some of the furniture so that the crew could fit inside. They needed to be filming Dominic interviewing a witness as he stood by the windowsill and right now there was a huge family dining table by the window and several family pictures stuck on the fridge. Chloe boxed up everything that couldn't appear while the team did the heavy lifting. They took down blinds to create more light and replaced the electric kettle with a steam one just to get that dramatic moment when the whistle blew. Chloe knew that some people barely recognised their own homes when they appeared on TV and it wasn't altogether surprising. Once cleared of all the clutter, photographs were taken to establish camera angles and Chloe was told they were good to go.

Outside, she found Andy loitering by the gate.

'Hello handsome,' she said giving him a kiss. 'To what do I owe the honour?'

'I have news,' he said taking hold of her hand as they walked back into the village. 'Well two pieces of news actually.'

'If it's about our secret hideaway, Roisin has already told me that it's been reassigned to a worthy cause.'

'I thought you would have done the same, just to keep your parents in the same village. You don't mind do you?'

Chloe shook her head and told him it was exactly what she would have done.

'What's the second piece of news?' she asked.

Andy stopped and reaching into his rucksack, pulled out a bundle of supermarket and department store Christmas catalogues and handed them to her.

'It's not news so much as a suggestion,' he said. 'I know that you're slightly nervous about leaving the big day up to me so I came up with an idea. Take a look through these and cut out the pictures of anything you fancy – food or decorations or anything – then leave the rest to me.'

'Like a mood board for a set design?' Chloe laughed.

'Exactly. I am learning to speak your language.'

'It's a lovely idea,' said Chloe. 'And it's just perfect for your control freak girlfriend.'

They walked back to Chloe's office and then with a quick kiss, Andy was gone leaving her with a huge smile on her face. It didn't last.

'Ms Walsh?'

A suited man stood in the doorway. He now walked forward to greet her with his hand outstretched. Chloe shook it as he introduced himself as being from the Union of Film Professionals.

'We represent the interests of both actors and crew members,' he explained handing her his card. 'In particular, we provide insurance in the event of an incident on set that may prevent them from working. Most people don't realise it but this can be a very precarious business.'

Chloe nodded along as he spoke not quite sure what he wanted and whether it was actually her he really needed to speak to.

'Nice to meet you,' she said. 'I don't think I would really need the union. I doubt I count as a film professional.'

The man explained that he wasn't trying to recruit her but he had been called to investigate the safety of the location.

'My sources tell me there has been an incident of food poisoning and a deadly weapon going astray.'

'Sources? Deadly weapon?' Chloe wasn't sure which to address first.

'Yes, a dagger,' replied the man. 'All weapons should be locked up in a secure location before and after any filming.'

Chloe looked around to see if this was some sort of joke and there was a hidden camera fixed on her. When no one leapt out laughing and when the man kept the deadly earnest expression on his face, she decided this was for real.

'We've had a tip-off from a concerned individual,' continued the man.

Chloe stood open-mouthed thinking if there had previously been any doubt that someone was trying to sabotage the shoot beforehand, there certainly wasn't now. She explained that the dagger in question was simply a replica and not at all deadly and that the food poisoning had not occurred on location.

'Nevertheless,' replied the union official. 'I do have to conduct some enquiries to declare the site safe for my members.'

'How long will that take?' asked Chloe trying not to sound as exasperated as she felt.

'As long as it needs to,' came the reply. 'And until I have completed my enquiries there can be no further filming.'

Chapter Twenty-One

Chloe opened her mouth to protest and tell this very officious man that she couldn't quite believe what was happening but the events of the past few days flashed through her head so she closed it again quickly. The truth was that after all the strange incidents she actually could believe it and protesting would do her no good whatsoever. The appearance of the official also confirmed that this hadn't just been a case of misplaced set items; someone had made the effort to report a fake dagger for goodness' sake, they simply had to be trying to jeopardise either the show or the village itself. Chloe pulled her shoulders back and stood tall; after all, she was the location manager and she was responsible for making sure the set was safe so this was her problem to help sort out.

'I understand,' she told the official. 'And I also want everything in Serenity to be absolutely safe for all parties concerned so I will assist you in every single way I can. Now where do we start?'

Chloe was going to play this absolutely by the book. It wasn't just the filming of *The Montgomery Mysteries* at risk, it was the reputation of the entire village if they were declared an unsafe film location. The official asked to be given somewhere to work and check all the permits. Chloe took him to her desk, told him he was welcome to work there during his investigation and gave him all the paperwork he needed. She settled him down with a cup of coffee then asked his permission to talk to the crew about the pause in shooting and the official was happy to let her go while he started his preliminary work.

'I will need you later to give me a tour of the locations used and the scenes where the complaints were made,' added the official as Chloe was walking out of the door.

'Absolutely,' replied Chloe forcing a smile that she hoped said supportive rather than scared – which is how she really felt. 'Just call me whenever you're ready and I'll be straight back.'

Chloe gathered the cast and crew together to give them the news and watched as their faces filled with the frustration of the delay. Animated discussion quickly followed.

'I can't hang around indefinitely you know. I do have another booking that I have to make pre-Christmas,' Lucinda was saying to Kareem as Chloe approached. Having only really seen the actress as the spiritual softly spoken character she played, it was strange meeting the real Lucinda standing with one hand on her hip and the other finger jabbing the producer in the chest. He seemed to accept it without flinching and Chloe guessed that dealing with haughty actors was simply part of his job.

'And we'll move heaven and earth to make sure you get to it,' he said as Lucinda turned and flounced off muttering that he'd better had or there'd be trouble.

Chloe gave Kareem a look of empathy and stood next to him. He put his hand around her shoulder and she leant into him giving him a friendly squeeze that said – we're in this together. Chloe had become good friends with the producer since first meeting him and she really wanted the very best for him. They stood quietly for a moment and then Kareem exhaled loudly.

'Come on, we'd better get on with the reschedule,' he said.

They walked over to Riley who was in the director's

tent with some of his team, listening to their instructions and nodding at what they heard. As Chloe and Kareem approached, Riley waved his team off.

'Someone is playing with us aren't they?' he said.

'I think so,' Kareem said. 'I've never actually heard of the union coming out to a location spontaneously so someone had to have called them.'

'Someone did,' said Chloe. 'He said "sources" had informed him.'

'So we find the source and we nail the culprit,' bellowed a voice behind them startling all three. They turned and saw Maggie who was now dressed as Columbo in a long raincoat.

Chloe looked at her and mouthed *What are you up to?*

'I know I look ridiculous,' said Maggie. 'But I'm serious about catching this saboteur and there's no harm in keeping everyone's spirits up while I do it is there?'

'I guess not,' said Kareem. 'And it made me smile.'

'Good,' replied Maggie. 'I read in an interview once that Peter Falk becomes the character as soon as he puts on that raincoat so you never know, if I look more like a detective, I might get results faster. I tried Miss Marple but as you can imagine, I couldn't pass for anyone that old and besides, she's so plain and dowdy. Why does no one invent an attractive femme-fatale detective?'

'They probably wouldn't blend in to the background,' suggested Riley. 'So they wouldn't be able to overhear conversations.'

Maggie raised her eyebrows as if she thought this was a very good point and one she was considering very carefully. Chloe knew there was a real danger of the next hour being hijacked by Maggie if they didn't send her on her way immediately.

'As you're in costume and ready for action, why don't you go and listen in to conversations in the pub,' said Chloe. 'I think most people have retreated there and I know you hear everything that goes on.'

'I'm on it,' replied Maggie lumbering off in character.

'Well at least she provided some light relief,' said Kareem. 'I think we needed that to break the tension today but we really should get on and discuss our options.'

Both Riley and Chloe nodded their agreement and they sat down spreading out the shooting schedule. Around them, the village was suddenly eerily quiet. There were no extras hanging around waiting to be called, no crew bustling everywhere setting up the next shots, no catering truck open for business and serving long queues. It was silent except for the sound of the seagulls.

'Okay,' started Kareem. 'We don't know how long the official is going to be here but the good news is that we were going to have our mid-shoot break the day after tomorrow so we may have just brought it forward a day. If we can answer all the questions we need to today, have a break tomorrow, then perhaps we'll get his sign off and can restart the following day.'

Chloe and Riley nodded along to what he was saying.

'There's no guarantee this guy will want to be hurried along,' Riley cautioned. 'So we have to make our efforts look as if they're all for his benefit.'

'Which of course they absolutely are,' added Chloe getting a nod from her co-conspirators.

Together they looked at the remaining scenes to be shot and moved things around to try and fit more into the remaining days just in case the delay went on for any longer.

'I need to try and get all Lucinda's scenes in first,' said Kareem. 'I don't think anyone else has a pre-Christmas booking so we're safe with the other actors.'

'And we really do need to start the Midwinter Festival on time,' said Chloe. 'I hate to put pressure on everyone but there is so much organised and it's too late to move it.'

'Okay – I think that's all we can move,' said Riley standing up and signalling that the time for talking was over. 'Let's see what we need to do for our official. I want to be back shouting Lights, Camera, Action as soon as I possibly can.'

'We all do,' said Chloe taking leave and heading back to the official.

The official was finishing off the paperwork section of his enquiry as they arrived and seemed satisfied with all the permits and insurances in place. Chloe breathed a sigh of relief on hearing this. She was fastidious about these things usually but there was always the chance that something had slipped through the net. Fortunately it hadn't. The official had a list of the complaints he'd been asked to address so they started by walking him to the chocolate shop that had been the museum and showing him the dagger. He made his notes as they explained everything but said nothing. This guy wasn't giving anything away. Next up they rang the extras agency and explained the problems and the solution they'd come up with. Chloe had fortunately registered every villager with the extras agency so that they would be covered and although this had been a real faff at the time, she was very glad she'd done so now. The official asked to walk along the coastline and through the rock pools where the character Poppy had been found. Chloe offered to take him but he asked whether Kareem would accompany him as he had some private questions for the producer.

Chloe knew that he'd be asking Kareem whether he had any doubts about the location and she felt sure the producer would sing their praises but nevertheless, as she watched them walking along the sand, Chloe nibbled off at least one fingernail.

'The word is,' muttered a voice, 'that someone tipped them off.'

Obviously it was Maggie giving an update on her investigations.

'I know that,' Chloe said impatiently. 'The official told me there had been a complaint. The thing I don't know is who complained and why.'

'Hold your horses, I was just getting there,' Maggie tutted. 'So first of all, I thought it might be Sophie from the hairdressers because she's been gossiping with absolutely everyone. She told her mum's friend that the shoot was being delayed because of the extras and she told her nan's pedicurist that they'd lost a dagger. I mean to say, if gossiping were an Olympic sport that woman could represent her country.'

Chloe wondered whether Maggie ever saw the irony in anything she ever said.

'So I thought that maybe they'd put it on Facebook or something,' she continued. 'That way, some busybody could have read about it and told the union.'

Chloe opened her mouth to comment but Maggie raised a finger to let her know she hadn't finished.

'Then I got talking to one of the runners, lovely lad hoping to make documentaries one day. Anyway, he said that it couldn't be hearsay because to respond like they have, the union would have to get a call or email from someone who was a member and they'd have to itemise dates and times. Which means ...'

Maggie paused dramatically.

'It was an inside job.'

Chloe clamped her hands over her face then drew them up through her hair in sheer frustration.

'Maggie,' she practically yelled. 'I know all this. I know it had to come from someone official. The question remains who and why? So if you don't have anything to tell me then perhaps you'd be better off back at the bar.'

'You are impatient,' said Maggie. 'Every detective has a grand reveal don't they. So Mrs Fluster-pants, I rang the union and said I wanted to add something onto the list of issues.'

Chloe's heart dropped like a stone as she waited dreading whatever the landlady had done.

'I said I knew they were investigating and I wanted my complaint looked into at the same time,' she continued. 'The lady on the phone said that wasn't possible and I had to register as a new complainant because they all get a case number or something. So I asked her, how do you know I didn't make the original one? And she said, because it was a *man* who made the original one.'

Chloe was listening now although they'd only eliminated half the population with this new piece of information.

'And apparently,' continued Maggie. 'This isn't the first time there have been complaints about the show.'

'Really?' said Chloe. Now this was news.

'That's right. The lady on the phone said they always get some complaint but until now they haven't been serious enough to look into. This time with a dagger and poison mentioned, they had no choice.'

Chloe felt slightly guilty about the relief this news

brought; it meant that whoever called in the officials had something against the show rather than Serenity Bay.

'So my next line of enquiry is to ask Kareem and Riley about the other complaints to see if there's a connection,' said Maggie. 'I'll have your culprit in no time.'

Maggie folded her arms in a very self-satisfied way and Chloe nodded her thanks. Despite not being very much further forward, they had something to go on. The landlady left to continue her investigations and Chloe waited for Kareem to return with the union official. They accompanied him back to the desk and left him completing his paperwork.

'What happens next?' asked Chloe.

'He's happy that the actress was in no danger over by the rock pools so now he goes back with his findings, reports to his supervisor and makes his recommendation. We can't get started until we get written notification of that recommendation. He might have additional measures he wants us to implement.'

'Did he give you any indication what the recommendation will be?'

'Nope,' said Kareem. 'He kept everything very close to his chest but we can't do any more now. He's seen everything, we've answered all his questions and now we sit tight. I hate just waiting around and so will Riley.'

'Then let's not just sit here. We're in this stunningly beautiful place and we've been forced to take some downtime. Let's make the most of it,' said Chloe.

Chapter Twenty-Two

Chloe knew that contractually, over the two week shoot, the crew had to have a day off. She had already planned to provide leisure activities where they were wanted but she also knew that the majority of the crew were heading into the city to buy Christmas presents or simply enjoy themselves. The stars couldn't really do that as they'd be recognised and hounded throughout their trip so main cast were staying in the village. Chloe had arranged for them to have a little "Serenity Bay Reviver" at the wellness retreat. As soon as the day off had been brought forward by circumstances, Chloe checked that Roisin was ready for them and the next morning the stars of the show along with Riley and Kareem arrived at the farmhouse looking forward to a day of revitalisation. Or at least some of them did.

'I really do think this is the most enormous waste of time and that you lot,' said Lucinda wagging a finger at Kareem and Riley, 'could be pursuing this official whoever he is or at least getting on with some editing. We could be learning lines not messing about.'

Riley reassured Lucinda that everything that could be done had been done and that they were simply bringing forward the scheduled break.

'This downtime is pretty unavoidable,' he said. 'Although if you don't know your lines then please do stay and do a read through with one of the crew.'

Lucinda harrumphed while Tegan gave out a little snort of laughter.

'I for one am really looking forward to this,' Tegan said

after getting a stern glare from her co-star. 'Now what do you have in store for us today?'

Roisin took centre stage and with a big smile on her face, started speaking.

'One of the things that everyone on this shoot seems to have learned is that you can't always plan ahead and you certainly can't control the future.'

Several murmurs of 'here, here' and 'you can say that again' rang around the room.

'This is a resource we all need in life – the ability to adapt,' she continued. 'If we can face change constructively and calmly, we'll all become more resilient and learn just how capable we are. So for this reason, I'm not going to tell you everything we have in store, I just want you to embrace each activity as it comes.'

This time the murmur was more like nervous excitement. Chloe knew exactly what Roisin and Lloyd had in store but if she hadn't then she too might have been slightly wary of what was going to happen to all these celebrities.

'We will be safe won't we?' asked Kareem.

'You will,' Roisin said with her palms pressed together in prayer mode as she nodded her assurance.

'And the shoot won't be jeopardised will it?' asked Riley.

'It most certainly will not,' she said.

'Will it be cold?' asked Ewan raising a giggle of laughter and getting a shove from Tegan.

'I'm afraid it probably will get a little chilly,' said Chloe. 'But we do have extra layers for you all.'

Chloe handed out the extra sweaters and down jackets they'd gathered guessing that the celebrities wouldn't have these things in their travel wardrobes, if at all. Dominic opted to keep his fedora on rather than accept a warmer beanie hat.

'I don't think Dominic Montgomery wears beanies—'he smiled—'even on his day off.'

He looked up and Chloe turned to follow his line of sight noticing her mother in the doorway of the farmhouse kitchen.

'Are you coming with us?' Dominic called out. Theresa strolled towards them looking at both Chloe and Kareem for permission to accept but they had no chance to reply as Tegan barged over to her and handed her a thick scarf.

'Of course you are,' she said. 'I can't have my confidant sitting here all alone being a warm and cosy Billy No-Mates while we're outside freezing our bits off. If we have to do this, then so do you.'

Chloe sighed with resignation as Theresa was drafted into the group and then just as the celebrities were getting restless and wanting to get on with the day, Lloyd turned up with a an old school style minibus and now chatting excitedly, the celebrities were jostled into it.

'This is like going on a class trip isn't it,' said Tegan.

'I bet you were one of the naughty ones on the back seat,' replied Harry with a wry grin on his face. Tegan simply winked in response.

Once they were all seated and on their way, Chloe looked around at the primetime TV stars wedged into their little minibus and imagined that none of them had been in such lowly transport since their school days. They were taking to it with varying degrees of enthusiasm. Tegan sat in the middle of the bus, next to Theresa and she seemed to have a hip flask with her. The two were sipping from it and giggling. Dominic and Jeremy sat behind them with their arms over the backs of the ladies chairs as if they were all on a singles coach trip and they were trying to chat them up. Lucinda and Ewan each sat alone with their arms wrapped closely around them as if afraid to touch the fabric of their seats. Harry was with Riley and the two nodded along independently to whatever music was playing through their ear-pods, Lizzie and DS Campbell seemed to have script notes in front of them and Chloe sat with Kareem hoping the day would go as well as they thought it might.

'Do you remember when you first came to Serenity Bay?' asked Chloe. Kareem nodded.

'I was shooting an advert wasn't I? And you taught me to surf – or Andy did. It was magical but please tell me you're not expecting these guys to put on wetsuits in this weather? I think Ewan would have a heart attack.'

Chloe smiled, it was still difficult to separate the fearsome historical writer Ewan was playing from the big scaredy-cat that he was in real life.

'No wetsuits or surfing.'

The coach drove a small way up the Northumberland coast and then stopped in a car park opposite a long causeway that led to a dramatic conical shaped island with a castle at the top. The chattering stopped on the minibus as everyone stared out of the window.

'Wow,' said Dominic. 'This is Holy Island isn't it?'

'It is,' Roisin said, 'and it's an important part of our heritage. The Vikings raided the Island on the eighth of June 793 AD. It's also where St Cuthbert is buried and it's considered the birthplace of Christianity.'

'It's also stunningly beautiful,' added Chloe.

Lloyd leapt down from the driver's seat and opened the door for everyone to jump out.

'Are you trying to insinuate that you're not driving us up to the island?' asked Lucinda. Everyone else had jumped out but she seemed glued to her seat.

At that moment Andy turned up in his van with several bikes loaded up.

'We're not driving,' said Lloyd. 'You guys are cycling over the causeway and up to the island. Have fun.'

And with that he drove off.

'He is coming back isn't he?' asked Ewan.

'Live in this moment,' replied Roisin. 'Now everyone finds the bike that Andy has picked for you. It will soon warm up when you're pedalling and trust me, it isn't far.'

There were a few moments of sorting everyone out with the right size bike and then Roisin led them across the sand and onto the causeway.

Although Chloe had seen it several times, this was actually the first time she'd ever cycled across it and knowing that you're on a road which is only safe to cross for a few hours a day was both exciting and nerve-wracking. In only a few hours this path would be completely submerged beneath the North Sea and there were always stories in the local press about tourists who'd mistimed the crossing and attempted to get across only to find the tide coming in quicker than they'd thought.

'Okay everyone,' shouted Roisin. 'Follow me.'

Chloe would follow last and watched as the TV stars got onto the bikes and wobbled along initially before remembering how to cycle and starting to speed up. She'd watched so many of the retreat guests pick up a bike for the first time in many years and it was always a delight to watch the nervous concentration turn into joyous realisation that they were turning the pedals and flying along. Fortunately it was quite a calm day without any wind but everyone was wearing the thick cycling gloves Lloyd had packed and it really wasn't a very long ride although it felt like a true adventure. By the time everyone reached the entrance to the ancient priory on the island every single person had rosy red cheeks and a big smile.

'Phew,' said Jeremy. 'I haven't done anything like that in years. I kept thinking the sea was closing in behind me and I had to pedal faster.'

'Completely invigorating wasn't it?' said Dominic. 'I feel bloody marvellous – what about you Ewan? Did you enjoy it?'

Ewan said nothing; he was staring beyond the priory over at Lindisfarne Castle perched on top of the hill.

'Look at this place, there is history everywhere,' he murmured in awe. 'This is definitely the kind of setting my character would have written about isn't it?'

His long legs seemed fired up as he started striding around the priory while the others followed albeit at a much slower pace.

Tegan and Theresa were only just in front of Chloe, sauntering along behind everyone deep in hip-flask fuelled conversation. Chloe wasn't trying to listen in but they weren't exactly being quiet.

'I know darling,' exclaimed Tegan, 'and she's absolutely right – one does need to take chances in life. Seize the day and all that. If I hadn't taken part in that celebrity cooking show, I'd have no work now and I can't cook to save my life.'

They cackled loudly and it was quite infectious so Chloe couldn't help but laugh along with them. They turned around.

'Oh sweetheart, I didn't know you were there,' said Chloe's mum with a broad smile and a slightly glazed expression. 'We were just talking about Kylie.'

'Marvellous woman, simply marvellous,' continued Tegan, taking another swig from this seemingly bottomless flask and handing it over to Theresa who did the same. They then went back to their conversation and Chloe hung back a little just to be sure that she didn't have to get involved. The way these two were going, it probably wouldn't be long before one of them broke into song.

They reached a tourist attraction board which outlined everything there was to see on the island and the actors started fanning out to visit the thing that most interested them. They were told the meet up time and place – one o'clock at the castle. Chloe watched them as they went and as she could have predicted, Tegan, Theresa and Dominic headed straight for the famous winery to test the mead so she stayed close to them. The winery guide recognised the actors immediately and asked for a selfie which was given although Tegan did negotiate "a sample for a selfie" causing Chloe to roll her eyes in an apology at the guide. After the pictures the guide explained the history of the winery and how the word "honeymoon" was a Viking import – it came from their custom of newlyweds staying in bed and drinking mead for a month to increase their chances of a fulfilled and happy marriage.

'It would certainly have helped mine.' Tegan laughed. 'Being drunk for the whole time!'

Dominic politely declined the second sample and having checked that he was happy to make sure the ladies didn't get into too much trouble and that they'd make the meet-up, Chloe left to find the others.

DS Campbell and Lizzie headed to the beaches and dunes hoping to catch sight of some of the birds the island was famous for. Lucinda, Jeremy and Roisin were in the Priory enjoying its peace and reading about the early history of the building and its role in the establishment of Christianity. They looked quietly contemplative so Chloe left them and headed out to the road and up the steep hill to the castle where she knew she'd find Riley, Kareem and Ewan. Having trotted quickly along the road and then taken the hill at speed, she arrived at the lookout point where the guys were standing, absolutely breathless but boy, was it worth it.

'Look at that,' said Riley. 'Just imagine standing here as a young monk seeing a fleet of Viking long ships approaching. It must have seemed like a message from God at that point in time.'

The distant sea was still and a shade of brushed silver that matched the low sky making the horizon difficult to discern. From here you could imagine that the earth was flat and that the boats had come from a piece of land just out of sight. Chloe had pictured the scene Riley described many times; since moving to live on the Northumberland coast she'd stared across that sea on calm days and in raging storms wondering about the people who'd had the courage and the imagination to cross it.

'It makes you wonder how they knew they'd reach another land,' said Ewan almost echoing her thoughts. 'They had no maps, no guarantees – they just set off and knew they'd cope with whatever happened.'

Kareem laughed slightly as if he'd realised something.

'Which I'm guessing is the reason Roisin brought us here? To realise that we can cope with anything that comes our way?'

'Kinda.' Chloe gave him a wink. 'Though I'm hoping we never have to cope with a Viking invasion!'

On the dot of one o'clock, Roisin appeared with Jeremy and Lucinda while staggering behind them were the hip-flask ladies with Dominic propping them up in the middle. Roisin asked everyone to stand in a line and look out at the sea; then she asked them to close their eyes and let their other senses take over.

'What can you smell, hear, feel and taste?' she asked.

The group fell silent and all that could be heard were the waves, the gulls and gentle breathing. Until Tegan let out a very loud hiccup and Theresa giggled making everyone else do the same.

'I guess it's time to go.' Roisin smiled, inviting everyone to turn around and face inland in the direction they'd come. They contentedly walked back from the castle, into the village, where all the cottages were now lit up with tiny fairy lights around the rooftops and windows; they glittered in the fading light and somehow made everything seem warmer. The large Christmas tree in the square was bedecked with coloured lights and hundreds of homemade angels made by the village children and on each one, they'd written a wish or a hope for the future. The celebrities stopped for a moment to read some of them and pop some money in the collection box for the local lifeboats. They then made their way back towards the causeway and suddenly stopped.

'This doesn't look like the way we came,' said Dominic. 'Something's different.'

It took a moment for anyone to say anything. Then Ewan got it.

'The causeway,' he said pointing at the place it should have been. 'It's completely covered. The tide has come in.'

'How do we get back?' cried Lucinda.

Chapter Twenty-Three

'Do you mean to tell us that we've been standing here staring out at the blooming sea when all that time the tide has been coming in?' roared DS Campbell, his cheeks red with anger rather than rosy.

'Why did no one take the precaution of looking at the crossing times?' added Lucinda. 'How long are we going to be stuck here?'

'There's no real need to worry. I seem to remember reading that the causeway is crossable every six hours or so,' Lizzie said. 'It's not as if we'll be stuck here forever.'

'Six hours?' exclaimed Lucinda. 'It'll be pitch black in less than three and I'm already freezing cold.'

Riley stepped forward and was about to say something but Kareem put his hand gently on the director's arm and said calmly, 'Don't worry, Roisin will have a plan.'

Roisin nodded her thanks and asked everyone not to worry – she did indeed have a plan.

'I'm sorry to have startled you so much. I simply wanted to use this day off to help everyone,' she said very gently as not everyone looked entirely convinced. 'In life, we can make plans and have adventures and for most of the time we feel good about ourselves. We feel glad that we took the risk and we have faith in our abilities. Then something happens out of the blue and doubt descends. Our first instinct is to doubt ourselves, abandon our plans and the things that make us feel good completely.'

'Flight or fight,' murmured Lizzie.

'Exactly,' said Roisin. 'Now you've had your shoot disrupted so we made the most of it. We came here and it has surpassed your expectations. You went from wanting to stay at Serenity Bay and learning lines that you already knew to being glad you came here. Now, when you have realised that your way back to your familiar harbour is blocked, your fear responses have re-emerged.'

'I've certainly never felt such a wide range of emotions in such a short space of time,' said Dominic. 'I'll certainly be able to draw on that in future.'

'But will you be able to show them with all that Botox,' cackled Tegan and everyone, including Dominic began to laugh.

'Mindfulness isn't just about relaxing into good moments,' continued Roisin. 'It's about taking stock when you have a bump in the road or when the road itself has actually disappeared under water.'

There was another murmur of laughter and Chloe noted that Roisin's serene tones had succeeded in calming everyone down.

'I want you to take a moment now and note how you feel. How your body feels and what your mind is saying,' said Roisin. 'It doesn't matter what that emotion is and I'm not going to ask you to express it but just acknowledge it.'

Everyone seemed to take a deep breath at the same time and most people closed their eyes. Chloe watched them following Roisin's instructions, some subconsciously nodding as if recognising their feelings for the first time. Roisin called them gently out of the reflection after a few moments.

'Thank you for doing that,' she said. 'Now has anyone worked out how we're going to get home?'

'If we're not waiting for the causeway to clear,' said Riley, 'then surely we have to go by boat?'

'Indeed we do,' said Roisin smiling. 'Now if everyone

will just follow me, we have one of the Serenity Bay trip cruisers waiting to take us back.'

There was a little whoop of delight and Jeremy said, 'Well I don't mind shouting from the rooftops that the emotion I'm feeling at those words is sheer relief.'

He got an affirmatory pat on the back from Riley as they made their way down the hill to the harbour. When they got there a little blue and white boat decked with fairy lights across the bow was waiting to take them home.

Inside the cabin, the crew of the boat handed out blankets and mugs of hot chocolate and once the celebrities were snuggled up with hands cupped around the warming drinks, a jovial atmosphere began to emerge.

'I have to say,' said Dominic opening the window by his seat and turning his face to the weakening winter sun. 'As much as I enjoyed recalling my childhood on that bicycle, this is a much better way to travel.'

'Such a splendid day – I only wish I'd kept a tot of brandy back for this chocolate.' Tegan drained her cup and rolled up a corner of the blanket like a pillow, putting it on Theresa's arm before falling asleep. Chloe watched as her mother tilted her head, rested it on the actress's and closed her eyes too; the pair seemed to have become very good friends in a short space of time.

Fortunately for everyone, the sea was kind to them on the return and for those who stayed awake despite the soporific roll of the waves, the views were stunning. As they motored further away from Holy Island, the silhouette of the castle grew darker and the sky started to take on the pale gold of the early sunset. The myriad of seabirds the area was famous for knew that the light would soon be gone and flitted through the skies, crying out in a final encore.

'It was a bit of a risk.' Riley leant forward in his seat to say to Chloe. 'But, now that we're safely on our way back, I have to admit it was worth it. If I'd stayed in Serenity I would have been marching around fretting and refreshing my email all day and it wouldn't have done any good. Now with just a few hours out, I feel rested and roaring to go. All we need is the nod from our friendly official.'

Chloe nodded and told him she felt exactly the same. At that moment, as if the heavens had heard their words and decided to smile on them, the powers of the universe sent a ping notification to three phones all at once. Kareem, Riley and Chloe looked at each other anxiously and then at the message – the official had found nothing amiss and the location was cleared to recommence filming. They all exhaled at the same time and a broad smile broke out on each of their faces; they high-fived each other.

'I'm guessing you've had good news,' said Roisin as she watched them.

'The best news,' replied Chloe.

'And talk about perfect timing,' added Kareem. 'We've had a fabulous day out – the crew and actors are refreshed and now we get the go ahead to resume filming.'

'Everyone ...' Riley stood up and called out across the cabin, waking most of the occupants. 'We're back in business – filming resumes tomorrow morning 7 a.m. sharp.'

'Brilliant news!' shouted Jeremy raising his mug and going to clink it with DS Campbell. The ex-detective simply tutted and went back to staring out of the window leaving it up to Lizzie to raise her empty mug and join the actor in celebrating the good news.

When the boat pulled up into Serenity Bay, Lloyd was

waiting on the harbour with the minibus ready to take everyone back to their respective accommodation.

'It sounded as if a party boat was pulling up.' He laughed holding out his hand to steady Tegan and Theresa as they tottered down the short gangway.

'Life is a party darling, or at least it should be,' replied Tegan. 'Shall we head to The Fiddler's Arms and have one for the road, Theresa?'

'At this time in the afternoon?' shouted Kareem, getting a wave of dismissal from his lead actress.

'I'll tell Maggie to get them out by dinner time and I promise to come back and bring them home at a decent hour,' Lloyd reassured him.

Chloe joined Kareem and Riley back at the office to ensure that everything and everyone would be ready to begin the shoot in the morning. The extras she called were particularly excited that filming was resuming and many Chloe spoke to mentioned a sense of sadness that any problems had happened at Serenity Bay – almost as if they themselves had let the production company down.

'That's exactly how I felt,' Chloe told person after person. 'But don't worry, it wasn't our fault and we're back on track now.'

It was after seven when Chloe finished and having ensured that she had done everything humanly possible to make sure the shoot would start on time and be on full throttle for the whole day, she left her office and headed back to the pub where, true to his word, Lloyd was cajoling Theresa and Tegan into the minibus to drive them back to the farmhouse. Maggie was standing at the doorway with her arms folded.

'She's a bad influence on your mother that one,' she said. 'And she flirts with anything in trousers.'

Chloe snorted quietly and suspected that the flirting was probably more of the problem. Maggie liked to be the alpha female and Tegan probably wasn't playing these unwritten rules. Chloe thanked Maggie for looking after her mother and turned to Lloyd as he finished fastening the ladies' seat belts and locking the doors firmly.

'Can I jump on board?' asked Chloe getting an 'of course' in reply.

She wanted to see Roisin again. The mindfulness exercises she'd done today had been great for the actors but Chloe hadn't been able to relax into it as she'd felt obliged to keep an eye on her entourage just in case they really didn't want to participate. Now that most of the problems were fixed, Chloe needed Roisin's help to relax so that she could simply stop dreading the festive season.

'I can certainly help with that,' said Roisin as Chloe explained herself.

Chloe sat down with the farmhouse guests for dinner as Roisin and Lloyd served up a delicious Parmigiana with home-made rosemary focaccia. With the aroma of the herbs and the deliciousness of the melted cheese over fresh vegetables, they could have been in central Tuscany rather than rural Northumberland.

'Good food is one of life's great joys,' said Tegan savouring a mouthful and looking as if she were in a state of bliss.

After dinner, they took a short leisurely walk to help the food digest and then Lloyd suggested that he look after Tegan and Theresa for the rest of the evening and try to encourage them to have an early night. Roisin and Chloe retired to the yoga room.

'So tell me what's bothering you,' said Roisin gently.

'I'm trying not to worry about Christmas, I really

am. Andy has been fabulous. He's promised to deliver everything I want and asked me to leave it completely up to him but even the thought of that makes me tense.'

'Do you want to do all of the organisation yourself?'

'No,' replied Chloe. 'Absolutely not – Andy adores Christmas and I would worry that I'd get it wrong – I'd make it the worst Christmas he's ever had.'

'Okay, so we definitely have to get you focussing on the moment.' Roisin smiled encouragingly. 'Come on let's start with some yoga.'

Chloe joined her friend sitting cross-legged on their yoga mats and followed her as she began by gently stretching her neck to one side and then the other, taking deep breaths in and out as she moved. Chloe felt herself relaxing almost immediately and Roisin asked her to lie down on her back and stretch out.

'Raise your hands above your head and point your toes,' said Roisin. 'Now push them to either end of the room so your spine grows two inches taller.'

Chloe did as she was asked, stretching her body and feeling every muscle elongate. Gnarly knots and tight tendons groaned as they relaxed and Chloe felt as if her back was melting into the floor like a marshmallow into hot chocolate. They lay there for a few moments longer with Roisin quietly asking Chloe to breath in to the count of five and breath out for the same length of time.

'Now,' said Roisin softly. 'I want you to think about how your body feels, whether there are any aches or pains you notice.'

Chloe thought her voice was almost ethereal as if her friend might be floating on the ceiling.

'If there are any aches or pains then gently touch them now.'

Chloe lifted a totally relaxed hand and crossed it over to her shoulder which had been tense.

'Thank that pain for reminding you to move more throughout the day and know that you can let it go by stretching.'

Chloe mentally let the ache go and felt her shoulders drop even further.

'Now I'd like you to search your body and find out where the anxiety is sitting,' said Roisin.

Chloe felt a little tension rear its head as she didn't really want to do this but she did as she was told and realised the anxiety was sitting in one particular spot – in the centre of her chest just below her ribs. She put her hand on it and her hand felt warm.

'I want you to know that it's just a feeling, like that shoulder ache and it can be eased away just as easily,' said Roisin. 'You're pointing to your solar plexus and it's often associated with the colour yellow so I want you to picture it as a dandelion. It seems real and bright but if you take a deep breath and blow, you'll see it turn into a pale clock of seeds and one by one they fly away.'

Chloe did as she was told and could visualise a bright yellow glow disappearing and turning into a gentle collection of seeds vanishing into the air as she blew. Her entire body also seemed to calm down with each exhale.

'Know that whenever you want to, you can close your eyes, blow those seeds away and relax.'

With that last blow, Chloe knew that she really was about to melt into her mat and simply let it happen.

Chapter Twenty-Four

'Woah this place is on fire today,' said Andy as he approached the director's tent with a coffee for Chloe. He was wearing a different Christmas hat and Chloe wondered whether everyone in the village had knitted something for him. 'Yesterday seems to have done everyone the power of good.'

Chloe stepped up to give him a kiss before taking the coffee and looked around at what he was watching. The village really was buzzing. Riley and Kareem had been up with the crew since the crack of dawn and every scene they were filming today was set up and ready to go. All they had to do was move actors and cameras.

'I really think it did do everyone good – the people who had the time to get their shopping done seem enormously relieved and everyone who came with us to Holy Island keep telling me how invigorating and inspiring it was,' said Chloe. 'I even think they've forgiven us for making them think they were stranded.'

'I'm sure they'll be telling everyone about it over their Christmas lunch. Talking of which, do you have any instructions for me yet?' Andy grinned.

Chloe recalled the session with Roisin the day before and felt that yellow glow of anxiety appear just below her ribs. She pictured it, then calmly blew it away before looking up at Andy.

'You know what?' she said. 'I think you're the expert here so I will be happy with whatever you would like to do.'

Andy raised his eyebrows in disbelief but Chloe simply

kissed him on the nose and added, 'As long as you're there that's all that matters.'

Riley called everyone to their places so Andy kissed her goodbye and said he'd look in later when her dad arrived.

It was a big day in many ways; the shoot would be particularly full-on with some of the bigger scenes shot today, everyone had to be particularly vigilant to ensure that nothing went wrong and in her own personal life, Chloe's dad was finally coming to Serenity Bay and perhaps her parents would reconcile. Chloe took out her notepad and scribbled; she doubted her father would remember to bring flowers or champagne but she could at least buy the bubbly from Maggie and give it to her dad to present.

She exhaled again, blowing away another pang of anxiety. She knew she couldn't control the future and dwelling on things that might never happen was of no help to anyone. Chloe smiled to herself and thought that the session with Roisin had worked wonders. She'd fallen into a deep state of relaxed slumber yesterday and her friend had let her lie in peace until Chloe opened her eyes naturally. It had only been twenty minutes but had felt incredible – a real power nap. Chloe had walked home to the pub, taken the sandwich offered by Maggie upstairs and after a warm shower had tucked herself in and enjoyed the best night's sleep in a very long time.

'Okay let's have quiet.' Riley was calling out, jolting Chloe back to the moment. 'And action.'

Jeremy was working at his office in Serenity Publishing when his phone beeped with a notification. He picked it up, seeing that an unknown number had sent a text message: Bookshop tonight. I know your secret

Horrified, Jeremy slammed the phone face down and

then looked around suspiciously to check whether anyone was watching him.

'Hmm, maybe I've got these odds wrong,' said Maggie from her usual spot – just behind the director's tent almost keeping out of the way. 'Jeremy was arrested but then they let him go. Now we know he has a secret, so have they got it wrong and he's not really innocent?'

Everyone ignored her. They were in the moment and completely focussed on the work. The crew scurried round to the next scene while Riley briefed Jeremy.

'Now is not the time, Maggie,' whispered Chloe. 'I'll come and see you later.'

Maggie put her nose in the air as if she'd been affronted and stepped back a little, her arms folded in indignation. She told any villager who passed by that the odds on it being Jeremy were coming down soon so they'd better get their bets in.

Next Jeremy was seen walking into the dark bookshop. He tried the light switch but it wasn't working. The only light was the moon through the windows casting a path through the rows of books. Jeremy followed the light and then suddenly there was the sound of a chair being scraped backwards. Jeremy jumped and called out to ask who was there. No one responded.

'I don't know what you think you know,' Jeremy called out into the darkness. There was another sound, like a heavy book being dropped onto a table. Jeremy scrambled in his pockets for his phone and nervously fumbled to put the torchlight on. He moved it around the store but there was no one there. Then the light caught the tails of a coat vanishing around one of the shelves and the sound of the bell above the main door rang out. Jeremy ran towards the noise, the camera staying in spot, watching his retreat.

There was a loud thud and Jeremy cried out. The camera moved to show Jeremy lying face down on the ground and a blood stain emerging from near his head. In the next scene shot, Ewan walked past the bookshop and saw the door slightly ajar. He peered inside and called out but getting no response, walked in towards the light of the phone. He discovered Jeremy's body and gasped.

'That Ewan could have just come from inside the bookshop couldn't he?' murmured Maggie getting no response from anyone.

The crew really were motoring today and with the village extras in place creating a crowd scene, medics arrived and stretchered Jeremy out of the bookshop and into an ambulance. It drove off with sirens flashing.

'Oh hang on then,' said Maggie as everyone took their lunch break. 'That wasn't a body bag – it means he's still alive doesn't it?'

Chloe knew all the questions now were rhetorical, as if Maggie were sitting on her own couch on a Sunday evening following the story and trying to guess the outcome. She smiled and winked at the landlady as the next scene began.

The remaining authors were sitting in the village hall which was decorated and ready for the awards ceremony with rows of chairs facing the stage at the front.

'What on earth do we do now?' said Tegan pacing around the floor. The large sunglasses her character wore were providing a vital service today – Chloe knew the actress and her mother had continued to quaff cocktails into the evening so there had been distinctly dark circles under Tegan's eyes as they began the scene. 'I only came to this godforsaken place for the bloody award and if it's not going to happen then I for one am not hanging around.'

'I don't imagine any of us will be able to leave,' said

Dominic continuing the scene and taking a seat in the front row labelled "Reserved" while Agatha lay down in front of him. 'This is an active investigation and Ewan was the one to find Jeremy. The local police will want to question him.'

Ewan shuddered. 'It was horrible. I've never seen so much blood or a real body.'

'Your books are full of blood and wars and warriors slashing each other with swords and spears,' mocked Tegan. 'And you can't stand the sight of one man on the floor – face down?'

'You weren't there,' replied Ewan sheepishly. 'It was very dark and very scary.'

'And it wasn't even a body,' continued Tegan now standing throwing her arms in the air. 'He's very much alive – as you would have known if you'd checked his pulse.'

Another shudder from Ewan. 'Oh no, I couldn't have touched him.'

Tegan looked across at Dominic and shook her head in despair. She plonked down on the seat beside him and sighed.

Just then, the action moved to the back of the hall where the door swung open and Portia marched in with the local police detective.

'He's going to be okay,' cried Portia. 'I'm so relieved. I don't think I could take any more after Poppy.'

Dominic stood up and put his arms around a weeping Portia. 'Has he said what happened?' he asked over at the police detective.

'Only that he got a text from an unknown user asking to meet him at the bookshop.'

'Well that sounds decidedly dodgy,' said Tegan. 'Why

on earth did he go? I wouldn't have gone to meet a stranger.'

'He said he thought it might have been one of you authors,' replied the police detective. 'He doesn't have all your numbers programmed in.'

'And when he got there,' continued Dominic, 'I'm presuming that someone came out of the shadows and hit him from behind?'

'Almost,' replied the police detective. 'They actually hit him on the front of the head. There was a huge risk that they'd be seen so we can only presume that they were intending to kill him.'

There was a gasp from Portia but Tegan just sighed and said, 'Well that much was obvious wasn't it? So, what happens next? Are these awards actually happening? Or should we all go home?'

'Jeremy would really like the awards to go ahead,' said Portia. 'He's going to be discharged in twenty-four hours if things look okay and he feels that it would be disrespectful to both Bart and Poppy to cancel now. The awards meant so much to them.'

'Don't worry,' said Dominic, 'we'll be here for them. The show must go on.'

'And cut,' shouted Riley. At his words the actors relaxed, the scene was cleared and rigs were moved ready for the next shot.

'I told Lizzie that scene wouldn't work. Imagine a copper coming to your house and telling you all the evidence he had then not even asking you a question – honestly, I'd kick this guy off the force.'

Chloe realised that DS Campbell always waited until Riley was out of earshot before complaining about the show. To her his actions felt very passive-aggressive and definitely disloyal. Still, he was a member of the production team and even if he wasn't being professional, she would be and simply smiled at him.

'I would never have called your police force in the first place,' said Maggie as ever within eavesdropping distance. 'Not when Dominic's around anyway.'

DS Campbell glared daggers at Maggie and stormed off leaving Chloe pursing her lips and trying not to laugh.

'We shouldn't really upset the writers,' she said to Maggie. 'He's very proud of his police background.'

'Oh I hate it when people harp on about what they used to do.' Maggie waved a hand in dismissal. 'If they'd been any good they'd still be doing it.'

Riley called for quiet yet again and the team began on the final scenes to be shot that day. They filmed Jeremy being discharged from hospital with his head bandaged up, him arriving back at his cottage and Portia visiting him with a huge basket of fruit from all the authors at the festival. Chloe was incredibly impressed at the focus from everyone throughout the day.

'And that's a wrap for today,' shouted Riley slightly ahead of schedule. 'Thank you everyone. That was a tremendous day's work. Let's keep this energy up for the rest of the shoot.'

The pace had kept everyone on a high and everyone applauded these words before the crew began jumping onto their wrap-up tasks and the actors headed back to their accommodation.

Chloe looked at her watch – her dad should be arriving soon. He had promised to stop at the pub first and together with Andy the three of them would walk down to the farmhouse to surprise her mum. She knew it was the control freak coming out in her but she really just wanted to be sure that he looked presentable and picked up the champagne to take with him. With Maggie she headed back to the pub.

'How is Theresa going to feel about you all disturbing her retreat?' asked Maggie.

Chloe hadn't thought about it like that before.

'I mean,' continued Maggie, 'she's come here to get away from things hasn't she?'

'Given that I live here, it's a strange place to get away from things,' Chloe said. 'I'm sure she'll be delighted to see Dad again, especially bearing a glass of champagne.'

'If you say so,' Maggie said.

Back at the pub, Maggie put the champagne in the chiller and Chloe popped up to her room to freshen up. She didn't intend to hang around at the farm as she wanted to get them talking and then leave her parents to it. Chloe had a quick wash and threw on a clean jumper then walked back down the stairs. Andy was already there and they wrapped their arms around each other in a tight, end of day hug.

'I think this is him,' said Maggie peering out of the window.

Chloe let go of Andy and joined Maggie by the window – sure enough, a sensible executive saloon with cream seats had parked up at the back of the pub and her father was bent over the boot taking out a suitcase. Chloe leapt from the window and ran to the back door to welcome him in. He stood up and closed the boot waving at her and as she looked at her father, Chloe suddenly found it very difficult to keep the broad smile on her face from fading. Her cheeks ached from just holding it in place. Her father was tall and broad but seemed to have developed a stoop making him look frailer than she'd ever seen him. He'd also grown a silver grey beard and on a face that had been indoors all week, he just looked so very old.

'Dad,' she said giving him a hug while Andy took his bag in for him. Chloe so desperately wanted to tell him he was looking well but she simply couldn't so went for the truth. 'You look tired, was that conference fairly full on?'

'It was. And it didn't help that your mother decided to have a midlife crisis in the middle of it either. Still, we'll sort her out won't we?'

Chloe hated herself for it but she couldn't stop herself comparing her dad to Dominic. He was an actor, in character and usually in full make-up but he was also the man Theresa had spent most time with over the past fortnight. Her father looked like the black and white version to Dominic's technicolour.

'Now, let's get down to the farmhouse shall we?' her dad said.

'Would you like to change or freshen up first?' asked Chloe looking at the dark grey suit that seemed to join up with the beard to make a tall streak of dullness.

'No, I'm good.'

Chloe took her dad's arm and they walked slowly down the street towards the farmhouse. Andy picked up the champagne and strode alongside.

'You don't want to forget this, Geoff,' he said, handing over the bottle.

Chloe's dad looked at the label and shrugged. 'I'd rather have a pint of ale.'

They reached the farmhouse and Chloe knocked on the door rather than barge in. She wanted Roisin to open it and perhaps stage-manage the meeting. Roisin did open the door but with a flustered frown on her face.

'Hi Geoff,' she said to Chloe's dad. 'Come in, although we've got a bit of a strange situation on our hands.'

The three followed Roisin into the kitchen where Tegan was sitting having what looked like a Virgin Mary. Chloe looked around and then at Roisin.

'Theresa isn't here,' said Roisin. 'She was slightly hungover after yesterday so I just left her to sleep it off today. I was so busy with other things and I didn't think anything of it when I hadn't seen her all day. I went to check on her just now and she wasn't in her room. I tried her phone but got no answer. Then Tegan came back from the shoot.'

She held out her hand for Tegan to continue the story.

'Darlings, how was I to know her handsome husband was arriving today.' Tegan's palm was placed gently on her chest as she protested her innocence. 'I understand it was to be a surprise – well it certainly was to me.'

'So where is my mum?' asked Chloe.

'She told me last night that she has a friend in Edinburgh who she hasn't seen for years,' Tegan said. 'And I said that she should seize the day and make arrangements to see her immediately. So she did.'

'She's in Edinburgh?' asked Chloe.

'Yes, carpe diem and all that. Not to worry, it's only for a couple of days.' She turned her attention to Geoff and smoothed down his tie before adding, 'Now aren't you going to introduce me to this handsome man?'

Chapter Twenty-Five

As Tegan continued to flirt with her father, Chloe, Andy and Roisin stepped out of the kitchen and stood in the hallway whispering.

'What on earth are we going to do now?' asked Chloe. 'How can I get them back together if they're not physically in the same place?'

'And Tegan doesn't know the name of this friend? Could we find out? Is your mum on Facebook?'

Chloe shook her head to every one of Andy's questions. She didn't know who this person was, even whether they were male or female and she couldn't think of any way of finding out. Her shoulders dropped in utter defeat. She had hoped this evening would be the start of a reconciliation but it looked as if her parents were going to be driven even further apart. They heard a peel of laughter from the kitchen and the door opened.

Tegan called out, 'Roisin darling, would you care to tell us where you keep that delicious local ale? This gentleman is positively parched.'

Roisin left to attend to her guest and Andy followed her. As soon as Geoff was engaged in studying the labels of the ale bottles and discussing them with Andy, Tegan snuck away from the group and joined Chloe.

'Look, I'm really sorry that I didn't think to tell you about your mum,' she said in a conspiratorial whisper. 'I honestly didn't know this was going to happen.'

'Don't worry. There's no way you could have known and it's not your fault.'

'But maybe it's fortuitous,' continued Tegan. 'I hope

you don't mind me saying this but your father is looking a little bedraggled and it wouldn't have done their relationship any good for him to have met your mother like that.'

Chloe felt tears prickling at her eyes and had to wipe one away. She knew Tegan was right but to even think this of her own dad was wrong; she loved him dearly and it was a betrayal. Tegan placed an elegant hand on her arm.

'You see it too don't you?' asked Tegan.

Chloe nodded as the tears managed to escape and rolled down her cheeks.

'Don't worry darling,' Tegan said. 'I have a plan and by the time your mum gets back and meets her husband again, he'll be absolutely irresistible. And if Theresa doesn't want him, then I'll be first in the queue.'

Tegan gave her an exaggerated wink and Chloe gave a little snort of laughter but because she'd also been full to the brim with tears it turned into a rather snotty, messy affair. She apologised to the actress who simply reached into a pocket and pulled out a packet of clean tissues for her.

'Come on,' she said to Chloe. 'We all need a good night's sleep and tomorrow we start Operation Gorgeous Geoff.'

Chloe simply nodded. She wasn't sure what Tegan had in store for her dad but right now, she was just relieved to have someone else seeing the problem and offering to help. Tegan had her mum's ear so maybe if the actress even pretended to fancy her dad it would get her mum's attention. It all felt so complicated and after being on a high for so much of the day, the energy now was seeping from her body and she was just exhausted.

Chloe and Tegan rejoined the group in the kitchen where they politely discussed her dad's conference and the actress made light of Theresa's trip to Edinburgh. Geoff said he might as well head off to bed but Tegan begged him to stay with her.

'I have to do a read through for tomorrow,' she said. 'I'd love to perform for you.'

She walked her fingertips up his arm as she spoke and the outrageous flirtation seemed to do the job as Geoff said that he might as well watch a movie star in action. Tegan began to read from the script and asked Geoff to read Dominic's lines. Chloe sat quietly and watched as Tegan directed her father to be more assertive or louder or bolder. She wondered whether this was part of the plan to make her father irresistible and if so, whether it had any chance whatsoever of working. Andy and Chloe decided to leave them to it so said goodbye and walked back to the pub. On the way, she told her boyfriend about the conversation she'd had with Tegan.

'Well if anyone can give him a little sparkle, I imagine it's Tegan,' said Andy. 'You just have to watch the extras when they're around her – I'd never seen our local butcher offering to hold a handbag until she asked him.'

They both laughed and linked arms closely all the way to the pub. As they reached the doorway Chloe turned to him and wrapped her arms tightly around his body. It felt so safe and strong.

'I don't want to let go,' she said, 'not tonight.'

'It'll be a very tight squeeze in a single bed – but I will if you will.'

They headed up the stairs and negotiated the tiny amount of space. If Chloe stayed wrapped in his arms and didn't move an inch, they could just about fit on and might even get some sleep. Fortunately she didn't plan on moving a muscle.

'Night night,' she said, nestling into his chest and closing her sleepy eyes.

'Night my love,' Andy said softly, kissing the top of her head.

When Chloe woke she was alone in the bed. She sat up feeling slightly bereft and then she saw him. Andy had taken a pillow and was sleeping on the floor, wrapped in his coat and her dressing gown. Chloe knelt down beside him and kissed his lips – he woke up.

'Good morning sleeping beauty,' she said. 'Have you been on the floor all night?'

'Most of it'—he yawned—'I think you must have been having a wild dream. You were throwing your arms all over the place. It was a lot safer down here.'

'I'm sorry,' said Chloe lying down beside him as Andy pulled her in close. 'If it's any consolation, I think I slept really well.'

Chloe propped herself up on her arm and looking down at her boyfriend, who was fabulously handsome even after a night without sleep, kissed him again.

'We should be getting down to breakfast,' she said. 'We've both got big days ahead.'

'I should have left a message on the bar to let Maggie know I'd be staying.'

'Oh don't worry about Maggie. Nothing gets past her, she'll know you're here.'

After calling Roisin and checking that all was well at the farmhouse, they went downstairs into the dining room, and as Chloe had predicted there was already a place set for Andy.

'I've put extra bacon on your plate, Andy,' said Maggie giving him a nudge as she served them. 'In case you worked up an appetite.'

Chloe shook her head and Andy actually blushed slightly as he thanked her. Seemingly unconcerned that the couple might want some privacy, Maggie pulled up a chair and sat down beside them as they ate.

'So do you think now that official bloke is gone, that's the end of the conspiracy to disrupt the show?' She selected a piece of toast from their rack and buttered it for herself. 'If whoever called that union knows they failed, what more can they do? I very much doubt they'll show their face now anyway so I'm not sure that you need me investigating any more.'

Having moved her attention back to sorting out her parents, Chloe had almost forgotten that the disruption had been caused by someone calling the union and with Maggie's words it came racing back to the fore.

'Oh I think we always need you being vigilant,' she heard Andy saying. 'In fact I was wondering why those two over there have so much to talk about this early in the morning. Maybe you could fill their cups and find out what they're saying?'

Maggie tapped the side of her nose and left to loiter beside the table of two members of the crew.

'Thank you,' said Chloe. 'I really didn't need to be reminded that we're not out of the woods yet.'

'No problem. I don't want any delays to the shoot either and having Maggie monitoring everyone's movements can't do us any harm.'

He checked his watch and, grabbing a final piece of toast, stood up and said, 'I have to go. I'm getting the plans for the hospital visit and light switch-on finalised this morning.'

Chloe blew him a kiss as he wrestled his jacket on and headed for the door. She stretched her arms out wide and yawned.

'Ready for another big day?' Kareem laughed as she sat with her mouth wide open from the yawn. Chloe smiled and replied that she was born ready.

On set, Chloe found Tegan having the last touches of make-up applied. The actress waved her over and shooed the make-up artist away.

'Day one of Operation GG,' said Tegan. 'I've shortened it by the way – gorgeous Geoff took far too long to say. Roisin is giving him a low carb breakfast to counteract all that awful conference food and Lloyd is giving him a bit of a workout.'

'My dad hates exercise,' replied Chloe imagining him puffing and panting along the beach. 'Besides which he has been ill recently.'

'Oh Lloyd knows what he's doing. I'm assured that he's asked Geoff to help him freshen up the outbuildings so he'll be getting the exercise without realising it.' Tegan gave Chloe a reassuring squeeze of the hand. 'Clever don't you think?'

Chloe nodded. Her dad might dislike exercise but he did like a project and she knew that Lloyd would look after him.

Tegan was called to take up her position outside the museum where Bart had been killed. As soon as Riley called action, she began flirting with the young policeman stationed outside.

'Are you as bored as I am? Stuck in this village with nothing to do?'

She ran a pink-nailed fingertip down the front of the officer's uniform as he cleared his throat awkwardly.

'They say that if you come here on holiday, you really should visit the museum but I'm guessing that's out of bounds isn't it?'

'It is madam,' croaked the officer.

'But surely it wouldn't do any harm for little old me to take a peak? Unless of course you think I'm a deadly assassin.'

She circled her finger on one of the buttons suggestively. 'Well I suppose my heroines often die of love.'

The young officer took a nervous step to one side and held up the police tape nodding her in. Chloe knew DS Campbell and Lizzie were elsewhere making script amendments but she imagined he wouldn't be very happy with this either.

The scene moved to inside the museum with Tegan walking around the dark rooms running her fingers along dusty shelves. She picked up a stuffed seagull and grimaced at it before putting it back with it's head facing the wall.

'Can't have you staring at me,' she said.

Next she moved over to an ornately carved writing desk and sat down at it, opening drawers and rifling through papers. She ran a finger over a relief carving of an acorn and as she did, a secret drawer opened.

'Oh my, what have we here?'

She reached inside and pulled out a little copper coloured key. Tegan looked around the desk but couldn't see anywhere it might fit. She stood up and looked around the room but just then the main detective came into the museum and told her she had to leave, that the officer had no right to let her come in. Tegan quietly pocketed the key and shrugged.

'I think I've seen everything there is to see anyway,' she said, bopping the detective's nose lightly with her finger as she sauntered past him out of the door.

'And cut,' shouted Riley. 'Good work everyone.'

'We need you to have a prompt lunch break then get onto this afternoon's shoot exactly on time,' said Kareem as the crew bustled around moving the equipment to the next location.

Chloe used the break to ring Roisin and hear that her dad was getting on stormingly well with Lloyd and had already lost some of that grey conference pallor he'd arrived with.

'That's good to hear. Call me at any time if anything untoward happens or if you hear from my mum.'

Roisin promised she would and with that it was time to start the next scene. Chloe got back into position just as Riley called for quiet and the stars of the show moved into position.

Dominic and Agatha were the next of the cast to slip under the police tape, this time into the bookshop. The soft padding of the dog's paws led the way as she sniffed books and seemed to get a scent.

'This was the way he walked is it girl?' said Dominic, inspecting shelves to see if they held any clues. Agatha disappeared out of shot and then started barking. Dominic walked towards her to the spot where the blood had been on the floor. Beside the stain was a little yellow police marker.

'Well I think I could have found this by myself.' Dominic laughed, rubbing the dog's head affectionately.

Agatha barked again, her head pointing upwards. She was barking at something beside Dominic's head – he looked up and touched a wrought sconce sticking out of the edge of the shelf. He brought his fingers back, rubbing them gently and looking at the red substance now staining them.

'Well done girl,' he said to Agatha. 'I think we've found our weapon and I now know that we need to ask Jeremy a couple of questions.'

Agatha barked in agreement and wagged her tail.

Chapter Twenty-Six

When Chloe walked back into the pub after the shoot, Maggie was at the other side of the room with her back to the door, sashaying to some music. She was wearing a rather tight red sweater dress, holding a pepper grinder like a microphone and singing her own version of the twelve days of Christmas. In this version her true love gave her something very naughty instead of a partridge in a pear tree. Chloe burst out laughing and Maggie swung around to face her. Chloe didn't know what to look at first – the glitter bomb of a snowman on the front of the dress or Maggie's shocked expression on seeing her.

'I didn't realise anyone was listening,' she said.

'I guessed that.'

Maggie put down the grinder and told Chloe that she had some important news. 'Your Christmas present,' she hissed. 'It's arriving tomorrow.' To check she wasn't being overheard, Maggie moved her eyes from left to right to glance around the room without moving her head. Chloe found the effect very creepy, like one of those portraits in a stately home that follows you around the room.

'I don't need to know that Maggie.' Chloe calmly blew away the tiny shard of anxiety that reared its head. 'If Andy wants to surprise me then that's what I want too.'

'Suit yourself,' said Maggie. 'Your first Christmas alone together and you want it perfect? Then I hope he loves his jumper.'

She said jumper as if it were something ridiculous and Chloe couldn't help but picture that yellow glow of stress pulsing in her body, threatening to grow larger and brighter. She had to escape Maggie and pull herself together. Chloe said she was going to change and left, taking the stairs two at a time, barging into her room and throwing herself down on the bed.

The floor was still piled with the dressing gown and pillow that Andy had used last night. Chloe picked up the pillow and hugged it close, inhaling its aroma. She thought back to the session with Roisin and took deep breaths before exhaling slowly and deeply. Eventually the anxiety turned into clouds of dandelion seeds and she relaxed, for a very brief moment anyway.

Chloe sat up on the bed and knew that simply eradicating the anxiety wasn't the answer. She couldn't arrive at Christmas day feeling wonderful about herself but having nothing for the man she loved and now the big day was a little over a week away. Shopping wasn't the answer; she wouldn't find anything for Andy in a store. She had to think more laterally and watch her boyfriend. True, she rarely took her eyes off the gorgeous man but she had to look deeper and really see who he was and what would make his day wonderful.

Full of calm resolve, Chloe did a quick wash and change then headed back down to the pub which was now filling with customers. As she entered the bar, Maggie approached her with a glass of wine.

'I'm sorry,' she said, handing the liquid apology to her. 'I overstepped the mark there didn't I?'

Chloe took the glass and sipped the warming burgundy – this certainly wasn't something usually served to customers; it was delicious and Chloe told Maggie that.

'It's from my own collection,' Maggie said. 'I really didn't mean to upset you – I was only trying to motivate you. There isn't much time.'

Chloe sat on a stool at the bar and ran a finger around the rim of the glass. She looked up at Maggie who still wore a frown of concern.

'Thank you,' she said. 'I know you meant well but I'm still completely at a loss as to what to do to make this Christmas special for Andy. He deserves a special day.'

'He certainly does – I've never seen the Midwinter Festival so well organised.'

She leaned in to Chloe and lowered her voice. 'And although you said you didn't want to know this, he is delivering your gift tomorrow afternoon and wants me to keep out of sight too – just in case you change your mind.'

Chloe sighed and knew that her landlady was back to her old self. She watched as Maggie laughed with a customer and served a couple of pints. The pub was still the only place in Serenity Bay that looked Christmassy and as soon as anyone walked through the doors, a big smile usually broke out on their faces. You really couldn't help but look around in wonder at the smorgasbord of decorations. The only addition since the beginning of the shoot was a new set of Christmas lights strewn around the specials aka sweepstake board. They were big red holly berries which flashed on and off as they highlighted the odds on each character being the murderer. The poor waiting staff had been forced to memorise all the specials ever since Maggie had decided to start taking bets.

'I see Tegan is still the favourite,' said Chloe nodding to the chalked up list of suspects. 'Are people actually betting on this?'

'Too right they are,' replied Maggie. 'And I've promised all the proceeds will pay for a big buffet at New Year – it should be quite a spread at this rate. Do you want to place a bet?'

'I'm guessing you haven't forgotten that I have the script and know whodunit?' said Chloe.

'It was worth a try.' Maggie shrugged. 'You might have given the game away.'

Kareem walked through the door and waved at them before heading up to his room.

'I still think the other funny business had something to do with Kareem you know,' said Maggie. 'You said it was quite a big promotion for him and that had to hurt someone. Do you happen to know whether there were many contenders for the job he got?'

'No,' Chloe said. 'How would I know something like that? I wouldn't even think to ask him. Why?'

'I've just been thinking through our other mystery – the saga of the saboteur. Although at first I thought it could be linked to all three of you – Riley, Kareem and you. I've now narrowed it down to Kareem. If he beat someone else to this job then he might be the reason all this is happening. The person causing all the trouble might be feeling sore because Kareem got the job.'

'But surely, the other applicants would all be TV producers too and Kareem would notice if one of his contemporaries were hanging around the set,' replied Chloe.

'Not if he were in disguise.' Maggie wagged her finger as if pointing out something truly revelatory. 'I've seen movies where a person wears a prosthetic nose, coloured lenses, false teeth – their own mothers didn't recognise them.'

'I'm pretty sure this show doesn't have that kind of budget,' said Chloe keeping a straight face. 'But I'm pleased to see you're still investigating. I hope that calling in the union was the big attempt to derail the shoot and having failed, they'll give up now.'

'Hmm, I wouldn't be too sure about that, but don't worry I'm still on the case – blending into the background and working incognito.'

Chloe looked at the dress and opened her mouth to say something about standing out like a sore thumb but then looked up at the pub in all its festive glory and decided that yep, in these surroundings Maggie did actually blend into the background. She checked her watch and hopped off the bar stool.

'I have to go,' she said finishing her wine. 'I need to see how my dad's getting on now that Tegan is looking after him. She's going to glam him up so that he's irresistible to my mum when she gets back.'

'I hope it works out,' said Maggie and Chloe thanked her.

'Well if your mum gets back together with your dad,' she continued, 'then it puts Dominic back on the market doesn't it?'

'Gee thanks, and here I was thinking you were concerned.'

'I am, but let's face it – it would be a bit weird if your mum went off with Dominic and the only man left was your dad. I'd be your stepmum. Although you already live here so maybe …'

'Enough!' cried Chloe shaking her head violently to try and dislodge the image of Maggie and her father. 'I'm going.'

The temperature outside had dropped dramatically in a very short space of time and even wrapped up, Chloe felt the biting chill of winter as she walked as quickly as she could to the farmhouse.

'Brrrr, its freezing out there,' she said as she peeled off the layers once inside. Roisin led Chloe into the kitchen where the blast of warmth pulsed through her almost immediately. The fire was on and sitting around the old wooden kitchen table Lloyd, Tegan and her father had big smiles on their faces as they sorted through a pile of clothes stacked on top. Roisin pulled a chair out for Chloe and then sat back down in the rocking chair by the fire that her grandmother always used. In the big butler sink, dishes were stacked ready to be rinsed and piled into the dishwasher – there was never any hurry in this house and it always felt warm and relaxed. Chloe hoped that one day, she'd create a place like this for herself and Andy – somewhere everyone felt welcome. She looked over at her father who after one day here was indeed looking better. He still looked tired but it seemed like a physical tiredness from a day's work rather than the draining greyness he'd arrived with. Tegan had been right – perhaps her mother's impromptu trip was a blessing.

'So what's going on here then?' asked Chloe trying to match her voice to the upbeat tone around the table.

'You're just in time darling,' said Tegan. 'We're about to have a fashion show.'

'Wonderful and I'm guessing these fine gentlemen are our catwalk models?' Chloe said noting that the clothes were all men's.

'Absolutely,' continued Tegan. 'I have told Geoff that grey does absolutely nothing for him and I have banned him from wearing it ever again.'

Tegan placed her hand on Geoff's arm and he gave her a comedic half-smile. Chloe thought that the actress was probably the only person she'd met who could give such direct and damning fashion advice and not get her dad's back up.

'I've stolen these from the costume department,'

whispered Tegan. 'We have to get them back in the morning but right now we're going to use them to show Geoff what his colours should be.'

Tegan picked out a selection of tops and thrust them in Geoff's direction. 'Now go and change,' she ordered.

Geoff took the clothes, saluted Tegan and left the room with Lloyd.

A few moments later Lloyd peered around the door and asked if everyone was ready. The ladies nodded and Tegan found some sexy strutting music on her phone. First through the door was Lloyd wearing a lumberjack shirt that really did nothing for him. He sauntered round the room and on reaching Roisin, pulled the shirt off his shoulder and winked at her to whoops of delight. Next through the door was Geoff in a midnight blue shirt – his sauntering was far more clumsy and to Chloe's relief he didn't attempt the off the shoulder thing. However, the blue suited him – he looked good.

'Now that colour brings out your eyes,' said Tegan standing beside him and turning him to face the mirror. 'Can you see that?'

Geoff looked at himself and nodded.

'Come on then, next outfits,' called Tegan pushing him back out the door.

The evening went on with the boys parading both the sublime and the ridiculous. At the end, Tegan laid out the colours that had worked best on her father. It was a surprising collection of blues, forest greens and a Tuscan orange – Chloe couldn't imagine her father ever choosing any of these on his own.

'Can you seriously see me in this lot?' Geoff said to his daughter, confirming her thoughts.

Tegan strode up to him and taking him by the shoulders

stood her father in front of the mirror again and made him put on his grey suit. Everyone in the room could see how his face dropped in those clothes. Then the actress overlaid the new colours to show him how much better he looked and without changing his facial expression, his face seemed to smile.

'Now I have an early call tomorrow,' Tegan said very firmly to Geoff. 'But after that I am free all afternoon and we are going to use that time to go shopping. We are going to buy you some gorgeous new clothes and we are going to throw away anything grey forever. Do I make myself clear?'

Geoff nodded, still looking at himself in the mirror and stroking his beard. Chloe watched him and felt that it was almost as if he was truly seeing himself for the first time in ages.

'Now darling,' Tegan said turning to Chloe. 'I will need your help smuggling all of this back into costume.'

Chapter Twenty-Seven

The next day, the camera tracked Lucinda as she approached the village hall. Behind her the sun had barely risen and the creak of the heavy wooden door was the loudest sound in the village as she opened it and crept inside. The hall was still set up for the awards ceremony with rows of chairs facing the stage and Lucinda slid over to the right hand side of the room then tiptoed down to a door at the side of the stage. With one more cautious look behind her, she opened that door and disappeared inside. The camera angle jolted back to the main front door as it opened again and this time, Ewan slipped in looking as furtive as Lucinda had and obviously believing himself alone. He too made for the door at the side of the stage.

With a set change, the point of view moved to inside the backstage room. Lucinda lit up the room with her phone and from the light, took in the layout. It was a surprisingly decadent room for a village hall office with walnut cabinets, heavy velvet curtains, a rosewood coffee table and burgundy leather armchairs. A small desk and chair sat in the corner with a laptop cable but no laptop while across the walls, posters from previous village hall performances hung alongside framed news articles about the festival and its organiser. These were accompanied by black and white autographed headshots of world famous actors who would never have even heard of a village as small as this let alone visited it. At the far end of the room was a shelf where glass trophies engraved with the words *Serenity Publishing Award* stood waiting for the ceremony beside pristine copies of Jeremy's novels. Chloe appraised the set and knew that viewers watching the show would instantly see that the person who had made this office his own certainly had serious delusions of grandeur.

Lucinda got to work searching the office; she put her phone on the desk so that the light shone out, then she began opening drawers and taking books off the shelves before shaking them in case they held the secret between their pages. She looked behind the picture frames hoping for a hidden safe and then knelt down to tug at a handle on the walnut cabinet. It wouldn't budge. She heard a noise and hid behind the door, grabbing an award and holding it above her head. The door opened and Lucinda was about to bring the heavy glass statue down on the head of the entrant until she saw who it was.

'You,' she said. 'What are you doing here?'

'I could ask you the same thing,' replied Ewan taking the award from her and weighing it in his hand. 'You could have killed me with that, or was that the plan?'

He put the award back up on the shelf and Lucinda stood, arms folded.

'I've had nothing to do with all these deaths,' she said. 'How was I to know you'd be here? You on the other hand probably saw me and followed me in – should I be afraid right now?'

'Only of losing when they declare the winner tomorrow night.' Ewan was studying the room. 'Let's face it, that's what we're both here for – to find out the awards results. If I'm not going to win, I don't want to sit around in a room and smile as if I'm pleased for whoever gets the gong.'

'Me neither,' said Lucinda. 'I've searched everywhere but I can't see where he would have hidden the envelope. The cabinet's locked so I'm presuming it's in there.'

Ewan knelt down and pulled the handle which held fast.

He took a credit card from his wallet and tried to push the lock mechanism but only succeeded in bending his card out of shape.

'It works in the movies. Maybe we need Dominic here.'

'Either that or you need the key,' said a voice behind them causing them both to jump.

It was Tegan holding the little key she'd found in the museum.

'Step aside my darlings,' she said as they cleared a space for her. 'And by the way, that's what I'll be saying when I go up for that award tomorrow.'

She held the key aloft as if it were the flame of Olympia and then inserted it into the lock. It didn't fit. She wiggled it around, took it out, wiped it and tried again. Still no luck.

'It's not the right key,' said Lucinda.

'That's because it's not a key,' said a fourth voice.

The other three authors turned to see Dominic standing, arms folded. He held out an open palm to Tegan.

'If I may,' he said and she handed the key to him.

He twisted the top and it came off in his hand to reveal a USB drive.

'Well I never,' said Ewan. 'We did have the right key – we just didn't know how to use it.'

'His laptop,' cried Tegan excitedly. 'We need his laptop or computer or something.'

Everyone except Dominic started hurriedly re-searching the room throwing papers aside and generally making a real mess.

'Guys,' said Dominic holding both his hands up telling them to calm down. 'I'm pretty sure the police will have taken all Jeremy's devices as evidence.'

The camera panned out as all the authors stopped what

they were doing and then Chloe noticed that on the far side of the room behind the door, tucked between some foolscap folders but definitely visible, was a small laptop. She pointed it out to Riley who yelled, 'Cut.'

'How the hell did that get there?' he said kicking a chair over in frustration.

Once again the set manager promised that the laptop had not been there when the set was signed off.

'I don't believe this,' Kareem muttered. 'I thought we'd dealt with it but it seems that whoever is sabotaging this shoot is at it again.'

'And now they're adding items to scenes rather than removing them,' said Chloe. 'That's going to be harder to spot.'

The only shot featuring that side of the room was the one where Lucinda had been hiding behind the door so Riley checked the footage and they re-filmed the moment. It didn't take long but Chloe knew it wasn't the delay that would frustrate the crew, it was the fact that their nemesis was still at large.

'It's back to man-marking everything I think,' said Kareem and Chloe nodded, having already decided that was the only way to move forward.

The morning's shoot ended only slightly over time and the team took a break for lunch. Chloe walked back to the pub to recruit some villagers to watch over the sets but had only got halfway when Maggie came rushing out blocking her path.

'You can't come any further,' she said holding her arms out wide. 'There's an important delivery being made.'

'He's in the pub now?' asked Chloe.

'Not in the pub,' said Maggie nodding towards the garage at the back of the car park. The garage itself wasn't visible but the van backing towards the door was – it was Andy's.

'He's had to back the van right up to the doorway,' said Maggie with her eyes almost popping out of her head. 'It must be *enormous*.'

Chloe shook her head and sighed before stepping around Maggie and continuing on to the pub.

'I told you last night, Maggie, this is supposed to be a surprise,' she called as she strode. 'So please stop spying on Andy. I really don't want to know.'

'You might have said that, but did you really mean it?' shouted Maggie as she ran to catch up.

'Yes Maggie – I meant it,' asserted Chloe opening the pub door, going in and letting it close on the landlady.

'I'll forgive you for that,' said Maggie as she entered the pub, smoothing down her hair. 'You're obviously upset about something. What's happened now?'

Chloe explained that they weren't out of the woods yet with regard to the saboteur and the landlady listened with her lips tightly pursed.

When Chloe had finished, Maggie leant in and whispered, 'Have you heard of the Dark Web?'

Chloe dropped her head into her hands. 'Maggie, really we don't have time for this.'

'I'm serious,' she said with an extremely earnest expression on her face. 'I didn't think it was real but apparently it is. You can get some nasty stuff on there.'

'And how does this concern the show?'

'I'm not ready to tell you,' said Maggie calmly and without her usual dramatics for once. 'I'm going to have a word with my Nick first but I think I might have found out what's going on.'

Maggie left to serve a customer without saying any more

which left Chloe feeling slightly dumbstruck. She was so used to hearing her bizarre suggestions in full and lurid detail that to be left hanging was an unusual sensation. Nevertheless she had work to do and started calling round the villagers to see if anyone was free to perform guard duties. She recruited a few willing souls who joined her for the afternoon's shoot and to Chloe's relief, everything went smoothly. Later, as she came down from her room after the tiring day, Tegan accosted her in the bar.

'Darling,' she said flouncing up to Chloe. 'I have a wonderful idea, come with me.'

She grabbed Chloe's arm and dragged her back out of the pub then down the road to the farmhouse.

'You know those rather strange cardboard cut-outs of policemen that you see in store windows?' asked the actress.

'Yes.' Chloe nodded. 'They're supposed to deter burglars and I have to say that on the few occasions I've seen them out of the corner of my eye, I've been sure there was someone standing there.'

'Precisely,' said Tegan.

'Are you suggesting that we get cut-outs to guard the sets?' asked Chloe. 'Because I think that whoever is doing this is pretty close to the show so they'd know fairly quickly that the guards weren't real.'

'Yes, yes – I do realise all of that and it's not what I'm suggesting.' Tegan waved Chloe's concern off with a flick of her fingers. 'But I was thinking about those cut-outs when I came up with an even better plan. I do believe I have the answer to all of our problems.'

They reached the farmhouse and walked into the kitchen where Chloe was told to sit down.

'Now,' started Tegan, 'what if we brought in a top-end Russian security guard?'

'It would probably scare the pants off them.'

'Precisely and there'd be no more funny business that's for sure,' said Tegan slapping her hand down on the table.

'There's one small problem,' said Chloe. 'Where are we going to get a Russian security guard?'

Tegan cleared her throat and kept her gaze downwards.

'As a young actress one gets asked to do many things and as one is desperate for money, one often does them.'

Tegan paused then got up to get a glass of water from the fridge. With her back still facing Chloe she continued. 'I'm not proud of this but when I was starting out, I was asked to do a private performance for a top Russian businessman living in London. He wanted me to do the Jamie Lee Curtis pole dance from the film *True Lies* – have you seen it?'

Chloe shook her head.

'It's very ... erotic,' said Tegan. 'I told myself that Jamie had done it on the big screen so what harm was replicating it? Anyway, the businessman assigned me a security guard while I was staying at his villa. A brute of a man with a gentle heart – Uri he was called. He could see I was still wet behind the ears and took pity on me. He looked after me and after the dance, drove me home not leaving until I was safely inside. We kept in touch.'

Chloe could barely follow everything that was being told to her and she wondered how this had never made the news. Tegan's love life was always making headlines.

'Anyway, when we finished the shoot today, I called him. I thought he might be able to get the private jet up here and join us tomorrow but by an incredible stroke of good fortune, the businessman was already in the area and agreed to release him. He's just arrived.'

Tegan turned to the door and shouted, 'Uri, can you come in please?'

Chloe sat back in fearful anticipation as the door opened. A man wearing heavy steel-capped boots and black combat trousers walked in. Chloe took him in from the ground upwards. He wore a black leather biker's jacket, a thick black polo neck jumper and he punched his fist in murderous black gloves. He had a hammer and sickle tattoo on his neck and wore a black hat pulled down over most of his head and dark sunglasses which wrapped around his face. This was a man who did not want to be recognised – but the beard gave it away.

'Dad.' Chloe sighed in relief as Tegan and her father burst out laughing.

'You were almost fooled weren't you?' asked Geoff and Chloe had to admit that she was.

'Think about it,' said Tegan. 'None of the actors know Geoff anyway. After I've had make-up deal with that grey tuft, he'll look fearsome and in this costume he'll be all the more terrifying, perhaps enough to make our saboteur think twice. It would be like one of those cardboard cut-outs only far more effective.'

'It might work.' Chloe laughed as the shock left her body. 'You had me fooled. All that stuff about the businessman – I was utterly and completely taken in. I believed every word you said, Tegan.'

The actress plumped her hair and shrugged her shoulders. 'What can I say – I'm a bloody good actress you know.'

Chapter Twenty-Eight

'I hope Riley will go for it. After all, it does kill two birds with one stone,' said Tegan in eager but hushed tones as Chloe's father left the room to put his normal clothes back on.

'I have always found that acting out a role helps you take on some of the qualities of that character,' continued Tegan. 'Your dear father has lost a little of his self-confidence so having people believe he's someone to be feared and respected will do him the world of good. And he'll be out walking in the fresh air all day, standing tall and being generally active. Lloyd thinks it will be fabulous exercise for him. Did you know that simply holding your stomach in actually works the muscles too?'

Chloe pulled her abdominal muscles in tightly as the actress spoke and could imagine that having to stand like that all day would be a workout and besides which, she trusted Lloyd's judgement. If he thought this was good exercise for her father then it most probably would be. Nevertheless, she still had real doubts about the overall plan.

'But what if it backfires?' she asked. 'If someone recognises him or doubts your backstory then he'll be laughed out of court and that won't do his self-esteem any good at all. He'll be a laughing stock.'

'We'll put a bandana over the rest of his face to hide the beard and the thing is Chloe, no one is expecting your dad to turn up on set so they'll believe what we tell them to. It's an odd thing about people – tell them not to drink the water and they tend not to.'

Chloe murmured, unconvinced.

'And as for the backstory,' continued Tegan. 'Darling, the whole nation thinks I'm such a floozy, they won't doubt for one minute that I've had a dodgy Russian interaction in my murky past. That's the advantage of being me – everyone always thinks the worst.'

Tegan gave a husky laugh as she said these words and Chloe couldn't help but smile broadly at the actress. She had probably been the same as everyone else when Tegan arrived – seeing a glamorous woman and thinking her airheaded and self-centred but here she was helping her father when she didn't need to. Chloe nodded and they were shaking hands on the deal when her dad walked back in.

'What do you think, Chlo?' he asked his face full of life and fun. 'Can you see me as a top Russian bodyguard? Someone Bond might have to tackle on his way to General Koskov?'

'I certainly can,' replied Chloe not wishing to do anything to erase the smile on his face. It was broad and genuine, and Chloe hadn't seen him looking so spirited in a long time.

'I could learn some Russian phrases—'

He was interrupted by a panicked, 'No!' from Tegan.

The actress led Geoff to the table and sat him down.

'Now Geoffrey, I'm your director in this movie and it is imperative that you do exactly as I say. You must remain the strong silent type. People will be far more afraid of you if you do not engage with them at all. Think about the guards at Buckingham Palace – curious toddlers drop ice-creams on their boots, beautiful young women drape themselves across the guards taking selfies but they do not budge. And you must not either. There is only one word you have to learn and it is the only line you will ever have in this production. That word is *"Nyet"* – No.'

'Nyet,' said Geoff in a deep stern voice.

'Deeper,' instructed Tegan. 'You are a lethal killer – now sound like one.'

'Nyet, nyet, nyet,' practised Geoff getting further into character the more times he said it.

Chloe knew that Tegan was trying to minimise the chances of her dad giving the game away so left them to their rehearsal. It was the most bizarre plan and who knows, it might just work. Stranger things had happened and she certainly hoped so for the sake of the show and her father.

The following day, Tegan pulled up on the main street in a taxi with a tall broad man dressed entirely in black. Everyone turned to face her as she strode towards the set with her bodyguard following her at a respectable distance.

'Who's that?' whispered Lizzie.

'I have no idea,' replied Kareem. 'You haven't written a thug into the story without telling us have you?'

Chloe held her breath nervously; so far so good. Kareem was probably the only member of the crew who'd ever seen her father for any length of time and he hadn't recognised him. Not that she was surprised – Tegan had added the bandana which now covered the lower part of his face. With the dark glasses and hat, a person would have to be able to identify Geoff's nose to guess who it actually was.

'Darlings,' announced Tegan. 'I have come up with a solution to our problems. Uri here guarded me when I was on a private commission in Moscow. I trust him implicitly and he has agreed to watch over our set until we are finished.'

'A private commission?' Dominic laughed. 'I wonder what type of commission that was.'

'A well paid one.' Tegan didn't miss a beat.

Kareem went to shake hands with Uri but the bodyguard stood arms folded and simply said, 'Nyet.' The producer backed away sheepishly.

Chloe could have burst out laughing if there wasn't so much at stake. Tegan asked Riley where Uri was needed and then instructed her bodyguard accordingly. Uri strode off menacingly.

'I heard the Terminator had arrived on set,' said a voice behind Chloe which turned out to be Maggie. 'I had to see it for myself. Tegan really does know the most extraordinary range of people doesn't she? They're saying he saved her life once – wouldn't mind him giving me a bit of mouth-to-mouth.'

'Maggie!' exclaimed Chloe picturing her father with the landlady and feeling nauseous as a result.

'Just saying. There's something about a man in uniform.'

'Just as long as he does the job and stops all the delays so everyone leaves on time.' The voice belonged to Andy this time. 'So where is he?'

'You've just missed him,' Maggie said. 'He was a bit of a brute.'

Chloe was relieved that she didn't have to say anything to her boyfriend. She was certain she wouldn't be able to lie to him, but if he didn't ask the right questions …

'So I hear,' continued Andy. 'I thought I'd come down to see what all the fuss was about. We have three days before the festival opening and it'll be a rush to get things set up even then so I hope he's up to the job.'

'No pressure then,' Chloe said, giving him a friendly punch to the arm before he went on his way.

Riley called for the set to be cleared and asked Chloe to help with removing all the villagers who'd come down to look at Tegan's bodyguard. Chloe started politely asking people to leave but Maggie had other ideas and took it upon herself to shoo everyone away.

'Have you lot got nothing better to do?' she shouted. 'No jobs to go to? Get back home the lot of you, there's nothing to gawp at here.'

Chloe shook her head in despair but at least Maggie was getting the job done. Once the streets were clear, Chloe reminded Maggie that she had to leave the set too.

'Oh I won't be hanging around. Unlike that lot I do have important things to be getting on with.'

She flounced off and as she left, Chloe couldn't help but ponder who was better at the dramatic exit – Maggie or Tegan? It would certainly be a close-run battle.

Today they'd be shooting Dominic's scene at the police station and it would be taking place in the local primary school which had now broken up for the Christmas holidays. There'd been a great many jokes in the community about some of the teachers being as strict as police sergeants while DS Campbell had gone in the other direction saying that the venue was particularly appropriate as Dominic had as many detection skills as a small child.

As the cameras rolled, Dominic and Agatha strode up to the front desk and demanded to see the officer in charge of the Serenity case. The policeman on reception protested but Agatha barked at him relentlessly until he gave up and let the pair into the office. Dominic showed the detective in charge the USB stick found in Bart's museum.

'You didn't find this during your search because it was pretty well hidden,' said Dominic. 'I think it might hold some vital information.'

'I hope you didn't come by this illegally,' replied the detective. 'There's no point having good evidence if it's inadmissible.'

Beside Chloe, DS Campbell punched the air. Then he realised he was being watched and explained himself. 'I really fought to have that added,' he whispered. 'We can't keep riding roughshod over the proper procedures.'

Chloe nodded at him and went back to watching the filming.

'And there's no point having the means to catch a killer if we don't use it,' Dominic was saying.

The two men went over to a computer and inserted the USB stick in the side.

'Damn,' said Dominic. 'It looks as if it's encrypted. Can your cyber guys check it out?'

The detective nodded and took the USB stick while Dominic sat with his elbows on the desk thinking. When the detective returned, Dominic asked whether they'd found anything on Bart's laptop.

'Well that was easy to open – he had no passwords or security set up – but there was nothing unusual on it,' the detective said. 'No suspicious emails, no threats, no social media accounts. He looks to have been a quiet museum curator who pretty much kept himself to himself with his head in his books.'

'No one is that straightforward,' said Dominic. 'There has to have been something for someone to want him dead. And then we find this – why would he have an encrypted file if there's nothing on it? Can I take a look at his laptop while we're waiting for the USB stick to be unlocked?'

The detective sighed but relented. 'Be my guest. But you won't find anything.'

He handed Dominic the laptop still sealed in a protective

plastic bag and Dominic promised to bring it back in the morning.

Later in the day, they would change location and film Dominic in his house poring over the contents of the laptop and finding the manuscript of a book – *A Literary History of Serenity Bay* – written by Bart. Today however, the crew were filming all the scenes that were taking place in the school aka police station as Andy needed this location clear as soon as possible to house all the decorations and equipment for the festival. So minutes after promising to return the laptop in the morning, Dominic was back at the front desk asking for the detective.

'Did you actually read the documents on this laptop?' he asked when the detective appeared.

'Of course we did, we're not amateurs.'

'Including the manuscript? All of it?' pressed Dominic.

'Are you kidding?' The detective sighing heavily. 'One hundred and fifty thousand words about dead poets and writers? We're trying to solve a murder not win the local pub quiz.'

At that moment, a young man appeared with the USB stick that Dominic had found saying that they'd finally unlocked the contents. All three huddled around a PC while the young guy pulled up the contents of the stick.

'It's the same manuscript,' said Dominic. 'But why would Bart want to store it on an encrypted flashdrive if anyone getting hold of his laptop could read it?'

'Who knows.' The detective ran his hands over his head. 'I guess you'd better tell me what's in it.'

'You're right – it's mainly about local writers and it's not particularly interesting. I think Bart was trying to ingratiate himself with Jeremy, perhaps trying to secure a nomination at next year's awards because there's a lot about his ancestor – Walter Kingsley.'

Dominic stopped in his tracks and studied the document with a furrowed brow.

'How does any of that help us solve the case?' the detective was asking, his arms folded impatiently.

Dominic looked up at him. 'I'm not sure but this manuscript isn't the same as the one I read on the laptop.'

'How do you know?'

'You said it – the one on the laptop is one hundred and fifty thousand words long and this is a hundred and sixty thousand. It's the latest version and must contain some new research. We have to read those final ten thousand words.'

'Knock yourself out.' The detective sighed, bringing the scene to an end.

'And cut,' called Riley. 'That's a wrap – good work everyone.'

When Chloe left the director's tent and checked her phone she saw that she'd had lots of calls from the local media. She strolled away to listen to her messages and as she reached the main street, she could see that she didn't need to call them, the media were already here.

'What can I do for you?' she asked a group of waiting journalists who stood with mics and cameras at the ready.

'Is it true that you've brought in a Russian bodyguard to stop the details of whodunit getting out?'

Chapter Twenty-Nine

Chloe couldn't lie to the journalists for fear of losing their trust for future articles. She stood for a moment that felt like years trying desperately to think of something she could tell them. She could feel their stares and was aware that they'd started looking at her strangely when happily Tegan stepped in to save the day.

'I'm afraid Chloe is not permitted to answer your questions,' said the actress. 'This is all my doing and although I would love to tell you the whole story, now is not the time. Suffice to say we have some concerns about security on set and we have now taken actions to help resolve them.'

All credit to the actress, thought Chloe – she hasn't told a word of a lie. She gathered herself together and continued the address to the journalists.

'We have a few days until the end of the shoot and we're hoping it will be without incident. Then Serenity Bay will be hosting its Midwinter Festival – to which you are all invited.'

The journalists seemed to stop scribbling at that point – the opening of a local fayre wasn't nearly as juicy as the story they thought they'd get.

'And just prior to the opening of the Festival,' Tegan announced glancing up at Chloe in such a way to let her know this hadn't been agreed beforehand. 'I will be holding a press conference plus one-to-one interviews and I will tell you the whole story behind the Russian bodyguard. Believe me – you will want to be here for that one.'

With a coquettish twirl, Tegan was gone. Chloe

promised everyone that she would be in touch to reserve their place at the conference and book in an interview with Tegan. Finally after ensuring she had every name and contact number, the journalists moved on and Chloe ran to find Tegan who was sitting having her make-up done.

'I hope you don't mind me doing that,' said Tegan as the make-up artist touched up her eyes. 'I thought it might get you off the hook.'

'Thank you,' Chloe said with feeling. 'It really did. I wasn't sure what to say but you have just promised to stick around after the shoot. Can you commit to that?'

Tegan nodded as the artist now attempted to do her lipstick. The actress shooed her away and dabbed her lips with a tissue before attempting to speak.

'Yes,' she said in a tone that suggested she had even surprised herself. 'I'm enjoying myself here and I'd like to see the festival. If I can help it along by ensuring the press turn up for the opening then I'm happy to do so. That is if I'm not treading on any toes?'

'You're certainly not and we'd be delighted to have you there. I can't wait to tell Andy.'

Chloe skipped off eager to let her boyfriend know that there was guaranteed press interest in the festival which would probably led to lots more visitors. She found him at the cricket club which was being used to store all the gifts people had donated for the local children's hospital.

'Wow,' said Chloe. 'That's an impressive collection of gifts – the hospital will be delighted.'

'I know,' said Andy standing back to look at the huge number of boxes. 'I have to say the production company have been brilliant. We've raised enough to have a sing-a-long at the retirement home too. Maggie's going to lead that one.'

'Poor residents, what did they do to deserve that?'

Andy smiled and Chloe could see that he was genuinely happy with what had been achieved.

'I can't wait to see their faces when Father Christmas turns up with Agatha as Rudolph,' he said. 'They're going to love her aren't they?'

Chloe nodded then wrapped her arms around her gorgeous boyfriend and in that moment knew that this was making his perfect Christmas – bringing happiness to others. She simply had to ensure she did everything possible to help him achieve that.

'I'll come back after the shoot and help you wrap all these gifts,' she said giving him a goodbye kiss.

Back on set, everyone was getting into position for the next scene. This was a crowd shot involving the villagers and Chloe was amused to see that as they walked along the main street to their places, they all took a very wide berth when they approached her father aka Uri. He stood like an immovable object as people scurried past him, almost afraid to meet his stare from behind those black glasses.

'You know,' said Maggie from her semi-permanent position just behind Chloe. 'There's something vaguely familiar about Uri. We did have some Russian visitors in the summer – I wonder if he's related to them.'

'It's unlikely.' Chloe decided it was the safest response. Maggie was about to say something more but Chloe pressed her fingers to her lips as Riley called for quiet on set.

Portia pushed Jeremy in his wheelchair down the main street to abundant cheers from the crowds. They held banners saying "The Show Must Go On", "Welcome Back" and "Who Won Jeremy?" The villagers had been directed to act overjoyed on seeing the head of Serenity Publishing and they did exactly as they were told. Chloe thought it a highly unlikely reaction to his return and then smiled at herself as she realised that of all the things that were unlikely in this show, this was the one she'd chosen to notice. Not the detective dog or the implausible number of murders.

At the head of the crowd stood the four authors who were also giving Jeremy a round of applause. Agatha held a small bouquet of flowers in her mouth and on Dominic's instruction trotted up to the wheelchair and sat down in front of it offering the bouquet to Jeremy. Tegan tilted her head to the side and smiled as if finding this utterly charming. Then she walked to the back of the wheelchair and shoving Portia to one side with a flick of the hips, proceeded to push the chair through the crowd, waving at them as she did. The camera caught the glare between the two women. Jeremy was wheeled to the entrance of the village hall and the crowd followed behind; once there, Tegan swung the chair around so that he was facing everyone and Ewan handed him a cane. With all the drama of a Shakespearian performance, Jeremy put his hand on top of the cane and pushed down on it urging his body upwards. After a false attempt there was another sharp intake of breath from the crowd and this time, using all the strength he could muster, Jeremy pushed himself up and was standing. The crowd applauded as he held a hand aloft and placed it on the door of the hall.

'I shall not be defeated,' he declared. 'These awards must go on and I shall walk onto that stage.'

Portia strode up and barged past Tegan to take his other arm as Jeremy disappeared into the hall with the authors following.

'That Portia character is a bit feisty isn't she?' said Maggie as the crew scurried around getting ready for the next scene. 'And she's not even in my sweepstake – I'd best sort that one out.'

She left the set to head back to the pub while the shoot continued without incident.

After filming had finished, Chloe returned to the cricket club and wrapped at least fifty gifts, putting a big bow and a gift tag on each one. Andy had already written them all out and each one said "With love from Santa Paws". It had been a long but very productive day when Chloe walked back to The Fiddler's Arms so she made her way straight upstairs and threw herself down on the bed. She was exhausted and had that feeling of things being so close and yet still so far away; one final push and they'd be there.

They were nearly at the end of the shoot. They were nearly at the launch of the festival. And she was so near to Christmas morning and waking up with the man she loved. It was so close, Chloe could almost touch it. A day of being with Andy and no interruptions – the mere thought of it gave her a warm and fuzzy feeling but it wasn't time for relaxing – not yet. She had to schedule the interviews Tegan had promised and ensure the invites were sent out for the press conference. Chloe went into the bathroom and splashed her face with water to freshen up before sitting back on the bed and opening up her laptop to begin the work.

About an hour later, as Chloe was finishing the invitations there was a knock on the door and before she had the chance to get up and open it, Maggie poked her head round.

'Good,' she said. 'You're up.'

Maggie came in carrying her own laptop and sat down on the bed beside Chloe.

'I had a Skype call with Nick last night and was telling him about everything that's been going on. Honestly – I think he's so excited about all the shenanigans here, he might even come home early. Anyway, he offered to do some searching on the internet and within hours, he rang me back – I think he's found something.' She sounded serious and lay the computer down for Chloe to see.

'LACC?' said Chloe reading the website address.

'It stands for the League Against Cosy Crime,' explained Maggie. 'It's a social media group of people who hate it and think it's an affront to society.'

'Why would they think that?' asked Chloe.

'I've been reading through their posts,' Maggie said, 'and they have a point. They think it presents an unrealistic expectation – that crime will always be solved.'

'Hmm, I think most viewers know that it's just a piece of entertainment,' said Chloe. 'So have they said anything about *The Montgomery Mysteries?*'

'Oh there's a whole section on it.' Maggie clicked a tab, bringing up a discussion which Chloe read quickly through.

'Wow,' she said widening her eyes, 'they really don't like it.'

'*Crime fighting dog sniffs out murder weapon,*' she started reading aloud from the page. '*Author finds suspect's button in field of hay – CPS would love that.*'

'I remember that episode,' said Maggie. 'He was very lucky to find it – the police force missed it completely.'

'I think that's the point they're making,' said Chloe. 'Who'd have thought that people could get so wound up about a TV show that they form a protest group against it? Why not just watch something else?'

'People are strange,' said Maggie. 'Anyway, I think these league members are the people behind all our disruptions.'

Chloe sat back dumbfounded.

'Why?' she said eventually. It felt incredulous to Chloe but at the same time so ridiculous it might just be true. 'And how do you have access to all of this? Isn't it a closed group?'

'After Nick found it, I joined,' replied Maggie looking very proud of herself. 'Nick set me up a false identity – I'm the Angel of Death.'

'Oh Maggie. I hope you know what you're doing, these people might seem a little eccentric but they can be dangerous.'

'I'll be careful,' she assured. 'Look at this, there's someone on here who calls themselves the Lone Wolf and they say it is their mission to bring down the show. They've apparently written to the network and demanded that they stop showing it but obviously the network refused so now this Lone Wolf person has decided to try and stop it being filmed. The whole social media group are egging him or her on.'

Chloe picked up Maggie's laptop and started scrolling through the Lone Wolf's conversation. This person really did have it in for the show and hinted at having already tried to disrupt things. They were clever though and nothing they said helped reveal who it was or if they'd even been near the set.

'It might be all bluster,' said Chloe. 'I haven't noticed anyone unusual loitering around the set.'

At that moment the laptop pinged with a notification to say someone had posted something new. The women positioned the laptop so they could both see it. One of the members had forwarded a link from the local press mentioning the new Russian bodyguard. Another commented that it would be impossible to disrupt filming with him around. Maggie instantly took hold of the laptop and started typing.

'What have you said?' asked Chloe trying to peer over Maggie's shoulder.

'That I have access to the shoot and I know a way round the bodyguard but I need help.' Maggie rubbed her hands in glee.

Almost instantly the Lone Wolf responded.

'What's he said?' asked Chloe watching Maggie's eyes go from left to right as she scanned the message.

'He says he has one final idea but needs the bodyguard distracted,' said Maggie. 'He wants to meet up.'

One final idea? Chloe's heart pounded, only a short while ago she'd thought they were close to finishing the show but now it seemed they were still very far away. And it looked as if it was Serenity Bay's slightly cookie landlady who was going to save the day.

Chapter Thirty

Over the next couple of days, Chloe was on tenterhooks. She studied everyone on set extra closely to try and establish whether they were this Lone Wolf person. What would they look like? Would they wear one of those howling wolf T-shirts or a wolf brand of clothing? Did anyone have a tattoo that she hadn't seen before? Chloe didn't notice just how much she was staring at every single person until one of the crew asked if he had something on his back. Then she realised that she'd been looking at the logo on his hoodie for far too long trying to work out whether it was a wolf or a dragon. The Lone Wolf hadn't contacted Maggie yet so they didn't know the hour he would strike or if this group were even real. Happily, with Uri still scaring the pants off everyone, the filming was still going smoothly and things were still looking good for finishing on time.

'This is it then,' said Kareem as he joined her for breakfast on the penultimate day. 'One more day of filming then we'll be out of your hair.'

Chloe smiled weakly at him. She was sitting with her elbow on the table and her fingernails firmly in her mouth – where they'd been ever since learning about the League Against Cosy Crime.

'I hope you weren't planning a manicure to celebrate,' said Maggie plonking plates of food in front of them. 'There'll be nothing left to varnish if you don't cut that out.'

Chloe sat on her hands and practised blowing that dandelion clock gently away as Kareem tucked in to the extra big portion of bacon and eggs that Maggie always seemed to make for him. He asked if Chloe was going to eat her toast and when she shook her head, he leant across and took a slice.

'I do like to see a man with a healthy appetite,' said Maggie looking extremely satisfied. 'I think it's very suspicious if a person doesn't like a good breakfast.'

Then as if suddenly contemplating what she'd said, she stroked her chin and started looking around the dining room.

'So if I can remember who hasn't accepted an extra portion, that might lead me to the Lone Wolf,' she said.

'Or maybe just someone who doesn't want to put on half a stone while they're here?' suggested Chloe getting a dismissive tut from the landlady as she left.

They hadn't told anyone else on set about the League and fortunately Kareem had been too engrossed in his breakfast to hear exactly what had been said although he evidently realised Maggie was still talking about her investigations.

'She can probably stop all that now,' he said after a big glug of coffee. 'Uri seems to have stopped whoever was nicking things from set. It probably was just a souvenir hunter.'

'Oh you know Maggie,' replied Chloe. 'She won't stop until she's been declared the saviour of the day – Uri or no Uri.'

'I've guessed who he is by the way.' Kareem smiled causing Chloe to splurt out her coffee and almost choke with laughter.

'Thank goodness,' she said when she'd recovered. 'I couldn't believe we were getting away with it. It was

Tegan's idea and I honestly didn't think it would work as well as it has.'

'He's pretty convincing,' continued Kareem, 'with that strong silent act. But I heard Tegan calling him Geoff as we finished filming the other day.'

'Did anyone else hear?'

Kareem shook his head. 'Your secret is safe with me. Now are you ready for the biggest day of filming?'

Chloe nodded.

'Maggie,' called Kareem as they stood up to leave. 'This is the last day to get those bets in – after today's session everyone will know who the killer is.'

He and Chloe both laughed at the panic-stricken look on the landlady's face. She scurried over to the specials board and started rubbing out the odds and writing up new ones.

'I'm pretty sure it's Tegan,' she mumbled as she wrote. 'But then it's never the obvious one so maybe I should go for the outsider – Ewan. Or maybe ...'

Outside the winter sun was bright and welcoming though the air was several degrees colder than it had been earlier in the week.

'I don't suppose you get snow on the coast,' said Kareem as he put on his thick gloves.

'Oh we do.' Chloe remembered the previous New Year's Eve. 'Although I do find it quite a strange sight, snow on top of sand.'

They walked past Uri who gave them a slight nod, to the village hall where all of the filming would take place today. The scene was the final evening of the festival and the awards dinner so the villagers, who were dressed up in their finery would all be sitting inside the hall as attendees of the dinner. They'd be checked to make sure they weren't carrying mobile phones which could either record the final scene or ring out during the shoot so in theory, no one could smuggle anything into the set. The streets of the village would also be fairly empty and Chloe wondered whether this gave more scope for the League to disrupt the show or less? Perhaps they were just a bunch of mischief makers who'd tried a couple of things but now realised that any further action would be just too difficult. Although she realised it was quite a selfish thought, Chloe couldn't help but hope that they'd move on and try to sabotage other episodes – ones that weren't being filmed in Serenity Bay.

The action began with the audience sitting at their round dinner tables chatting amongst themselves. Then a voice asked for quiet and a spotlight shone on the podium in the centre of the stage. Chloe thought the hall really did look wonderful, all dressed for these awards. The audience had walked in under an arch of rose gold balloons to a room where a glitter ball which had been newly installed reflected the spotlights and sent sparkles on the cut glass and silver crockery adorning the tables. Bunting with a calligraphy design was strewn along either side of the room, tall flower displays made a walkway to the stage where huge posters featuring each of the finalists smiling out hopefully, were hanging. At the top table reserved for the authors and organisers, dinner was being served but Dominic was missing. Tegan checked her watch and sighed.

'That man will be late for his own funeral – well I'm not waiting for him.'

She picked up her glass and toasted, 'To the winner – whoever *she* may be.' And the other authors laughed but followed her lead, taking a drink then tucking into their meal with the empty seat beside them.

A voice off-stage announced the moment that everyone had been waiting for: the final of the Serenity Publishing Literary Awards. The audience applauded and Jeremy hobbled onto the stage with his cane in hand.

'It can't be him can it? He was attacked and only just survived,' said Maggie. She was now such a feature of the director's tent no one even questioned her presence although Chloe had to shush her now.

'This year's event,' Jeremy was saying, 'has been marked by tragedy and some might say that it is in poor taste to proceed with these awards. I would remind those naysayers that art is tragedy and tragedy is art. Where would we be without *Romeo and Juliet*? *Anthony{Antony} and Cleopatra*? *Wuthering Heights*? Nowhere and that is why we must continue, we must honour our friends and celebrate in their memory. Ladies and gentlemen can I ask you to raise a toast to Bart and Portia.'

The room raised their glasses and murmured the toast. At the authors' table Lucinda rolled her eyes and downed her glass. Jeremy began presenting the smaller prizes acknowledging the work of the festival organisers, the bookshop, the people of the village who had supported the event and the sponsors without whom such a grand dinner would not be possible. It was the stuff of every single award ceremony that viewers would recognise and as Jeremy droned on, the authors got more and more twitchy.

'If he starts thanking his mother I'm out of here,' said Harry. 'It's typical of Dominic to miss all this guff.'

Dramatic music played and Jeremy invited Portia onto the stage with him.

'And now the moment you have all been waiting for,' he said. 'The crescendo to the celebrations, the highlight of our evening, the Serenity Publishing Award for the best book launched this year.'

He burbled on about his ancestor, his love of books and then took the opportunity to make an announcement.

'I'm sure that you will all be interested to learn that I too am dipping into the realms of fiction with a novel of my own, based on my great-great grandfather's life which will launch next year. It focusses ...'

Jeremy continued to use the ceremony as his own publicity stunt while the camera caught the growing expressions of impatience from everyone. The shoot was going well until Maggie's phone vibrated. She'd turned off the ringtone but the buzz was still loud enough for the team in the tent to hear and Chloe shoved her outside as quickly as she could so as not to disturb anyone.

'You shouldn't have a phone anywhere near set,' scolded Chloe once they were outside.

'But it's him,' replied Maggie with a startled look on her face. 'He says he's ready to act.'

Chloe's whole body went icy cold and she stood frozen to the spot. Everything was going so well and she'd relaxed into assuming the threat was over. She pulled herself together and asked Maggie what he wanted from her.

'He wants me to distract Uri for the next hour,' she said.

'The next hour? That's when Jeremy will announce the winner,' said Chloe thinking through the scene and picturing all the ways anyone could disrupt it. Given the saboteur's previous attempts, it was likely that something critical would be missing from the set when the actor came to use it.

'The golden envelope,' said Chloe. 'He has to be after the envelope.'

'Is that the next scene?' asked Maggie. 'That would mean he has to be in there already.'

'No,' replied Chloe. 'The next scene is Dominic barging into the ceremony to solve the crime and then after the break, the awards are filmed. He's probably going to take the envelope during the break. Let's speak to Uri, I mean Dad.'

Chloe clamped her hand over her mouth after blurting that out while Maggie stared at Chloe – her own mouth open so wide she looked as though she might swallow Chloe whole.

'I knew I recognised him from somewhere,' she croaked after recovering from the shock.

'Never mind. We have to warn him.'

Her dad was standing guard outside the hall striding up and down.

'Dad,' yelled Chloe getting no reaction until she added, 'It's okay – Maggie knows.'

They explained the situation and told him to stand at the door of the hall and not to let anyone either in or out until she told him to. Prior to the break, Chloe would get the golden envelope and keep tight hold of it until filming resumed.

'Maggie, just in case he watched you, you have to stand here with Uri and be seen to be flirting with him,' Chloe instructed and Maggie saluted her.

Chloe took one more look up and down the street but it really was deserted. Dominic would be in his changing room waiting for his scene but she was pretty sure he wouldn't be trying to disrupt his own show. She stepped back inside the tent where filming had continued to go smoothly and they were setting up for Dominic's big entrance. On stage, Jeremy was announcing the shortlist and the camera was moving in close to show the author reactions.

'And for his most recent work *A Perfect Revenge* and of course a lifetime of making us guess whodunit – Dominic Montgomery.'

The extras applauded but then noticed that Dominic's chair was still empty. Everyone started looking round and the camera panned to the door of the hall, waiting for Dominic to burst through. Except he didn't.

'Can someone please find out where our leading man is?' yelled Riley.

Chloe felt her knees go weak. Had she got it wrong? Was Dominic the target?

Just then they heard a kerfuffle on the other side of the door and Chloe rushed up, throwing it open. Outside her dad was trying to stop a frantic looking Dominic from getting in.

'Can you tell this oaf to get his hands off me?' Dominic was yelling.

'Oh D- Uri – we didn't mean you to stop the actors getting in,' said Chloe freeing Dominic from her dad's clutches.

Riley sighed and shook his head. 'Can we get back to the business in hand please?'

'No,' shouted Dominic. 'That's just it – we can't. It's Agatha – she's been dognapped.'

Chapter Thirty-One

'What?'

The news infiltrated the village more quickly than a mist coming in off the sea and that single incredulous word was on everyone's lips but it was Riley who voiced it the loudest.

'What do you mean she's been *dognapped*?' he demanded.

'I went to collect her from her trainer for this scene,' explained Dominic. 'He said that Agatha had already been collected by a member of the crew a little while ago.'

'The dognapper struck while we were all inside,' said Chloe. 'We were guarding the wrong thing.'

'Her handler is utterly beside himself,' continued Dominic. 'Thinking that something awful could have happened to her and he just handed her over.'

'No one would hurt her surely?' said Kareem. 'It's probably a ransom job – Agatha is probably quite valuable.'

'She's not just valuable,' Andy suddenly burst into the group looking both angry and determined. 'Who would hurt a dog? The person who did this is not going to get away with it!'

Chloe saw that her boyfriend was looking more than ready to punch the culprit. Andy spent all of his time outdoors and had a great love of Mother Nature and all animals. He really did abhor any mistreatment of anything that put its trust in mankind. Andy began agitating to set up a search party but Chloe put a calming hand on his arm.

'Let's think this through first,' she said. 'Agatha's trainer wouldn't have handed her over if he didn't recognise the member of the crew would he? Did he say who it was?'

'He didn't know the name,' replied Dominic. 'He said the man was well wrapped up and in a hurry so he didn't ask any questions.'

'But Agatha wouldn't have gone with a complete stranger,' added Kareem.

'One of my scarves is missing.' Dominic sighed. 'I didn't think anything of it as I don't need it for this scene with it being a black tie event, but our culprit could have taken it.'

'She is trained to do what she's told and it would have your scent on it so Agatha would have followed willingly.' Chloe shook her head in despair. 'Where on earth could she be?'

'Let's split up into groups with everyone taking a different part of the bay,' said Andy. 'Dominic – we'll need an item of your clothing for the head of each group so Agatha isn't afraid of us. We'll get permission from the residents to search every garage and shed just in case she's tied up in there. We won't leave a stone unturned.'

He strode into the village hall and up onto the stage. Looking out of place in his big down jacket and heavy boots, he quickly explained the plan, got each resident into a group and gave them different streets to search. He'd head one group, Dominic the other, Uri the third and Agatha's trainer the fourth. Kareem and Riley had to re-plan their schedule while Chloe would be the central point of contact for any news or sightings. Having given everyone their instructions, the villagers, dressed in their finery from the shoot, started combing the village.

Chloe took up her position at a table in The Fiddler's Arms. She rang the police telling them what had happened and that the village was searching for the dog at the moment. She could tell from the tone of the voice at the other end of the line that they didn't think a missing dog was much of a priority.

'Think of her as a TV star, not a dog,' Chloe tried to explain. 'It would be like losing Lassie.'

'Oh you'd never lose Lassie,' chortled the voice on the phone. 'She always comes home.'

Chloe calmly ended the call. There was no point upsetting the police – they might need them later. By then the media would have caught wind of what had happened and the force might just take it seriously. Chloe called around the heads of each group for an update but there was no news. It wasn't really surprising – Serenity Bay was a small village and wouldn't take long to search even if they went through everyone's sock drawer too. Maggie brought her over a glass of cranberry juice and the tartness of it was quite revitalising. She hadn't realised just how dehydrated and drained she'd felt.

'The Lone Wolf played us didn't he?' said Maggie taking a seat beside Chloe. 'He asked me to guard Uri knowing that it would focus our attention on the village hall while he made off with Agatha.'

'It looks that way. He must have known you were the Angel of Death.'

'How could he have known that?' asked Maggie.

'You do tend to have difficulty keeping secrets when you're excited about them,' said Chloe as politely as she could. 'Did you happen to mention it to anyone in the bar?'

Maggie stuck out her bottom lip as she thought about it and then slapped her hands over her face as she came to some realisation.

'Who?' asked Chloe.

'I was reading about cyber stuff,' Maggie explained. 'I didn't know whether joining this group would send off all sorts of alarms in the secret service – you hear these things don't you? A person happens to be talking about buying bath bombs on the phone but that voice recognition stuff only hears the word bomb and all of a sudden they're battering down the front door with an armed response unit.'

'I don't think that happens in real life.' Chloe really had to get Maggie away from espionage films.

'Well I can't afford to lose my licence so I thought I'd ask about it.'

'Who did you ask?'

The cogs whirred and Chloe said the name at the same time as Maggie.

'That ex-policeman.'

Chloe stood up and started pacing around the bar. 'Of course, how did we not guess this earlier? He was constantly complaining about the show and how inaccurate it is. He probably applied for the job as the script consultant just to try and disrupt it.'

'And no one would have suspected anything if they found him taking an item of Dominic's from costume,' said Maggie.

'He wasn't there when we set up the search groups and he had access to every set prior to filming,' added Chloe. 'And even if Agatha's handler didn't know his name, he would have been vaguely familiar as someone that had been on set these past weeks.'

'What a complete and utter ...' started Maggie.

'No time for that,' said Chloe. 'We might know whodunit but we haven't found Agatha yet and that's the most important thing. Now where could he have taken her?'

Chloe called in the groups and gave her update – she asked that Lizzie return to the pub to try and work out DS Campbell's movements.

'Please believe me,' pleaded Lizzie as she burst through the door of the pub. 'I had nothing to do with this. I'd never endanger Agatha or the show in any way.'

'We know that, but have you any idea where he could be?' asked Andy following closely behind the scriptwriter. She shook her head and said she really didn't know.

'If I were playing a character like that,' said Dominic, 'I wouldn't be able to resist boasting about my accomplishment. He calls himself the Lone Wolf and he has succeeded whereas all of the other members of this group have failed. A narcissist like him couldn't resist telling people.'

Maggie opened her laptop and logged on to the LACC.

'You're right,' she said. 'There's a post saying that the production team will never be able to finish this episode now.'

She swung the screen round for everyone to see. It was a shot of Agatha tied to a huge tree trunk of driftwood on an empty beach. The person taking the picture was evidently some distance from her but the well-trained dog simply sat and waited.

'It breaks my heart,' said Andy. 'She's sitting there, behaving beautifully and doing exactly what she's been told while that swine betrays her trust.'

Chloe put her hand on Andy's arm to comfort him.

'But where is she?' said Dominic. 'The photo doesn't give much away and there are miles and miles of sandy beaches around here. It could be anywhere.'

'Andy,' said Chloe. 'You know this coastline better than anyone, do you recognise it?'

Andy looked more closely at the photograph and exclaimed, 'Actually, I do. I saw that piece of driftwood only this week when you were all having your day off. He's taken Agatha to Holy Island.'

Quickly he searched for the safe crossing times and then leapt up. 'The causeway has closed and won't be open until morning,' he read out.

'What are we going to do?' asked Dominic.

'There's no road access but we have to get her now. That beach is nowhere near the main village so she might not be spotted and she can't be out all night, she'll freeze.' Andy fished his phone out and made a call.

'I've borrowed a speedboat,' he said as he put the phone away. 'We'll get to the beach by sea.' Andy pushed his way through everyone and ran down towards the harbour.

'I'll come with you,' shouted Uri chasing after him.

Chloe called the coastguard and told them there was a dog tied up on the beach and asked that someone find her. Then she called one of the pubs on the island and asked if Agatha could stay with them until Andy arrived. She could have kicked herself as she realised that they'd probably given the idea to DS Campbell with their trip out to the island. There was no point in dwelling on that now and little else they could do but sit and wait.

Kareem and Riley were huddled in discussion and when they emerged, they asked everyone if they would be comfortable continuing with the shots that were still possible so they didn't lose any more time than necessary. Probably wanting to keep their minds off things, the crew, cast and extras all agreed to resume the shoot filming. They already had Jeremy reading out the nominees then the scene was about to move to Dominic bursting in with Agatha and revealing the murderer. They'd have to leave this scene for later when Agatha was hopefully back safely but they could film the next one which was Jeremy and Portia being marched out of the hall in handcuffs and Tegan jumping up onto the stage to grab the golden envelope from the podium.

'I'm not going to let that bloody man ruin the ceremony,' Tegan's character declared to the audience of extras. 'This dress cost me a fortune.'

She opened the envelope and her face wrinkled in annoyance. 'Bloody space ships and Martians,' she said in disgust. 'Harry darling – the gong's yours.'

She thrust the glass trophy at the sci-fi writer and marched off the stage. Harry stood behind the podium holding the prize aloft as the audience applauded. Riley called it a wrap for the day. They managed to film anything that didn't include Agatha and although she wouldn't have been in the scene anyway, her absence left a heavy gloom on the set. Outside, after what seemed like an eternity Chloe got a call from Andy to say that they had Agatha on board and were returning to the bay. He'd also had word that DS Kevin Campbell had been apprehended speeding away from the village and the arresting officer – who was both a *Montgomery Mysteries* fan and dog lover – planned to throw the book at him. Chloe relayed the news to everyone in the village hall and the cheer that erupted could have been heard in the next village.

'The shoot's going well then?' said the voice behind Chloe. 'Everyone seems to be enjoying themselves.'

Chloe turned to see her mother looking very perky. Before she'd had the chance to give her a hug, Tegan rushed up and did exactly that.

'Theresa,' cried the actress kissing her on both cheeks. 'Thank goodness you're back – you look marvellous.'

'Thank you. I feel like myself again. It was just the break I needed. Have I missed anything here?'

'Just a little.' Chloe gave her mum a huge hug, thoroughly relieved to have her back home.

'They're here,' shouted Dominic giving Theresa a friendly wave then running up towards the harbour.

The whole ensemble followed him and Chloe grabbed her mother's hand dragging her towards the approaching speedboat.

It was like something from a Bond film. The two heroes spun the boat around making waves in the shallow water, Agatha sat upright in the back seat wearing a little yellow life jacket and wagging her tail. Her trainer ran down the beach as Uri leapt out of the boat; Andy lifted Agatha and passed her over to Uri who carried her through the water to dry land. He put her down on the sand and the dog ran straight to her owner licking his face enthusiastically. Uri turned back to the boat and helped secure it as Andy jumped out, punching the air in victory.

'Gosh,' said Theresa. 'Who is that action man with Andy?'

Chloe winked at her and said, 'Come and meet him.'

She led her mum to the two men and as she pulled Andy's face towards her and kissed him as if she hadn't seen him for years, Uri turned to his wife and pulled off his glasses, hat and mask.

'Geoff,' exclaimed Theresa. 'Is that really you?'

Her husband put an arm around her waist and pulled her towards him. 'Nyet tonight,' he said before tipping her back in his arms and kissing her passionately.

The crowd on the beach cheered as Maggie invited

everyone back to The Fiddler's Arms, adding very pointedly that just because everyone was celebrating – it did *not* mean that anything was on the house.

Chapter Thirty-Two

The big day finally arrived. After a frantic period of filming the denouement, trucks carried production equipment out of the village passing one bringing the enormous Christmas tree in, along with the crane that hoisted it into position at the centre of the village. It really was fabulous and now everyone was gathering around it ready for the big switch-on.

All the cast and crew had found themselves full of nervous energy after Agatha's rescue and the final scene was laced with relief and happiness. Dominic and his faithful companion burst into the village hall as they were supposed to, Dominic held out a hand and told Jeremy to stop the ceremony then proceeded to announce to the room that the publisher had murdered Bart. Chloe watched Maggie as the scene unfolded, the landlady frowning and scribbling on a little piece of paper.

'I'm seeing how much I have to pay out,' she whispered. Chloe smiled to herself knowing what was coming next and nudged Maggie to watch the rest of the scene.

Dominic stood on stage as the police officers who'd arrived with him handcuffed Jeremy. Then Agatha barked and the super sleuth thanked her.

'Agatha is right,' said Dominic. 'There is more news. Jeremy is guilty of Bart's murder but he did not kill Poppy.'

The extras gasped. Dominic went on to explain that Bart had discovered that Jeremy was not in fact an ancestor of Walter Kingsley and had no right to be publishing his works. The museum curator had written about it in the research paper that was stored on the memory stick. Bart had told Poppy and she, unfortunately, had told someone else.

'Please arrest that person now, Agatha,' Dominic instructed as the dog trotted over to the top table. As she approached, Portia scraped her chair back and tried to make a run for it but Agatha had hold of the hem of her dress in her teeth and wouldn't let go. The police officers quickly cuffed the bookshop owner too.

'You see Portia was in love with Jeremy and would have done anything to keep their cosy arrangement,' explained Dominic. 'Jeremy brought book-lovers to the village and Portia sold the books. It was a perfect arrangement until Bart moved in.'

Maggie punched the air in victory.

'I knew it,' she declared as the filming was wrapped up. 'Didn't I say that a woman normally poisons her victims but wouldn't do the stabbing?'

'You did,' Chloe agreed. 'It was indeed one of your theories. So who's won the sweepstake?'

'Well no one actually named the two of them together,' said Maggie. 'So I guess the whole lot goes to the New Year buffet. It'll be quite a spread – which is just as well.'

'Why?' asked Chloe.

'Nick called me last night,' Maggie said with the biggest smile on her face. 'He's on his way home for Christmas and has been telling his travelling mates all about the mystery we've had here so they're all joining us for New Year. A full house! I can't wait.'

'Oh that's brilliant news, Maggie.'

The production company had been such a feature of the village for the past few weeks, it was almost sad to see them go and Chloe knew that Maggie would have felt it particularly hard if she'd gone from a full pub to an empty one. Chloe walked up to Riley and Kareem and kissed them both on the cheek, wishing them a Happy Christmas, then they, along with almost everyone else, left Serenity Bay and for a moment there was quiet in the village.

But not any longer, now there was a buzz as everyone waited for the lights. Tegan and Dominic had stayed to do the switch-on and their presence, together with the dognapping tale which made it into the national news, had drawn a huge crowd of tourists which delighted all the local shopkeepers. Tonight, genuine stallholders had taken the place of the fake murder mystery ones and the air was filled with the aroma of mulled wine and roasting chestnuts. Visitors had started to arrive in the early afternoon and Chloe had quickly created a tour showing the film locations and she was particularly delighted when so many people chose to pick up those last minute stocking fillers from the chocolate shop. Tony had made his themed chocolates and they flew off the shelves, especially the little Agatha shaped ones. He gave Chloe a nod of thanks as the final tour group of the day left his shop.

The actors were now making their way to the huge lever that would mark the official start of Christmas. Chloe looked around for Andy; he'd said he would just be a couple of minutes and that he had to collect something but that was twenty minutes ago. At this rate he'd miss the switch-on. Her mum and dad were right at the front snuggling together like young lovers and Chloe's heart simply melted to see them like that. The friend her mother had visited was on her fourth divorce and apparently Theresa had realised she didn't want that kind of freedom. She'd confided in Tegan that she knew she loved Geoff, she just wished he'd be a little more adventurous. Tegan had played a blinder; while under the cover of his Uri costume, she'd had the make-up guys shave the grey beard, trim the bushy eyebrows and give him a great haircut that made his salt and pepper colouring look almost trendy. So when Theresa unwrapped the action man she saw on the beach, she declared it was like getting an early Christmas present. They hadn't let go of each other ever since.

Maggie stood on the makeshift stage beside Tegan and Dominic. Before the switch on, Chloe had told her the couple were genuinely an item – just in case the landlady was still hankering after the leading man.

'Oh I guessed that ages ago,' she'd replied. 'I couldn't be doing with a man who spends his life in make-up anyway. They're very welcome to each other as far as I'm concerned.'

So, as Maggie thanked everyone for coming and then asked the actors to do the honours, the only thing Chloe had to worry about was whether her boyfriend was actually going to see any of this. The crowd started counting down.

'Ten, nine, eight ...'

Chloe again looked frantically for Andy – he really was going to miss it. Where on earth was he? The countdown reached one and the actors pulled the lever causing a mini flash that the special effects team had created and then it happened – first the lights strewn from lamp post to lamp post lit up along the promenade as if coming to life one by one – silver and gold snowflakes twinkled above everyone's heads from one end of the village to the next. Then on the tree, starting from the bottom, every row lit up one at a time until it reached the very top where an enormous star shone out as the village cheered. It was magnificent. The crowd applauded and were moving to disperse when Tegan called out over the microphone.

'Wait what's that I hear?'

She put her hand to her ear theatrically and over the speaker came the sound of sleigh bells and a hearty, 'Ho, Ho, Ho.'

Chloe frowned and looked at Maggie who shrugged that she had no idea what was happening either.

Then he appeared. Father Christmas in his sleigh. Well obviously not *the* Father Christmas but Andy, in a big white beard and a padded red suit. Chloe clasped her hands to her face in surprise and delight. That's where he'd been. The sleigh was pulled, as he'd promised, by Agatha – with velvet antlers on her head and a collar with bells which jingled as she trotted along. Tegan announced that Father Christmas was on his way to the local hospital but if anyone wanted to donate a gift, he'd be happy to take it on his sleigh. She also said that donations to the dog rescue charity would be welcomed for any selfies.

Chloe waited until the excitement around seeing Agatha died down before going up to Andy and pulling his beard down for a kiss.

'This is where you were,' she said. 'I thought you were missing all the excitement but actually you were creating it.'

'It was too good an opportunity to miss,' he said. 'There'll be a lot of happy people at the hospital when they see all the gifts people have donated.'

Chloe looked up at her gorgeous man, he really was Mr Christmas and not just because he loved the insane jumpers and hats but because he believed in the true spirit of it. The moment he handed over those gifts and saw the smiling faces of the children would mean more to him than any gift. He looked down at her and stroked her cheek gently.

'So,' he said, 'what do you think of the beard?'

'Definitely prefer you without it.' Chloe laughed, kissing his soft warm lips and then pulling a whisker from her mouth. 'Yes – definitely prefer you without it.'

They stood for a moment watching everyone enjoying the Midwinter Festival. The cricket club choir were taking centre stage now, all dressed in green elf outfits. They began a medley of songs old and new which had the crowds joining in and bopping along.

'I was a bit concerned that we were starting Christmas too late,' said Andy. 'Everyone else seems to start celebrations in autumn, but now seeing this, I think we got it right. The panic buying is over and people can just relax can't they?'

Chloe nodded and exhaled deeply. Her panic was over and she'd decided on a Christmas gift for Andy. She just hoped she hadn't got it completely wrong. Andy said he'd better get going – he had to get the sleigh up to the hospital and then Agatha back to her trainer.

'Where did you get the sleigh?' asked Chloe inspecting it and seeing that it had a small electric motor so that Agatha wasn't actually pulling it, she was just trotting along in front of it.

'I had it built,' he said. 'It uses the motor of an e-bike and I had a friend mock up the rest. It had to be quite light but strong.'

'You managed to keep it a secret,' continued Chloe. 'Where on earth did you keep it?'

'Maggie's garage,' Andy said mischievously. 'I backed the van up right to the door so she couldn't see what it was. I think it drove her nuts.'

Chloe snorted and could picture Maggie's face when she told her what was really in her garage.

'You know she told me you were storing my Christmas present don't you?' she said with a huge grin on her face. 'She said it was so huge that you needed a garage to store it in.'

Andy laughed. 'Yeah, well I might have told her that to put her off the scent,' he said. 'She kept asking what I was planning to get you and you know Maggie, she can't keep a secret for love nor money. And I like surprises.'

Chloe nodded in agreement then kissed Andy goodbye as he left for the hospital.

'To surprises!' she called after him.

Chapter Thirty-Three

Chloe opened her eyes to a sprig of mistletoe being held above her head.

'Merry Christmas gorgeous,' said Andy leaning over her and kissing her gently. She responded by sleepily pulling him closer and softly pressing her lips to his forehead, nose then lips.

'How long have you been waiting for me to wake up?'

'Ever since Rudolf left.' Andy smiled. 'He said thanks for the carrot.'

Chloe's smile widened. They were staying at his little terraced cottage for the day and last night, her insanely enthusiastic boyfriend had persuaded her to leave out a mince pie and carrot by the fireplace – something she hadn't done since she was a small child.

'I hope Santa enjoyed his treat,' she replied.

'Alas,' said Andy shaking his head in mock regret. 'He's doing low carb this year – I had to eat it.'

He rolled over onto his back and Chloe sat astride him; he stroked her dark hair as it tumbled down towards him.

'You wanted to know what would make my perfect Christmas?' he said. 'It's this, waking up with you. I can't think of anywhere I'd rather be or anything I'd rather be doing.'

'I can,' said Chloe leaning over him and kissing his broad chest.

When they eventually got out of bed, Andy led Chloe to the kitchen which he'd decorated with lights. He popped on a Christmas playlist quietly in the background, sat her down at the table and poured her a glass of bucks fizz. They clinked glasses then he rustled up a couple of bacon sandwiches.

'Our new tradition is this – champagne for you and a butty for me,' he said as they both tucked in and Chloe realised she'd already worked up quite an appetite this morning.

'Hmm,' she mumbled, 'that was delicious. I like our new tradition. What's next?'

She looked around the kitchen and couldn't see any sign of a turkey or vegetables waiting to be peeled. Andy caught her looking.

'Our next new tradition is that neither of us work too hard on this day. We've both had a busy December so there'll be no cooking. To celebrate Nick coming home, Maggie is serving lunch for family and friends down at the Fiddler's so we can relax all day. That's okay isn't it?'

Despite having spent the last few weeks at the pub, Chloe realised that it really did feel right to be celebrating the day there.

'Roisin and Lloyd will be there too,' added Andy. 'As well as your mum and dad.'

'It sounds perfect,' Chloe said as Andy topped up her Bucks Fizz. 'No cooking and no washing up.'

'So ...' said Andy taking hold of her hand. 'Are you ready to do presents?'

She was. Chloe felt insanely excited and knew that even the pair of novelty pyjamas she was about to open would completely delight her right now. They took their champagne flutes and sat down on the rug in front of the fireplace.

'Can I go first?' asked Chloe getting an enthusiastic nod from Andy. 'Okay – small gift first.'

She reached under the tree and pulled out a beautifully wrapped gift. Andy pulled on the ribbon and carefully unwrapped the merino wool jumper.

'It's fabulous,' he said. 'I'll wear it to lunch.'

'You might find Lloyd in something similar.' Chloe explained the shopping trip she'd had with Roisin. 'And although I think you'll look gorgeous in it, I also know it's probably a bit too smart for you today so I've also bought you these.'

She handed him another collection of parcels which he took as much care opening. He tore a tiny corner of paper and a piece of fabric with a snowman poked out. Andy looked up at Chloe and grinned, tearing open the rest of the parcel. It contained socks and a scarf both decorated with snowmen and penguins dancing together. With a press of a button, the scarf played "Walking in a Winter Wonderland".

'It's hilarious,' said Andy wrapping the scarf around his neck. 'And I'm definitely wearing it to lunch.'

He kissed her and reached under the tree to retrieve a gift box that looked a lot larger than a pair of pyjamas. Chloe unwrapped the bow slowly and opened the lid. Inside there was another box and another bow. She looked up at Andy who looked as excited as she felt. Chloe unwrapped the next bow and then the next, getting to smaller and smaller boxes – ones that certainly weren't big enough to contain nightwear of any kind. Eventually she got to the smallest box; she shook it and heard something rattling inside. Andy shifted nervously as she pulled gently at the bow, almost afraid to open it. She lifted the lid cautiously and then looked puzzled at the contents: a little silver robin key ring. It was very cute but a slightly confusing choice. Andy cleared his throat and shifted slightly to sit in front of her.

'It's to hold this key,' he said holding one out to her. 'I want us to wake up together every morning. And I don't mean on a blow-up mattress in the Surfshack.'

Chloe's heart was pounding so this joke gave them both the chance to laugh a little and clear the electric tension in the air. Andy took hold of both Chloe's hands.

'I want us to move in together,' he continued as Chloe's whole body filled with joy. 'I know this place is a little small for us both and so ...'

He swallowed and continued.

'So I have spoken to the owners of Harbour Cottage and if you say yes, they won't put it on the market – they will sell it only to us.'

Andy paused looking intently at Chloe who sat with her hand pressed to her mouth unable to speak. Tears were forming at the corners of her eyes and all she could do was nod, nod enthusiastically and grab hold of Andy in a tight hug.

'Yes, yes and yes again! I love that house,' she squeaked when she eventually found her voice. 'It's just so perfect – the nooks and crannies, the view and the garden. And Andy it has a garden!'

She squeezed him even tighter until he begged permission to come up for air. He explained his conversation with the owners and how they could look at it objectively over the next week or two and then make a decision in the cold light of day.

'I don't need to look at it objectively,' said Chloe. 'I know every inch of it. And it has a garden.'

Andy looked puzzled. 'So you said – I didn't know you were so into gardening.'

'I'm not. Can I give you your main present now?'

He looked at her slightly suspiciously but nodded. Chloe picked a long slender box out of the branches of the tree.

'You hid that well,' said Andy as he weighed the box in his hand. 'It feels expensive.'

'You have no idea,' Chloe said, giving nothing away.

Andy seemed to take a lifetime to unwrap the small box during which time Chloe sat biting her fingers in excitement.

'Erm,' said Andy on seeing the contents. 'I'm not really into this kind of thing. Does it suit me?'

He picked up the leather dog collar inside and playfully placed it against his neck.

'It looks fabulous,' she said. 'But it's not for you.'

Chloe reached into the branches again and pulled out a golden envelope, handing it to her boyfriend.

'Did you steal this from the set?' asked Andy tearing it open.

'I certainly did.' Chloe giggled. 'Only a few days ago, this very envelope contained the name of the award-winning author.'

Andy pulled out the sheet of paper inside and unfolded it. His jaw dropped and he looked every bit as delighted as Chloe had just felt.

'Wh- What?' he stuttered.

Chloe sat alongside him and together they looked at the paper and the photograph of the cheeky mongrel on it.

'I saw how much you loved Agatha and I thought that you, well we, would be the perfect people to give a dog a loving home,' she said. 'We both love the outdoors, we work flexibly and the whole world now knows you're the person who rescued the most famous dog on TV.

'I went to the rescue centre and they've recommended

this chap – he's called Rusty. They don't let people take dogs home at Christmas but we can go there after the holidays and pick him up.'

'He's gorgeous,' said Andy. 'Now I know why you were so enthusiastic about the garden.'

Chloe nodded and watched her boyfriend looking lovingly at the mischievous looking mutt. She'd got the idea watching Andy on set with Agatha and had called the rescue centre just before the dognapping. Afterwards, she'd known that she'd done the right thing and Andy's expression now confirmed it.

'You know some people have trained their dogs to go out with them in their kayaks and on paddle boards,' he said. 'I wonder if Rusty fancies a go.'

'I'm sure if anyone can train him, you can,' said Chloe. 'I think this calls for more fizz.'

They walked back to the kitchen with little fingers linked and Chloe realised she simply couldn't be more in love. With that full to bursting sensation in her chest, she simply had to be the happiest person in the world right now. They refilled their glasses.

'To us, our new home and our new member of the family,' toasted Andy.

They sipped and then put their glasses down as Chloe pulled her boyfriend back to the bedroom.

'I think we still have time before Maggie serves lunch, don't we?' she asked.

'We'll make time,' replied Andy kissing her neck passionately. 'And I'd quite like to unwrap my most important gift one more time.'

Thank You

Dear Reader,

Thank you for choosing to read *Christmas at Serenity Bay* – I really hope you enjoyed it and that it's put you in the Christmas mood. I have to confess that I had a blast writing this story. I have a Chocolate Labrador (who is nowhere near as well trained as Agatha!) and the idea of my dog solving crimes kept me truly entertained. I also had to go to Holy Island several times to check the layout of the island and the tide times. It really is a spectacular place so if you ever get the chance, do visit it. And if, like Chloe, you're ever struggling with what to buy someone for Christmas – might I suggest a book as the ideal gift?!

If you've enjoyed reading *Christmas at Serenity Bay*, I hope you will leave a review for the book on Goodreads or the website where you bought the book. You can also follow me on Twitter for news on my other books (details on 'About the Author' page next).

Love Helen

x

About the Author

Helen Bridgett lives in the North East of England. Outside of writing feel good fiction, Helen loves the great outdoors and having a good laugh with friends over a glass of wine. Helen lives with her husband and their chocolate Labrador, Angus; all three can often be found walking the Northumberland coastline that inspired her novels, *Summer at Serenity Bay* and *Christmas at Serenity Bay*.

All Helen's novels feature strong female leads who are faced with situations that they have to resolve. Her goal is to create characters that you would want to get to know better in real life.

*To find out more about Helen,
follow her on social media:*

www.twitter.com/Helen_Bridgett
www.facebook.com/HelenBridgettAuthor/

More Ruby Fiction

From Helen Bridgett

Summer at Serenity Bay

What happens when you send a group of celebrities to a tiny seaside village?

Advertising executive Chloe Walsh thought she was visiting her friend Roisin to get away from it all, but little does she know her kooky friend has a master plan to breathe some life into her sleepy seaside village through a new wellness retreat – and she needs Chloe's skills.

So starts a community effort to put the retreat, Serenity Bay, on the map. Everyone from Andy at the Surf Shack to Tony at the chocolate shop is involved – even Roisin's Gran has a few ideas!

But Chloe strikes gold almost too soon, attracting the attention of a major production company. Now a colourful group of celebrities are preparing to descend on Serenity Bay to film a reality TV show. Is the village ready for the fun and scandal that are bound to follow?

Visit www.rubyfiction.com for details.

One by One

Professor Maxie Reddick Files

When practising what you preach is easier said than done …

Professor Maxie Reddick has her reasons for being sceptical of traditional policing methods, but, in between her criminology lecturing job and her Criminal Thoughts podcast, she stays firmly on the side lines of the crime solving world.

Then a young woman is brutally attacked, and suddenly it's essential that Maxie turns her words into actions; this is no longer an academic exercise – this is somebody's life.

But as she delves deeper, the case takes a sickening turn, which leads Maxie to the horrifying realisation that the attack might not have been a one-off. It seems there's a depraved individual out there seeking revenge, and they'll stop at nothing to get it … little by little … one by one.

Visit www.rubyfiction.com for details.

Wrong Sort of Girl

Professor Maxie Reddick Files

A young woman has gone missing. It's nearly Christmas. Why does hardly anyone seem to care?

Kelly Ingles' case should have been one to tug on the public's heartstrings: a young woman missing in the run-up to Christmas. But Kelly wasn't perfect – she liked to party, enjoyed a drink, didn't always make the best decisions. And when evidence of her drunken antics appears online, it becomes clear that Kelly might not just have been in the wrong place at the wrong time; she might also be the wrong sort of girl to encourage public sympathy. It's a case that's right up Maxie Reddick's street. As a criminology professor, she's made it her mission to challenge unconscious biases within the criminal justice system – the sort of biases that cause girls like Kelly to slip through the cracks. But can she get the police and public on board before it's too late?

Visit www.rubyfiction.com for details.

Introducing Ruby Fiction

Ruby Fiction is an imprint of Choc Lit Publishing. We're an award-winning independent publisher, creating a delicious selection of fiction.

See our selection here:
www.rubyfiction.com

Ruby Fiction brings you stories that inspire emotions.

We'd love to hear how you enjoyed
Christmas at Serenity Bay. Please visit
www.rubyfiction.com and give your feedback or
leave a review where you purchased this novel.

Ruby novels are selected by genuine readers like yourself. We only publish stories our Tasting Panel want to see in print. Our reviews and awards speak for themselves.

Could you be a Star Selector and join our Tasting Panel?
Would you like to play a role in choosing which novels
we decide to publish? Do you enjoy reading women's
fiction? Then you could be perfect for our Tasting Panel.

Visit here for more details …
www.choc-lit.com/join-the-choc-lit-tasting-panel

Keep in touch:
Sign up for our monthly newsletter Spread for all the latest
news and offers: www.spread.choc-lit.com. Follow us on
Twitter: @RubyFiction and Facebook: RubyFiction.

Stories that inspire emotions!